Ghosts

in Baker Street

Ghosts
in Baker Street

EDITED BY

Martin H. Greenberg • Jon Lellenberg • Daniel Stashower

CARROLL & GRAF PUBLISHERS
NEW YORK

GHOSTS IN BAKER STREET
New Tales of Sherlock Holmes

Carroll & Graf Publishers
An Imprint of Avalon Publishing Group Inc.
245 West 17th Street
11th Floor
New York, NY 10011

AVALON
publishing group incorporated

Library of Congress Cataloging-in-Publication Data is available.

ISBN-10: 0-7867-1400-X
ISBN-13: 978-0-78671-400-1

9 8 7 6 5 4 3 2 1

Printed in the United States of America
Distributed by Publishers Group West

CONTENTS

COPYRIGHTS

FOREWORD

John H. Watson, M.D.

MY FRIEND MR. SHERLOCK Holmes was always the most rational of men. His formal education was incomplete, due to his having moved from university classes without taking a degree to the eccentric medical and other studies in London that he chose to prepare himself for the role of the world's first consulting detective. But what education he did possess was in a very austere school of medical and other scientific thought. I always felt that he would have made a fine consulting physician, in fact, though his aloof and sometimes abrupt manner toward people, even his own clients, would have limited his success at the everyday practice of medicine. But when it came to a scientific outlook on things, there was no one who insisted more than he upon the evidence—not of his senses, for he knew well that they can mislead and deceive, but of the physical world.

My wife found this entertaining since Holmes reached the height of his powers and fame at the very time that the English ghost story, to which she was addicted (and not to my own small contributions to literature, I am compelled to admit), was reaching its zenith. So interested then were people in the possibility of ghosts and other psychic phenomena, that not only did the Society for Psychical Research come into being and flourish, but certain individuals set themselves up in London as "psychic detectives," who for an earthly fee would determine why one's house was haunted and lay the ghost.

For such men as these, and the views which made them possible,

Sherlock Holmes had nothing but scorn. I have related how he exclaimed, in the case I set down—long after we had both retired from our respective practices—as *The Adventure of the Sussex Vampire*: "This Agency stands flat-footed upon the ground, and there it must remain. The world is big enough for us. No ghosts need apply." And of course, events vindicated his view that the case brought us by a respectable firm of men of affairs under the *outré* heading of "Re: Vampires" would find its solution in mundane mischief. Less mundane, but equally due to mortal wickedness, was the case recorded as *The Hound of the Baskervilles*. Holmes never lost confidence during the shocking events of that case that he would find a rational explanation for the seeming revisitation of a legendary curse, even if I wondered about it when out on Dartmoor without him. And his annoyance with the "romanticism" with which he said I endowed my tale was mitigated only by his pride in bringing this remarkable case to a successful conclusion.

But there were other times when I was not so sure about these things; and neither, at certain dreadful or weird moments, I sincerely believe, was my friend. A few cases seemed to defy rational explanation, even in instances when my friend succeeded in bringing them to a satisfactory conclusion for his clients. He would never allow me to publish accounts of them, because once they were done, he insisted that there was a rational explanation which eluded him for certain phenomena, and he wished no one to believe that he accepted the supernatural as a possibility. So I made a furtive job of recording these cases, at moments when Holmes was out and I could do so without interruption or censure, and I locked them away in my old dispatch box that I kept in the vaults of a bank at Charing Cross.

There they have lain these many years. Now it will do no harm for the public to see them, for I am convinced that they do no disservice to my friend's memory, whatever may have been the truth of them. At all times, my friend acted for the right; and if there were cases not explainable in mundane terms, then we must all agree that the world is bigger than we are, bigger still than we know, and that some things may be beyond rational explanation.

The Devil and Sherlock Holmes

Loren D. Estleman

THE YEAR 1899 stands out of particular note in my memory, not because it was the last but one of the old century, but because it was the only time during my long and stimulating association with Sherlock Holmes that I came to call upon his unique services in the capacity of a client.

It was the last day of April, and because I had not yet made up my mind whether to invest in South African securities, I was refreshing my memory by way of recent numbers of the *Times* and the *Telegraph* about developments in the souring relationship between the Boers and the British in Johannesburg. The day was Sunday, and my professional consulting room presented the happy prospect of uninterrupted study outside the melancholy surroundings of my widower's quarters, as well as a haven from personal troubles of more recent vintage. I was, therefore, somewhat disgruntled to be forced to disinter myself from the pile of discarded sections to answer the bell.

"Ah, Watson," greeted Sherlock Holmes. "When I find you squandering your day of rest in conference with your cheque book, I wonder that I should have come in chains, to haunt you out of your miser's destiny."

I was always pleased to encounter my oldest of friends, and wrung his hand before I realised that he had once again trespassed upon my private reflections. It was not until I had relieved him of his hat, ulster, and stick, and we were comfortable in my worn chairs with glasses of brandy in hand to ward off the spring chill, that I asked him by what sorcery he'd divined my late activity.

"The printers' ink upon your hands, on a day when no newspapers are delivered, is evidence; the rest is surmise, based upon familiarity with the company and the one story that has claimed the interest of every journal in the country this past week. Having experienced war at first hand, you are scarcely an enthusiast of sword-rattling rhetoric; but you are a chronic investor who prides himself upon his determination to wrest every scrap of intelligence from a venture before he takes the plunge. The rest is simple arithmetic."

"You haven't lost your touch," said I, shaking my head.

"And yet I fear I shall, should I remain in this calm another week. There isn't a criminal with imagination left on our island. They have all emigrated to America to run for public office."

His voice was jocular, but he appeared drawn. I recognised with alarm the look of desperation which had driven him to unhealthy practices in the past. Instead, he had come to me. "Well, I don't propose to ask you to investigate the Uitlanders in South Africa," I remarked.

He threw his cigarette, which he had just lit, into the grate, in a gesture of irritation. "The fare would be a waste. Anyone with eyes in his head can see there will be war, and that it will be no holiday for Her Majesty's troops. Heed my advice and restrict your gambling to the turf."

Holmes was prickly company when he was agitated. Fortunately, I did not have to cast far to strike a subject that might distract him from his boredom, which in his case could be fatal. The situation had been nearly as much on my mind of late as the squabbling on the Ivory Coast. However, a cautious approach was required, as the circumstances were anathema to his icy faculties of reason.

"As a matter of fact," I teased, "I have been in the way of a matter that may present some features of interest. However, I hesitate to bring it up."

"Old fellow, this is no time in life to acquire discretion. It suits you little." He lifted his head, as a hound does when the wind shifts from the direction of a wood.

"My dear Holmes, let's pretend I said nothing. I know too well your opinions on the subject."

"What subject is that?" he barked. He was well and truly on the scent.

"The supernatural."

"Bah! Spare me your bogey tales."

He pretended disappointment, but I knew him better than to accent appearances. He could disguise his person from me, but not his smoldering curiosity.

"You know, perhaps, that I am a consulting physician to the staff of St. Porphyry's Hospital in Battersea?"

"I know St. Poor's," he said. "My testimony at the Assizes sent a murderer there, bypassing the scaffold, and there are at least two bank robbers jittering in front of the alienists who ought to be rotting in Reading Gaol."

I was annoyed. "St. Porphyry's is a leader in the modern treatment of lunacy. It's not a bolt-hole for scofflaws."

"I did not mean to suggest it was. Pray continue. This penchant for withholding the most important feature until the end may please the readers of your tales, but it exhausts my stores of patience."

"To be brief," said I, "there is a patient there at present who's convinced himself he's the Devil."

"That's on its way toward balancing the account. Bedlam has two Christs and a Moses."

"Have they succeeded in convincing anyone else?"

He saw my direction, and lit another cigarette with an air of exaggerated insouciance. "It's no revelation that this fellow's found some tormented souls in residence who agree with him."

"It isn't just some patients, Holmes," I said, springing my trap. "There are at least two nurses on the staff, and one doctor, who are absolutely unshakeable in the conviction that this fellow is Satan Incarnate."

WITHIN THE HOUR, we were aboard a coach bound for Battersea, the telegraph poles clicking past, quite in time with the working of

Holmes's brain. He hammered me with questions, seeking to string the morsels of information I'd already provided into a chronological narrative. It was an old trick of his, not unlike the process of mesmerisation: he worried me for every detail, and in so doing, caused me to recall incidents that had been related to me and that I had seen for myself and since forgotten.

My regular practice having stagnated, I had succumbed at last to persistent entreaties from my friend and colleague, Dr. James Menitor, chief alienist at St. Porphyry's, to observe the behavior of his more challenging patients twice a week and offer my opinion upon their treatment. In this I suspect he thought my close exposure to Holmes's detective techniques would prove useful, and I was rather too flattered by his determination, and intrigued by the diversion, to put him off any longer. Dr. Menitor was particularly eager to consult with me in the case of a patient known only as John Smith, at which point in my narration I was interrupted by a derisive snort from Holmes.

"A *nom de romance*," said he, "lacking even the virtue of originality. If I cannot have imagination in my criminals, let me at least have it in my lunatics."

"It was the staff who christened him thus, in lieu of any other identification. He was apprehended verbally accosting strollers along the Thames, and committed by Scotland Yard for observation. It seems he told the constable that he was engaged on his annual expedition to snare souls."

"I hadn't realised there was a season. When was this?"

"Three days ago. It was fortuitous you dropped in upon me when you did, for Mr. Smith has indicated he will be returning to the netherworld this night."

"*Walpurgisnacht,*" said Holmes.

"I beg your pardon?"

"A Teutonic superstition, not worthy of discussion in our scientific age, but possibly of interest to the deluded mind. Has your John Smith a foreign accent?"

"No. As a matter of fact, his speech is British upper class. I wonder that no one has reported him missing."

"In that case, I am guilty of a *non sequitur.* The date may not be significant. What has he done to support his claim apart from wandering the hospital corridors snatching at gnats?"

"I would that were the case. He has already nearly caused the death of one patient and jeopardised the career of a nurse whose professional behavior was impeccable before he arrived."

Holmes's eyes grew alight in the reflection of the match he had set to his pipe. Violence and disgrace were details dear to his detective's heart.

I continued my report. On his first day in residence, Smith was observed in close whispered conversation in the common room with a young man named Tom Turner, who suffered from the conviction that he was Socrates, the ancient Greek sage. Dr. Menitor had been pleased with Turner's progress since he'd been admitted six months previously, wearing a bedsheet wrapped about him in the manner of a toga, bent over and speaking in a voice cracked with age, when in fact he was barely four-and-twenty. He had of his own volition recently resumed contemporary dress, and had even commenced to score off his delusion with self-deprecating wit, an encouraging sign that sanity was returning.

All that changed after his encounter with John Smith.

Minutes after the pair separated, young Turner opened a supply closet and was prevented from ingesting the contents of a bottle of chlorine bleach only by strenuous intervention by a male orderly who happened to be passing. Placed in restraints in the infirmary, the young man raved in his cracked old voice that he must have his hemlock, else how could Socrates fulfill his destiny?

Confronted by Dr. Menitor, John Smith smiled blandly. "Good Physician," he said, "when he was Socrates, his acquaintance was worthy of pursuing, but as a plain pudding of the middle class, he was a bore. I am overstocked with Tom Turners, but my inventory of great philosophers is dangerously low."

"And what of the disgraced nurse?" Holmes asked me.

"Martha Brant has worked at St. Porphyry's for twenty years without so much as a spot on her record. It was her key to the supply closet Turner had in his possession when he was apprehended."

"Stolen?"

"Given, by her own account. When questioned, she confessed to removing the key from its ring and surrendering it to Turner. She insisted that she was commanded to do so by Smith. She became hysterical. Dr. Menitor was forced to sedate her with morphine and confine her to a private room, where she remains, attended by another nurse on the staff. Before she lost consciousness, Miss Brant insisted that Smith is the Prince of Lies, precisely as he claims."

"What has been done with Smith in the meantime?"

"At present, he is locked up in the criminal ward. However, that has not stopped him from exercising an unhealthy influence upon all of St. Porphyry's. Since his incarceration, a previously dependable orderly has been sacked for stealing food from the kitchen pantry and selling it to the owner of a public house in the neighbourhood, and restlessness among the patients has increased to the point where Menitor refuses to step outside his own consulting room without first placing a loaded revolver in his pocket. The orderlies have all been put on their guard, for an uprising is feared.

"It's for my friend I'm concerned, Holmes," I continued. "He has been forced to replace the nurse in charge of Miss Brant and assign her to less demanding duties elsewhere in the hospital; the poor girl has come to agree with her that Smith is the Devil. It's true that the girl's a devout Catholic, and given to belief in demonic obsession and the cleansing effects of exorcism. However, Miss Brant is a down-to-earth sort who was never before heard to express any opinion that was not well-founded in medical science. And when I was there yesterday, I found Menitor in a highly agitated state, and disinclined to rule out the Black Arts as a cause for his present miseries. I fear the situation has unhinged him. I hope you will consider me your client in this affair."

"Hmm." Holmes pulled at his pipe. "Under ordinary circumstances, I would dismiss this fellow Smith as nothing more than a talented student of the principles taught by the late Franz Mesmer. However, I doubt even that estimable doctor was capable of entrancing the entire population of a London hospital."

"It is more than that, Holmes. I've met the fellow, and I can state with absolute certainty that I've never encountered anyone who impressed me so thoroughly that he is the living embodiment of evil. This was before the Turner incident, and we exchanged nothing more than casual greetings; yet his mere presence filled me with dread."

"Insanity is a contagion, Watson. I've seen it before, and no amount of persuasion will force me to concede that prolonged exposure to it is less dangerous than an outbreak of smallpox. Do limit your visits to St. Poor's, lest you contract it as well. I have never been stimulated by your intellect, but I have come to rely upon your granite pragmatism. Common sense is not common, and wisdom is anything but conventional. You must guard them as if they were the crown jewels."

"Is it then your theory that this situation may be explained away as mass hysteria?"

"I refuse to theorise until I have made the acquaintance of Mr. John Smith."

St. Porphyry's Hospital was Georgian, but only insofar as it had been rebuilt from the ruins of the Reformation. Parts of it dated back to William the Conqueror, and I once knew an antiquarian who insisted it was constructed upon a Roman foundation. It had been by turns a redoubt, a prison, and an abbey, but the addition of some modern architectural features had softened somewhat the medieval gloom I felt whenever I entered its grounds.

The improved effect evaporated the moment the door opened. An agitated orderly conducted us down the narrow corridor that led past the common room—the heavy door to which was locked up tight—to Dr. Menitor's consulting room at the back. A stout rubber truncheon hung from a strap round his wrist, and he gripped it with knuckles white. The ancient walls seemed to murmur an unintelligible warning as we passed; it was the sound of the patients, muttering to themselves behind locked doors. This general confinement was by no means a common practice. It had been added since my last visit.

We found my friend in an advanced state of nervous excitement, worse than the one I had left him in less than twenty-four hours before. He appeared to have lost weight, and his fallen face was as white as his hair, which I had sworn still bore traces of its original dark colour at our parting. He shook our hands listlessly, dismissed the orderly with an air of distraction, and addressed my companion in a bleating tone I scarcely credited as his.

"I am honoured, Mr. Holmes," said he, "but I fear even your skills are no match for the fate that has befallen this institution to which I have dedicated my entire professional life. St. Porphyry's is damned."

"Has something happened since I left?" I asked, alarmed by his resignation.

"Two of my best orderlies have quit, and I've taken to arming the rest, much good has it done them. None will go near Room Six, even to push a plate of bread through the portal in the door. 'You cannot starve the Devil,' said one, when I attempted to upbraid him. And who am I to lay blame? I'd sooner face the Zulu Nation at Rorke's Drift than approach that colony of hell."

"Come, come." Holmes was impatient. "Consider: If Smith's assertion is genuine, no door fashioned by the hand of man can hold him. His continued presence there is proof enough he's either mad or a charlatan."

"You don't know him, Mr. Holmes. We're just his playthings. It pleases him at present to remain where he is and turn brave men into cowards and good women into familiars. When he tires of that, he'll slither out through the bars and bid the maws of the underworld to open and swallow us all." His voice rose to a shrill cackle that cut off suddenly, as by the sheer will of whatever reason he retained within him.

I went into action without waiting for Holmes's signal. I forced Menitor into a chair with my hand on his shoulder, strode to the cabinet where he kept a flask of brandy, poured a generous draught into a glass, and commanded him to drink. He drank off half in one motion. It seemed to fortify him; he took another sip and set the glass on the corner of his desk. Colour climbed his sallow cheeks.

"Thank you, John. I apologise, Mr. Holmes. I don't mind telling you I've questioned my own rationality throughout this affair. It's more comforting to believe myself mad than to accept the only other explanation that suggests itself."

Holmes's cold tones were as bracing as the spirits. "Only the sane question their sanity, Doctor. Perhaps when this business is concluded, you will agree to collaborate with me on a monograph about the unstable nature of the criminal mind in general. Certainly only an irrational individual would consider committing a felony as long as Sherlock Holmes is in practice."

"Bless you, sir, for the attempt, but I fear I've passed the point where an amusing remark will lift the bleakness from my soul. Smith has taken the hindmost, and that unfortunate is I."

At that moment, the clock upon the mantel struck the hour of six. Menitor started, his eyes bulging from his head. "Six hours left!" he moaned. "He's pledged to quit this world at midnight, and that we shall all accompany him."

"I, for one, never embark upon a long voyage without first taking the measure of the captain," Holmes said. "Where is the key to Room Six?"

A great deal of persuasion—and another injection of brandy—was necessary before Dr. Menitor would part with the key to the room in which John Smith had been shut. He wore it, like the poetic albatross, on a cord round his neck. Holmes took it from his hand and instructed me to stay behind with Menitor.

"I'm going with you," I told Holmes. "We've faced every other devil together. Why not the Dark Lord himself?"

"Your other friend needs you more."

"He will sleep. I slipped a solution of morphine into his second drink." In fact, Menitor was already insensate in his chair, with a more peaceful expression upon his face than he had worn in days.

Holmes nodded curtly. "Then by all means, let us deal with the devil we don't know."

The criminal ward occupied most of the ancient keep, with Room Six at the top. Sturdy bars in the windows separated the occupant from a hundred-foot drop to the flags below. I had brought my old service revolver, and Holmes instructed me to stand back with it cocked and in hand as he turned the key in the lock.

This precaution proved unnecessary, as we found the patient seated peacefully upon the cot that represented the room's only furnishing. He was dressed neatly but simply in the patched clothing that had been donated to the hospital by the city's charitable institutions, and the shoes he'd worn when he was brought there—shiny black patent leathers to match the formal dress from which all the tailor's labels had been removed.

In appearance, there was little about John Smith to support his demonic claim. He was fair, with a windblown mop of blonde curls, moustaches in need of trimming, and a sprinkling of golden whiskers to attest to his three days without a razor. He was a dozen or so pounds overweight. I should have judged his age to be about thirty, and yet there was a quality in his eyes, which were large, and of the palest blue imaginable, that suggested the bleakness of an uninhabited room, as if he had witnessed more than one lifetime and remained unchanged. There was, too, an attitude of mockery in his smile, outwardly polite and welcoming, that seemed to reduce everything and everyone he turned it upon to insignificance. I do not know if it was these features or the man himself that filled me with such dread and loathing. I closed the door and stationed myself with my back to it, the revolver in my pocket now, but still cocked in my hand.

"Mr. Sherlock Holmes," he greeted in his soft, modulated voice, gentled further by a West End accent. "The engravings in the public journals do you little justice. You have the brow of a philosopher."

"Indeed? A late gentleman of my acquaintance once remarked that there was less frontal development than he'd expected."

"Dear Professor Moriarty. Thank you for that unexpected gift. I did not have him down for another decade when you pitched him over those falls."

Holmes was unimpressed by this intelligence; the story of his last meeting with that blackguardly academic was well known to readers of the account I had published in *The Strand Magazine*. "Shall I address you familiarly as Lucifer, or as Your Dark Majesty?" Holmes asked evenly. "I'm ignorant as to the protocol."

"Smith will do. I find it difficult to keep track of all my titles myself. How did you make out on that Milverton affair, by the way? The Dreyfuss business had me distracted."

Holmes hesitated at this, and I was hard put to disguise my astonishment. The case of the late blackmailer Charles Augustus Milverton had only recently been concluded, in a most shocking
fashion, and its circumstances enjoined me from reporting it publicly for an indefinite period. Holmes's involvement was unknown
even to Scotland Yard.

He changed the subject, dissembling his own thoughts on Smith's
sources. "I have come to ask you what was your motive in attempting
to destroy Tom Turner," said he. "I shan't accept that fable you told
Dr. Menitor."

Smith smiled. "I must have my amusements. Arranging wars and
corrupting governments requires close concentration over long
periods. You have your quaint chemical experiments to divert you
from your labours upon your clients' behalf; I have my pursuit of
unprepossessing souls. Exquisite miniatures, I call them. One day I
hope to show you my display."

"It's a pity Turner escaped your net."

"Fortunately, St. Porphyry's offers a variety of other possibilities."
The patient appeared unmoved by Holmes's thrust.

"So I am told. A career ruined, another besmirched, and a third
severely straitened. Will you add violent insurrection to your
exhibit?"

"Alas, there may not be time. I depart at midnight."

"Do you miss home so much?"

"I am not going home just yet. If Menitor gave you that impression, he misunderstood me. This has been a pleasant holiday, but
there is work for me in Whitehall and upon the Continent. Your Foreign Secretary shows indications of being entirely too reasonable at
Bloemfontein, and the Kaiser is far too comfortable with his
country's borders. Also, the Americans have grown complacent with
the indestructibility of her Presidents. A trip abroad may be war-
ranted. It isn't as if the situation at home will go to hell in my
absence." He chuckled.

"Blighter!" I could no longer restrain myself.

Smith turned that infernal smile upon me, and with it those
vacant, soulless eyes. "I congratulate you, Doctor. In matters of

detective science you remain Holmes's trained baboon, but as a master of classic British understatement you have no peer."

"Your own grasp of the obvious comes close," Holmes observed. "How pedestrian that you should choose this of all nights to plan your escape."

"It's hardly an escape. It's pleased me to have stayed this long in residence. *Walpurgisnacht,* that brief excursion when the dead walk and witches convene, has a paralysing effect upon those who still credit it. However, it requires renewal from time to time. Perhaps after tonight, you will believe as well."

Holmes made a little bow. "I accept the challenge, Mr. Smith. We shall return at midnight."

"I shall look forward to it, Mr. Holmes."

Once outside the room, Holmes locked the door and led me down the first flight of stairs, a finger to his lips. On the landing he stopped. "We are out of his earshot now, Watson. What is your opinion?"

"I don't trust him, Holmes. Whatever devilry he has planned won't wait till midnight."

"I don't agree. In his way he considers himself an honourable fellow. Tricksters never cheat. It robs them of their triumph."

"However did he know about the Milverton case?"

"That was a bit of a knock up, was it not? Milverton may have had a partner after all—either Smith or one he's been in communication with. Smuggled intelligence is a parlor trick. Mind-readers and spiritualists have been using it for years. We shall ask him after the stroke of midnight. How long will Menitor sleep?"

"Until early morning, I should say."

"While he is incommoded, you are St. Poor's ranking medical authority. I advise you to place a guard upon Smith's door and another outside, at the base of the tower. I suspect our friend is too enamoured of his confidence skills to attempt anything so vulgar as an escape by force or an assault upon the bars of his window, to say nothing of the precipitous drop that awaits; still, one cannot be too careful. While we are waiting, I suggest we avail ourselves of the comforts of that public-house you mentioned earlier." Holmes's expression was eager. It carried no hint of the irritable ennui he had worn to my consulting room.

"YOU MUST THINK of it as if you'd borrowed from our century, and must repay the full amount," Holmes explained. "You would not return ninety-nine guineas and imagine that you had discharged your debt of one hundred. Therefore, you cannot consider that the twentieth century has begun until nineteen hundred has come and gone."

We had enjoyed a meal of bangers-and-mash at our corner table, and were now relaxing over whiskies and soda. Holmes had refused to discuss Smith since we had entered the public house.

"I understand it now that you have explained it," said I, "but I doubt your example will prevent all London from attending the pyrotechnics display over the Thames next January."

"Appearances are clever liars, much like friend Smith."

I saw then that he was ready to return to the subject of our visit to Battersea.

"Is it your theory, then, that he is posing as a madman?"

"I have not made up my mind. Madmen lie better than most, for they manage to convince themselves as well as their listeners. If he is posing, we shall know once midnight has passed and he is still in residence. A lunatic, once confronted with the evidence of his delusion, either becomes depressed or substitutes another for the one that has betrayed him. A liar attempts to explain it away. Conventional liars are invariably rational."

"But what is Smith's motive?"

"That remains to be seen. He may be acting in concert with an accomplice, distracting me from some other crime committed somewhere far away from this place to which we've been decoyed. I think that more likely than Smith enjoying making mischief and laying the guilt at Satan's door; in any case, that's what I hope. Any unscrupulous minister is capable of the latter. I am no connoisseur of the ordinary."

"What do you think he meant when he spoke of Africa and Germany and America?"

"If I were Beelzebub, or pretending to be, I couldn't think of better places for mischief."

The publican, a narrow, rat-faced fellow, looking just the sort who would purchase provisions from a hospital orderly with no questions asked, announced that the establishment was closing in a quarter of an hour.

"What need for watches, when we have merchants?" Holmes enquired. "Shall we watch the patient in Room Six unfold his leathery wings and fly to the sound of mortals in torment?"

AT THE DOOR the orderly, who was built along the lines of a prize-fighter and held his truncheon as if it were an extension of his right arm, reported that all was quiet. Holmes unlocked the door, I gripped my revolver, and we rejoined Smith, who apparently had not moved in our absence. He sat with his hands resting on his thighs and his mocking smile in place.

"How was the service?" he asked.

Holmes was unshaken by this assumption of our recent where-abouts. "You're inconsistent. If you indeed saw into our minds, you would know the answer to your question."

"You confuse me with my former Master. I am not omniscient."

"In that case, the service was indifferent, but the fare above the average. We would have brought you a sample, but it might slow your flight."

Smith chuckled once more, in a way that chilled me to the bone.

"I shall miss you, Holmes. I am sorry my holiday can't be extended. I should have admired to snare your soul. I could build a new display with it as the centre piece."

"You exalt me, Smith. Dr. Watson is the better catch. He has the fairest soul in all of England, and the noblest heart."

Smith stroked his chin thoughtfully, as if he expected to find a spade-shaped beard there. "I shall not be gone forever. If I return in a year, will you wager your friend's fair soul that I cannot vanquish you in a game of wits?"

"Twaddle!" I exclaimed, and looked to Holmes for support. But his reaction surprised and unnerved me. When he was amused, his own cold chuckle was nearly a match for Smith's. Instead, he appeared to grow a shade more pale, and raised a stubborn chin.

"You will forgive me if I decline the invitation," said he simply.

Smith shrugged. "It is one minute to midnight."

"You have no watch," I said.

"I told the time before there were clocks and watches."

I groped for the watch in my pocket, eager to prove him wrong, if only by seconds. Holmes stopped me with a nearly infinitesimal shake of his head. His eyes remained upon Smith. My hand tightened on the revolver in my pocket.

The first throb of Big Ben's iron bell penetrated the keep's thick wall.

We three remained absolutely motionless through those that followed. As the last chime tolled, John Smith turned his bland, evil smile upon us both, and lowered his chin to his chest.

That final solemn bong seemed, to reverberate long after it had passed. Silence followed, as complete as the grave.

"Right." Holmes stirred. "Wake up, Smith. St. Walporgis has fled, and you are still here."

Smith raised his head. Relief swept through me. I relaxed my grip upon my weapon.

The man seated on the cot blinked, looked around. "What is this place?" His gaze fell upon Holmes. "Who the devil are you?"

To this day, I still cannot encompass the change that took place in the man we knew as John Smith after Big Ben had finished its report. He was still the same figure, fair and blue-eyed and inclining toward stoutness, but the mocking smile had vanished and his eyes had become expressive, as if whoever had decamped from the room beyond had returned. Most unsettling of all, his upper-class British accent was gone, replaced by the somewhat nasal tones of an American of English stock.

"Stop staring at me, you clods, and tell me where you've taken me. Where are my clothes? By God, you'll answer to Lord Battlebroke before this day is out. He's expecting me for dinner."

The young man's story would not be shaken, even when Holmes admitted failure and sent for Inspector Lestrade, whose brutish technique for obtaining confessions made up to a great extent for his shortcomings as a practical investigator. It was eventually corroborated when Lord Battlebroke himself was summoned and confirmed the young man's identity as Jeffrey Vestle, son of the Boston industrialist Cornelius Vestle, who had dispatched him to London to request the hand of his lordship's daughter in marriage and merge their American fortune with noble blood. Young Vestle had failed to keep a dinner appointment three days before, and the police had been combing the charitable hospitals and mortuaries to determine whether he'd come to misfortune; private hospitals and lunatic asylums were at the bottom of their list.

Lestrade, in conference with Holmes and me in Dr. Menitor's consulting room, was shamefaced. "I daresay you have the advantage of me this one time, Mr. Holmes. I didn't recognise the fellow from the description."

Holmes was grave. "You won't hear it from me, Inspector. When the first stone is cast, you will not be the one it strikes."

Lestrade thanked him, although it was clear he knew not what to make of the remark, or of the grim humour in which it was delivered.

The mystery of the Devil of St. Porphyry's Hospital is a first in that I was Holmes's client, but it is a first also in that I have chosen to place it before the public without a solution. Dr. Menitor was satisfied, for with the departure of "John Smith" exited also the curse that seemed to have befallen his institution. Menitor erased the mark from Nurse Brant's record and reinstated the temporarily larcenous orderly—assigning their lapses to strain connected with overwork, as he had dismissed his own emotional crisis—and thanked Holmes and me profusely for our intervention. Holmes himself never refers to the case, except to hold it up as an example of *amnesia dysplasia*, a temporary loss of identity on young Vestle's part, complicated by dementia, and brought on by stress, possibly related to his forthcoming nuptials.

"I might, in his place, have been stricken similarly," he says. "I met Lady Battlebroke," but the humour rings hollow.

Holmes considers his role in the mystery that of a passive observer, and therefore not one of his successes. In this I am inclined to agree, but for a different reason.

I do not know that "John Smith" was the Devil having let Jeffrey Vestle's body for a brief holiday from his busy schedule; I do not know that Holmes's scientific explanation for the phenomenon—in which, I am bound to say, Dr. Menitor concurred—is not the correct one. I fervently hope it is. However, it does not explain how Smith/Vestle knew of the Milverton business, cloaked in secrecy as it was by the only two people who could give evidence. At the time of that affair, the young Bostonian was three thousand miles away in Massachusetts, and in no position to connect himself with either Milverton or his fate. I am at a loss to supply such a connection, and too sensitive of Holmes's avoidance of the issue to bring it up.

Lack of evidence is not evidence, and such evidence as I possess is at best circumstantial. Within months of Smith's leaving Vestle's body, the Bloemfontein Conference in South Africa came to grief over the British Foreign Secretary's refusal to back away from his political position and an ultimatum from Paul Krueger, precipitating our nation into a long and tragic armed conflict with the Boers. Less than two years later, on September 6, 1901, William McKinley, the American president, was fatally shot by a lone assassin in Buffalo, New York; and all the world knows what happened in August 1914, when Kaiser Wilhelm II invaded France, violating Belgium's neutrality and bringing Germany to war with England, and eventually to the world. That prediction of Smith's took longer to become reality, but its effects will be with us for another century at least.

Regardless of whether Sherlock Holmes sparred with the Devil or of whether the Devil exists, I know there is evil in our world. I know, too, that there is great good, and I found myself in the presence of both in Room Six at St. Poor's. For one fleeting moment, my friend put aside his pragmatic convictions and refused, even in jest, to gamble with Satan over my soul. I say again that he was the best and the wisest man I have ever known, and I challenge you, the reader, to suggest one better and wiser.

THE ADVENTURE OF
THE LIBRARIAN'S GHOST

Jon L. Breen

T HOUGH OSTENSIBLY RETIRED to a cottage on the Sussex
Downs and a quiet life of bee-keeping, my friend Sherlock
Holmes was periodically lured back to London in the first decade of
the twentieth century, sometimes in his role as consulting detective.
On some occasions, fewer than I might have liked, I was honored to
take up my old duties as his associate and chronicler. It was on a
rainy morning in the late autumn of 1909 that Holmes unexpectedly
appeared at my door and asked me to accompany him to one of
London's most exclusive private clubs for an interview with a
baronet. With my long-suffering wife's kind indulgence, I agreed.

When we had stated our business at the Preservation Club's
reception desk, an elderly servant led us through a maze of corridors to a small but comfortably furnished sitting room where Sir
Richard Bootcrafter awaited us. He was familiar to me through newspaper accounts as a plainspoken, constantly quoted, frequently witty
Member of Parliament. A tall, jovial, distinguished-looking man of
middle years with a well-trimmed grey moustache and keen blue
eyes, he greeted us with a politician's firm handshake, apologies for
asking us to brave the streets in such weather, and assurances that,
in this part of the Club at least, quiet conversation was permitted.

When we were all seated in plush armchairs with drinks at our elbows, Sir Richard began his story. Though clearly troubled, he clung tenaciously to a jocular manner.

"Mr. Holmes, Dr. Watson, let me put it simply. I am haunted by the family ghost. After lo these many years, he's back again."

Holmes raised an eyebrow but said nothing.

Sir Richard looked at him for a moment with pursed lips, then said, "No, not really *again*. At least not in *my* experience. Hang it all, not in anybody's experience. There are no ghosts, and there is no family ghost, but you see, a house as old and grand as mine is meant to have one. Therefore, some creative and accommodating relative generations back invented one for us. No idea which ancestor did the deed, probably some mischievous uncle who wanted to amuse and mildly frighten the children. There's no ghost, Mr. Holmes, no indeed." Sir Richard paused, took a swallow of his whisky, and resumed. "But then again, it seems there is." He ran his hand through his thick greying hair. "Why do I babble so? When I rise to speak in the Commons, I am known for my pithiness and organization as much as my oratorical skills, but on this matter . . . ."

"Perhaps I might suggest an outline for you, Sir Richard," Holmes offered. "First, give us the history of the fictitious family ghost. Then, tell us about its current manifestation."

"A sound plan." Sir Richard cleared his throat, as if to help him simulate his platform manner. "Bootcrafter Hall, my country house, is one of the most beautiful in all of England. In that, I flatter not myself but my ancestors. For centuries, they have been bringing to perfection the gardens, the furnishings, and the art collection, maintaining the charm of the place while judiciously adding modern conveniences as they become available. Of all the house's features, I believe my family is proudest of our library. Certainly, I am. It contains one of the finest private collections in all of England, and generation after generation of my family have made constant efforts to keep it that way. Its greatest strength is in historical and political subjects, as you might imagine, but it also covers the arts, the sciences, and every imaginable aspect of human endeavour."

"And does your ghost have something to do with the library?" Holmes prodded.

"It does, or he does—I'm not sure which designation is proper. Family folklore claims we are periodically haunted by the shade of one Chauncey Stocker, who, though not a member of the family, was the individual most responsible for establishing and building our library. He was initially employed by my ancestor Sir Edgar Boot-crafter some two hundred years ago. Truthfully, old Edgar cared nothing whatever for books and reading, being more inclined to the hunt and other country pursuits. But he charged his librarian with filling the floor-to-ceiling shelves with whatever ornate spines were most pleasing to the eye and suitable to the décor of the room. Edgar had no notion, you must realize, of ever taking a book down from the shelf and perusing its contents.

"When Edgar died in a fall from a horse, his son William inherited his title and fortune. William, in contrast to his father, was well read and politically astute. He admired Chauncey's careful selection of books and was even more impressed with his knowledge of their contents. Ask Chauncey a question of political thinking or strategy, and he could find the proper theory, sentiment, or fact on those shelves at a moment's notice. William encouraged him by doubling the library's annual budget.

"Tragically, William died young, his heart giving out at the end of a spirited speech in Parliament, and his younger brother Gavin, a much less impressive twig on the Bootcrafter family tree, took over. Gavin resented the money Chauncey Stocker was spending, and frankly hated the man. He surely would have fired Chauncey had not the rest of the family loved him so.

"One morning, Chauncey was found dead on the library floor, apparently after a fall from a high ladder. He had bled profusely from a wound to his head, which he had struck on a table. A copy of Plato's *Republic*, which he had been either taking down or replacing at the time of his fall, lay next to the body, sadly stained by the flow of blood from his wound. According to some family historians, Gavin had murdered him, but he was never charged, and I have never believed his motive could have been sufficient for such an act.

In all likelihood it was an accident, but of course when enough generations have passed since the event, murder makes a better story.

"Anyway, that much is fact. On to the ghost story. I don't know when it entered the family legend, but I surely wish it had not. Supposedly, whenever there is political turmoil in the land the ghost of Chauncey Stocker walks."

"He must do a deal of walking," I ventured.

Sir Richard smiled. "One would think he'd never rest, Dr. Watson. In any case, the story goes that the sound of heavily pacing footfalls would be heard coming from the library late at night, though of course if anyone came to investigate, no one would be seen. Sometime in his nocturnal pacing, however, the ghost would remove from the shelf, often violently, a book that was relevant to whatever political controversy was currently in the forefront. Often he would helpfully leave it open to a page on which he, in his supernatural wisdom, believed a solution could be found to sorting out the American colonies, or whatever the immediate problem was. According to some of the tales, he would circle or underline passages in red—red ink in some accounts, blood in others—depending on the sensitivity of the particular uncle telling the story. Often, but not always, the book selected would be that same copy of Plato's *Republic* he had been perusing at the time of his death. His other favourites were the philosophy of Aristotle and in later years, Gibbon's *Decline and Fall of the Roman Empire*.

"Over the years, the stories of his appearances would be told and retold. Dramatic details would be added to each telling. But no one ever claimed to have observed one of these manifestations firsthand, and there was no solid evidence any of them had actually happened. One might also wonder why one who revered books as Chauncey did would treat them so shabbily, throwing them about the room and defacing their pages with red fluid."

"The Plato was already damaged," I pointed out.

"True, but he did not stop at Plato. Or so goes the legend."

"I gather no such defaced books are extant?" Holmes said.

"Certainly not. None of the library's copies of Aristotle or Gibbon has any evidence of red marks or rough handling. And that copy of

Plato, assuming it actually existed, is no longer to be found. Actually, I once told the story of the family ghost to a collector of books on the occult, and he said he would pay a handsome price for that bloodied Plato. If I ever found it, I'd certainly sell it to him, especially after the annoyance that blasted legend is causing me. But then, maybe the bloodstains magically vanished. Some inventive adherents of our ghost story have claimed that Chauncey used ghost ink or ghost blood, which disappeared from the books whenever the particular political crisis had passed." Sir Richard shook his head and sighed. "No, gentlemen, it was all a joke. I always knew that, even as a child. Now, you must realize no one appreciates a good joke more than I. Indeed, some of my colleagues in Parliament find me excessively given to unseemly humor. But what has happened in the past few weeks—well, I daresay it may be a joke, most likely is, but I am well past the point of finding it amusing."

"Go on," Holmes said.

Sir Richard had paused. He seemed embarrassed but continued. "I myself have heard footsteps coming from the library on several nights. I have looked and found no one there. It seems impossible."

"Does this library not have more than one door?" Holmes asked.

"Three, actually."

"So a flesh and blood person impersonating a ghost could leave by one door as you enter by another."

"Yes, that is true, if they were quick. And there's a fourth possibility. Apart from the three conventional doors, one section of bookshelves swings about on a turntable to allow a secret entry from the kitchen downstairs. It was my ancestor Sir Edgar's invention for the convenience of the servants, though I can't think it appealed to Chauncey Stocker."

"Do the members of your household know about this secret entrance?"

"As far as I know, only the butler, Priam. It's an amusing story, actually. One afternoon some years ago when I was reading in the library, Priam came silently through the secret door, which I had never known about and which had not been used in years, to serve me a drink. I must have leapt thirty feet in the air. I found the incident and my discomfiture laughable afterwards, but Priam was so mortified at having startled me he swore he would never use that secret entry again. To my knowledge, he has not, nor has any other servant."

"Could this butler be your mysterious ghost?" I offered.

Sir Richard shook his head. "Unthinkable. He's been with the family for many years and would never do anything to embarrass us."

"Forgive me, Sir Richard," Holmes said, "but given all those modes of entry and egress, your use of the term *impossible* seems too strong."

"But I didn't mean physically impossible. I meant—I don't know—spiritually impossible. Impossible that the ghost should actually exist, certainly, and more to the point, impossible that anyone in my household, whether family or servant, should be doing this to me."

"Is this ghost offering political advice?" Holmes asked.

"If he is, I don't understand what it is. The first time I heard the mysterious footsteps was about a fortnight ago, when all the household had retired for the night. I investigated, found no one, frankly thought nothing of it, and went back to bed. In the morning, however, I entered the library to find that a world atlas was lying in the middle of the floor. The corners of its binding had been battered and some pages creased. It looked as if it had been thrown from the shelf by someone enraged. It lay open to a map of the world on which New Zealand had been circled."

"The North or the South Island?" I inquired.

"One big circle around both."

"In red?"

"Certainly. Since then there have been four more instances of mysterious footsteps in the night, never on consecutive nights, always with a night or two between. When I've investigated, whoever is doing it has eluded me."

"Have others in the house heard these noises?" Holmes asked.

"Oh, yes. I assure you I am not going mad, Mr. Holmes. Or if I am, I'm not going alone. Both my daughters have reported hearing the footsteps, as have some of the servants. Each time our ghost walked, I found a book on the floor the next morning. The second instance involved that same world atlas, except that this time it was open to a map of the United States of America with the State of

Wyoming circled in red. The third time, that poor atlas suffered yet another indignity and lay open to a map of Australia with the small State of Western Australia circled."

"And I daresay these red marks proved indelible?" Holmes suggested.

"They did, I'm sorry to say," Sir Richard replied with a faint smile.

"I believe I should put that atlas under lock and key," I said.

"I did remove it, Dr. Watson, and on the next manifestation, the ghost's vehicle of communication changed. A copy of *Through the Looking Glass* lay on the floor. This book and Lewis Carroll's other whimsical works were particular favorites of my late wife. We accumulated a variety of editions, some quite valuable. My younger daughter and I were most upset to see this one damaged."

"Was there something unique about this particular edition?" Holmes asked.

"It is far from the rarest, I'm thankful to say, but it was the first American edition of the book, published by Lee and Shephard in Boston in 1872. It is the only American edition we own."

"I believe Lewis Carroll was the pen name of Dr. Charles Ludwig Dodgson, the mathematician," I offered.

"Yes, that's correct," said Sir Richard absently.

"I recall he had a strong interest in the occult and spiritualism in the latter part of his life."

"Most interesting, Watson," Holmes said, "though probably quite irrelevant to our enquiries."

"Possibly so," I said, somewhat deflated.

"And was something circled in red in this copy of *Through the Looking Glass*?" Holmes asked.

"Yes," Sir Richard replied, "a passage of text early in the book. I believe I can quote it from memory. Alice is speaking to her cat." The baronet closed his eyes, cleared his throat, and recited, " 'Oh, Kitty, how nice it would be if we could only get through into Looking Glass House! I'm sure it's got, oh!, such beautiful things in it! Let's pretend there's a way of getting through into it, somehow, Kitty.' " He opened his eyes and added somewhat sheepishly, "No political significance I can gather from that. Can you, gentlemen?"

I shook my head. Holmes said nothing.

"After that incident," Sir Richard continued, "I took to locking up some of the most valuable first editions in a safe, but one can't lock up the whole library."

"Was that the most recent incident?" Holmes asked.

"No. The fifth instance occurred just two nights ago. This time, on entering the library in the morning I found on the floor a racing calendar, with the date and conditions of that year's Derby circled."

"For what year?" I asked.

"It was 1896, I believe, but I can't imagine how the date could be significant. The turf has not been one of our collecting interests, and the book is the only racing calendar in our library. I'm not even sure how we happen to own it. What can it mean?"

"You said the librarian's ghost was a joke to begin with," I ventured, determined to offer something helpful. "Someone in your household is merely continuing the joke. Apart from damage to the books, there seems to be little harm done."

"But, why, Dr. Watson? Why? Where is the point? My family and my servants all know that my patience on this matter is running thin. And anyway, no one in my household is given to such jokes." He paused in thought. "Well, with the possible exception of my younger brother Reggie. Never know what that idler might come up with. And my son Gilbert, who is entirely too much under his uncle's influence. But neither of them was present for all of the, er, manifestations."

"And who *was* present for all of them?" Holmes asked.

"Only my two daughters. Caroline, the elder, is frankly too much preoccupied with her social position and her young friends to enter into even such a marginally intellectual activity as throwing books about. Daphne, the younger, is more intelligent but far too proper and considerate of her family to do anything like this. To be truthful, she is so meek and retiring I sometimes worry about her. In any case, the last thing she would ever damage is one of our Lewis Carroll editions."

"And the servants?"

"No, no, I cannot believe it. Most have been with the family for a long time, and the younger ones are under far too close a watch to have the opportunity for such mischief. Priam and my housekeeper, Mrs. Crandall, control their staff, I assure you."

"Sir Richard, I believe it will be necessary for Dr. Watson and myself to visit your house, examine the library, and speak with the members of your household. Is that acceptable to you?"

"Certainly. I'll instruct them to give you every cooperation."

"Perhaps we shall have to spend a night in the library, eh, Holmes?" I offered.

The look Holmes gave me was unnecessarily scornful. "If we truly expected a ghost, Watson, that course would be brave, though foolhardy. But as we all agree this is not a wisp of ectoplasm but a flesh and blood trickster, such a plan would only guarantee the supposed ghost would not appear."

"Quite right," I muttered, somewhat abashed but unable to counter his reasoning.

Thus it was we found ourselves the following weekend in the Bootcrafter library, a massive room stacked floor to ceiling with books, their multicolored spines ranging from contemporary and drab to historic and ornate, serviced by a moveable ladder on each wall. It was as magnificent a collection, in as richly appointed a setting, as I could have imagined. The range of subjects represented, including some rare medical references, amazed me. I could have spent hours browsing on the shelves or reading in one of the comfortable armchairs, but we had more serious business.

After quietly demonstrating the secret entry point, located behind matched sets of Dickens and Trollope and deployed by a button under one of the shelves, Sir Richard showed us the damaged books, which Holmes examined closely. Then the baronet said, "Now you'll want to interview the principal servants and the family. If you don't mind, I'll bring you the servants first. They, after all, have work to do, and, though it pains me to say it, it will in no way detract from any useful activity for my brother and children to wait a bit longer."

When Priam and Mrs. Crandall entered the room, I noticed that the butler had a bandage on his right hand. Both servants agreed that they had heard the footsteps in the library on the nights in question, but merely assumed they were made by some member of the family. It was not their place to investigate, except when asked to do so by Sir Richard. On the occasions when that occurred, they were able to discover nothing helpful. When Holmes brought up the secret doorway, Priam kept his proper and respectful mask, but the way the veins in his neck stood out revealed it was a sore point with him.

"That means of entry is never used, Mr. Holmes," Priam said.

"*Could* it be used?"

"By a maid or footman who no longer desired continued employment in this house, certainly. That is, if they knew it was there, which to the best of my knowledge, they do not."

"But you knew, Mrs. Crandall?" Holmes asked, turning to the housekeeper.

"I knew, yes, indeed, and many's the time it could have come in most handy for serving." In response to a hard look from the butler, she added, "But of course, I told no one of its existence. Priam makes the rules below stairs. I don't have a vote."

Priam stiffened at the impertinence but said nothing. I suspected their colloquy would be a lively one when they left our company.

Holmes continued to question them about the particular incidents, but to no enlightenment I could discern. When Priam and Mrs. Crandall had been dismissed, Sir Richard left us to gather his family members "from their various idle pursuits," as he put it.

When Sir Richard had left the room, I murmured to Holmes, "That bandage on the butler's hand, Holmes. Could it mean something?"

"If you're thinking the marks in the books were made in blood, Watson, save that kind of dramatics for *The Strand Magazine.* The marks were made in red ink."

"Couldn't the butler's bandage have some other significance?" I said.

"Possibly. What other significance were you attributing to it?

It was just as well Sir Richard returned then with the other members of his family, for I did not have an answer.

Reggie Bootcrafter, the younger brother, and Gilbert, the son, resembled each other in their dandified dress and insistent insouciance more than either of them resembled Sir Richard. They proved to be as facetious and irresponsible as we'd been led to expect and, in their tiresome banter and wordplay, clearly believed themselves as amusing as characters in a West End farce.

"This is the library, Gilbert," Reggie said. "Jolly fine lot of dusty old tomes, what?"

"I *have* been here before, Uncle," Gilbert replied. "Last Christmas, I believe. Had a look at one of Dickens's ghost stories. Believe Father must have as well, eh?"

Sir Richard made a face, and his younger brother mimicked it. "I fear you're a terrible disappointment to your family, Gilbert," Reggie said with mock solemnity.

"They call me feckless, don't they, Uncle Reggie?" Gilbert said.

"That they do, Gilbert."

"And it's true, I am totally without feck!"

Holmes managed to question them about what they had heard on the nights in question. Reggie had been present on three of the occasions, Gilbert on the other two. Both swore they were sound sleepers but on at least one occasion each had been awakened, though not by the ghost.

"But by the time old Chauncey had his third go at the world atlas," Gilbert said aggrievedly, "Father made more noise than any ghost rousing the whole household."

"Do you believe in the ghost, Gilbert?" his uncle asked.

"Oh, but I must. When I take my place in the family seat in Parliament, I shall need old Chauncey to give me proper instruction, won't I?"

The pair obviously had nothing of value to tell us, and Holmes soon turned to the two daughters. Only the elder, Caroline, had appeared at all amused by her brother and uncle. She seemed a charming but quite empty-headed beauty. The younger daughter, Daphne, could not have been more different. She was painfully shy, and when she spoke, her voice was almost inaudible. Both daughters verified that they had been home on all five occasions that the ghost had done his work.

"How odd, really," said Caroline, "that I should have been there every time the supposed ghost appeared. I am so often away on overnight or weekend visits to family or friends."

"And did you hear the footsteps?" Holmes asked.

"Several times. My bedroom is situated directly above the library, and I sleep much more lightly than my brother or uncle." She looked their way with a dazzling smile. "Perhaps if I were allowed to join them in their after-dinner port, I, too, could sleep through any-thing short of Father shouting."

"Did you ever go to investigate?"

"Certainly not. I thought it was Father at first, until he began roaring the whole house awake and demanding answers. And if I did think it was a ghost, or some burglar up to mischief, I would be foolish to leave my room, would I not?"

Holmes turned to the younger sister. "Miss Daphne, you also were present every time the supposed ghost appeared. Was that also unusual?"

Caroline answered before her sister had the chance. "Daphne never leaves the house, Mr. Holmes," she said, almost with a note of accusation. "She never sees the sunlight."

"My sister exaggerates," Daphne said softly. "Three afternoons a week Aunt Clarissa sends her coach for me, and I travel to London so that she can give me my piano lessons."

"Aunt Clarissa!" Caroline said with a note of exasperation. "You sit alone in a coach to be transported from one dimly-lit, depressing room to another. You must get out into society, my dear girl. You mustn't think I fear the competition." The older sister's brilliant smile underlined the foolishness of such an idea.

Holmes's further questioning added nothing important that I could see, but when we left Bootcrafter Hall, I had some ideas of my own and was eager to discuss the case on the return train to London.

"I think the brother and the uncle are in it together, Holmes," I suggested. "They seem to spend a good deal of time in each other's company, and yet on the occasions the ghost appeared, there was always one of them in residence, but not the other. It looks to me a clear attempt to provide themselves with mutual alibis, does it not?"

Holmes merely grunted and said nothing of consequence for the

rest of the journey. I was more than a bit annoyed at his secretiveness. When we debarked at Victoria Station, he thanked me for
accompanying him but said the rest of his enquiries in the Bootcrafter matter were best pursued alone.

"In some outlandish disguise, no doubt," I said, somewhat ill-
temperedly.

Sensing my displeasure at his rejection, Holmes decided to throw
me a small bone to chew on. "Watson have you not discerned the
political issue on which the purported ghost wished to influence Sir
Richard?"

"No, Holmes, I confess it is no clearer than it was at the beginning."

"Then I suggest you carefully read your newspaper. And when it
is time to return to Bootcrafter Hall and give Sir Richard my conclusions, I hope you can again accompany me."

"If I can be of some use, certainly," I said, only slightly mollified.

AFTER A FORTNIGHT had passed, during which my perusal of the
political columns had made me none the wiser, the baronet again
received us in his library. I was almost as anxious as Sir Richard himself to hear Holmes's account, and was equally startled at what
seemed to be an irrelevant question.

"Tell us, Sir Richard, what is your opinion of the suffragette
movement?"

"My opinion of—Mr. Holmes, what does that have to do with the
matter at hand?"

"Perhaps nothing, and perhaps a great deal. Do you have a position on the question of votes for women?"

"I do, and it is well known. I respect and revere the gentle sex
too much to give them the vote. Placing them on the same plane
as men to whom they are, quite frankly, utterly superior in many
ways, would be bad for them, bad for us, bad for the nation, and
bad for the empire. Those rare women with definite political views
can and do influence their husbands' votes, and to give them their
own vote would be tantamount to doubling their franchise. That
great majority of women who are unconcerned with politics could
easily be misled by demagogues. As for the suffragettes, they are

tragically misguided. It pains me as a gentleman to see them jailed, to see them embark on hunger strikes, necessitating forced feeding. All most unpleasant, but, unhappily, they have made it necessary by their ill-considered actions. That is my opinion. My late wife shared it, I might add, and I'm pleased to say my daughters do as well. Now why, Mr. Holmes, do you bring up this irrelevant matter?"

"Votes for women, Sir Richard, constitute the very topic on which your ghost wishes to advise you."

"And how, pray tell, do you come to that conclusion?"

"The indications were there for anyone familiar with the world-wide movement for women's suffrage. First consider the geographic clues from your much-battered world atlas. The purported ghost circled New Zealand, one of the first countries to give votes to women; then Wyoming, the first of the United States to grant women the franchise; finally, Western Australia, one of two small states in that Commonwealth that extended the vote to women."

"Most unconvincing, Mr. Holmes. What about *Through the Looking Glass*? Where is the suffragette connection there? Was Lewis Carroll a proponent of votes for women? I seriously doubt it."

"Perhaps I can answer that, Father," said a faint voice from across the room. Sir Richard looked up with a start. The slight form of his younger daughter, Miss Daphne Bootcrafter, had appeared in the library, not by way of one of the three conventional doors but through the rotating section of shelves.

"Didn't you know about this means of access, Father?" she asked in response to his look of surprise. "The servants used to use it. There's a stairway to the kitchen—"

"Certainly I knew about it," Sir Richard snapped. "But I didn't realize you did. What is it, Daphne? We're discussing important matters here."

"Too important for a mere woman?" Her manner was timid as ever and her voice almost inaudible, but a crack of thunder could not have shocked her father more than those words.

"Do I gather you're the ghost?" Sir Richard asked after a moment, with his usual strained effort at jocularity.

Miss Daphne smiled and turned to Holmes. "I knew you would read the clues properly, Mr. Holmes. I am surprised that Father could not. You know why I chose the book I did?"

"You chose, from all the variant editions available in this room, the American edition of Lewis Carroll's sequel to *Alice in Wonderland*, a book which chronicles the further adventures of Alice. Among the women prominent in recent suffragette demonstrations is a young American woman named Alice Paul. It is not unreasonable to suppose the clue referred to her."

Miss Daphne nodded serenely. "They have not been so militant in America as my brave sisters here. But they will be, I think."

The baronet shook his head, as if to clear away cobwebs. "What— what is the meaning of this? Daphne, you are not a suffragette. Your mother would be ashamed."

"Not if she truly understood."

"Perhaps you will explain the meaning of the passage from *Through the Looking Glass* that was circled in red, Miss Bootcrafter?" Holmes suggested.

"Is that not what we women do, Mr. Holmes?" she asked softly, with the faintest smile. "Look in the looking glass? But I don't mean only to admire ourselves or to adjust our clothing or straighten our hair or consider the effect of our appearance on men, or on other women. I mean something a bit more than that." Her voice was gathering strength. "Do not women look into the looking glass and see, as Alice does in Lewis Carroll's story, another world? Oh, it is a world that looks the same as ours, contains the same furniture and the same pictures on the wall with the same faithful dog curled up by the fire, but we imagine it is somehow not the same. Indeed, we know very well it is not the same. Things are turned backwards, certainly, but the difference is more than that. You and I may occupy the same room, Father, breathe the same air, share the same family memories, have access to the same old tomes. But my room is not the same as your room. Your room is part of the world of men, Father, the world of men's privilege, the world where every object is the same, but your power over it, your power over yourself, your control over your own destiny is increased by the simple fact of your masculine gender. Women have looked through that looking glass too long, Father, and if we must, we shall break it to get what we demand, what we deserve, what is our birthright as God's creatures."

These last statements were made so fiercely, so loudly, with such an unaccustomed light in his daughter's eyes, that Sir Richard now took a step backward as if from a blow.

"Madness," he said almost inaudibly. "My daughter is mad." Having seen her unsettling transformation, I silently agreed.

"No, I am not mad, Father," she said more quietly, "though it suits you to think so. Angry, yes, determined, yes, ready to leave your house and take my proper place among my sisters, yes, not as an anonymous orator but as a full-scale fighter in the battle for women's rights. Do I long to be arrested? No. Do I want to be jailed? No. Do I pine after the hideous experience of being force-fed? No. But do I want to live one more day, one more hour before that mocking looking glass? No, no, no, a thousand times no!"

Her voice was strong, but not shrill or hysterical. She was not mad, I decided. Misled, perhaps, wrong, certainly, but not mad. I determined to ask my wife's opinion when we returned to London. And then again, perhaps not.

"Sir Richard," Sherlock Holmes said, "when I left this house a fortnight ago, I had some small inkling of what the messages from your family ghost might mean. I began to follow the activities of the suffragettes. I also visited the home of your sister-in-law, Clarissa Helmsworth. You are probably unaware that she is a covert supporter of the women's suffrage cause. I soon learned that on those days your daughter was transported to her aunt's house, it was not for piano lessons."

The baronet looked at his daughter, puzzlement on his face. "It was not?"

"I cannot play a note, Father," she said with quiet pride.

"Clarissa Helmsworth enlisted your daughter as an active member of the suffragette movement under a second identity. When she takes on this identity, she is especially gifted in speaking for the cause. Indeed, in the grip of her oratory, her whole personality changes to the extent that someone who knew her might be slow even to recognise her. This is not so unusual, Sir Richard. I have known actors who are quiet, reserved, even depressed in their everyday life, but become galvanized when they set foot on the stage. Your daughter is a natural orator, and valued as such by her fellow advocates of the suffrage cause."

"I could speak my mind before anonymous crowds," Daphne said, "but not in this house. Never in this house. Women do not speak in this house."

"Women speak constantly in this house," Sir Richard retorted, with a vestige of his customary humour.

"Not about anything that matters, Father."

"No," said Holmes, "here you remained a child, so oppressed by your outgoing siblings and the forceful personality of your father that you remained unable to speak your mind. The only way she saw to make her views known to you, Sir Richard, and even then indirectly, was through a resuscitation of the family ghost."

"The only way until now, Mr. Holmes," Daphne Bootcrafter said.

Her father was speechless for a moment. He seemed smaller somehow, drawn into himself. It was as if father and daughter had exchanged both roles and personalities before our very eyes. At that point, none of us had any idea what he would say, what he would do, or even how he would vote in future considerations of women's suffrage.

When he finally spoke, it was to ask a more mundane question. "You entered and left the library through the servants' secret door?"

"I did," she confirmed. "In that way, I would never be seen near any of the three proper doors, entering or leaving. When I told you I never left my room those evenings, you would believe me, knowing what a scared rabbit I am."

"But the stairway comes out in the kitchen. You would need an accomplice among the servants."

"No, I wouldn't," she protested. "I did it all on my own."

"Please feel free to tell the truth, Miss Daphne," said a voice from one of the "proper" doors. Mrs. Crandall entered the room. "It is not only upper-class women who would like the chance to cast a vote, Sir Richard."

Daphne crossed the room and embraced the housekeeper. Then

she turned toward her father and her face was suddenly suffused with compassion. "Oh, Father, I'm sorry it had to be this way. When I learned from Mr. Holmes that my secret would have to be revealed, far from being threatened, I suddenly felt free. Strange, isn't it? And I'm sorry about the books, especially the Alice book, but at least I was able to use one of the less valuable editions. And when I was using that stairway, I found something surprising." She walked to a table near the secret entry and picked up a very old and battered book. "Our earlier ghost, whoever it was, must have hidden this for future use under a loose board on the stairs. I think you will find it of some value and interest."

She handed the book to her father. It was an old and stained copy of Plato's *Republic*, and as he turned the pages, I looked over his shoulder. Several passages were circled in red. I sensed a lessening of tension between father and daughter, though I doubted they would ever agree on the question of votes for women.

"That racing calendar with the Derby conditions circled, Miss Bootcrafter," Holmes said. "Your final clue. That one I confess perplexes me."

She smiled faintly. "It perplexes me as well, Mr. Holmes. I have no idea what it means. One of my sisters in the cause suggested it to me. It doesn't matter who."

Holmes could be forgiven for not understanding that last clue, for clairvoyance was not one of his talents. Four years later, in June of 1913, we would all wonder if we had solved the mystery. It was the usual festive Derby Day at Epsom Race Course. As was often the case, the Royal Family was represented with an entry in the great race, a steed named Anmer, owned by the King himself and ridden by jockey Herbert Jones. As the enormous crowd watched the field round Tattenham Corner and enter the home stretch, a woman ducked under the rails, ran onto the course, and stopped in front of the King's onrushing horse. Horse and jockey survived the collision, but the woman, later identified as Miss Emily Davison, died of her injuries. Though some said she must have been mad, others found her action a daring and militant gesture in the cause of votes for women. The 1913 race was known from then on as the Suffragette Derby.

THE ADVENTURE OF
THE LATE ORANG OUTANG

Gillian Linscott

HOLMES—THE BRIGHTNESS of his eyes and sharp intelligence of his features set off by the light of dozens of candles in their silver holders, reflecting from decanters of some of the finest claret in the country—sat at the Principal's right hand. He had recently performed a service for the college of St. Simeon's which had saved its five-hundred-year-old reputation from one of the blackest scandals that ever threatened Oxford University. This dinner, along with the assurance that whenever he happened to be in Oxford he must count on St. Simeon's hospitality as a right, was an expression of the college's gratitude. A man less ascetic than Holmes in matters of food and drink might have been more likely to take advantage of the privilege. Even in a city where the dons did themselves well, St. Simeon's was proverbial. Its high intellectual attainments, the beauty of its buildings and gardens, and the rarity of the volumes in its library were equalled, if not surpassed, by the excellence of its cellars and the abilities of its cooks. Fellows elected to the college were assured a life tenure of luxury that Renaissance princes might have envied.

I'd been placed opposite Holmes, with an ancient fellow on my right who must have been ninety at least, uttered nothing but an indecipherable mumble when we were introduced, and applied himself to the six courses of our dinner with an enthusiasm at odds with his shrivelled appearance. The man on my left mentioned that the ancient fellow some fifty years before had written a famous work on the Etruscans. This other individual was a pleasant companion and drew me out on the subject of medical adventures and mishaps, quite overcoming my apprehension that I'd be at a disadvantage among such formidable minds.

My friend, of course, had entertained no such apprehensions. In a little lull in the conversation, as the servants slid plates of a final savoury course of angels-on-horseback in front of us, I heard him and the Principal discussing a passage on the relation between the body and spirit in *De Rerum Natura* by Lucretius. Although I'd once rated Holmes's knowledge of philosophy as nil, I had heard him speak approvingly of Lucretius; and now he seemed to be defending him against an attack by his host.

"You maintain that he is a mere narrow materialist. I say that is to his credit. Is it not the duty of any rational man to resist a theory incapable of being proved or disproved by evidence?"

A young man sitting a few places to my left leaned across the table towards Holmes and said quite loudly, "Indeed sir, you might say that Lucretius was not the kind of man to believe in ghosts."

Holmes looked taken aback for a moment and the Principal appeared annoyed. It was not an especially profound contribution, and the young man hadn't been invited to take part in the conversation. The Principal turned it aside with some easy remark, and the young man subsided, although it seemed to me that he looked unreasonably pleased with himself. He stood out among this assembly of mostly middle-aged or elderly men by being in his mid twenties, with dark hair and a wholesome appearance, as if he enjoyed plenty of fresh air. In fact, I'd taken him for the only young man at the table until I noticed a person of about the same age sitting on the opposite side of the table. He was fair-haired, less robust-looking than the other young man, with a pale finely-boned face and bright eyes. When I noticed him, he was staring at the dark young man who'd made the remark about ghosts with an expression that seemed to me one of disgust.

Soon after that the Principal rose and led us into the senior common room, where port and walnuts were laid out on small tables, leather armchairs waited, and—although it was June—oak logs blazed in a carved stone fireplace large enough to have stabled a gig. Conversation over port was less formal, with men dispersed in groups of armchairs and sofas. The largest group surrounded Holmes and the Principal, who were sitting by a window with the scent of roses from the fellows's garden mingling with the wood smoke from the fire. I noticed that the dark-haired young man formed part of it, while the fair-haired one stood on his own, leafing through a periodical on a table. I complimented my dinner companion on the excellence of St. Simeon's domestic arrangements.

"Thank you. I suspect that some of the comfort of our small commonwealth is owing to obduracy. You will have observed that most of the Oxford colleges have now broken the tradition of centuries, and the intentions of their founders, by allowing dons to marry. The result is that the dons cycle home in the evenings to their narrow houses in the suburbs, and college society suffers. We still insist on bachelorhood for our fellows."

"So if a man marries he must leave all this?"

"Indeed. I may say that, so far, few have been prepared to make the sacrifice, not surprisingly perhaps."

Having from my own experience more tender views on the state of matrimony, I did not pursue the point. The talk turned to college history and traditions. As it happened, it was the Principal himself who brought up the subject of ghosts again, though this time in the form of a humorous anecdote about a college scullion of four centuries ago who had been hanged for killing a steward with a meat cleaver, and who was allegedly encountered on winter midnights by the more highly strung undergraduates.

Others followed the Principal's example with Oxford ghost stories, all of them of a sceptical cast, involving skylarking undergraduates or superstitious college servants. Then the dark-haired young man, who'd been silent while the stories flowed, remarked that it was odd that one so rarely heard of animal ghosts. Everybody else objected and overwhelmed him with examples, from the black dog that presaged death for members of the Vaughan family on the Welsh borders, and headless coachmen driving teams of phantom horses, to Dick Turpin galloping through the night on Black Bess. The young man stood his ground.

"Yes, but all of those are ancillary to men. The black dog, for example, relates to the Vaughan family rather than his own dog-gishness. People who want us to believe in ghosts should explain why you never hear of a ghostly cow grazing in a field or a phantom dog chasing phantom rats."

Various objections followed. A man in a clerical collar said it was because animals had no souls. A sporting-looking don said the porter's dog was forever chasing imaginary rats. When the objections died down the young man made another remark in his clear and carrying voice.

"In fact, I know of only one ghost story relating to an animal simply as an animal and that is supposed to happen not far away from here. Peter could tell you about his ancestor and the ghostly orang outang."

Eyes turned to the fair-haired young man standing by the table. In the silence that followed his colleague's remark we all heard the small scrunching sound as his fingers closed on the pages he'd been reading or pretending to read. He said in an angry undertone, "Don't make a fool of yourself, Doughty."

The tension between the two young men brought something ugly into the room, at odds with the luxury and cultivation round us. I expected one of the older dons to step in and make peace, but gained the impression that they were all watching for the next move like men at some sporting event. I could see that Holmes, who'd been following the college stories with no more than half his attention, was suddenly alert.

"Peter is ashamed of his distinguished ancestor," the dark-haired man said. "You'd think he'd be proud to be descended from a true English eccentric who had a pet ghost."

The periodical fell to the floor. The fair-haired man gave an angry bow in the general direction of the Principal and stalked out of the room. There were murmurs of disapproval at his bad manners in leaving before the high table guests. Too late, the Principal tried to change the subject, but to my surprise Holmes was guilty of his own lapse of manners in refusing to let him.

"You'll forgive me, sir, but I must confess to an unsatisfied curiosity about this spectral anthropoid. Perhaps, if you'll allow it, our friend will tell us more."

The Principal clearly didn't like it, but the service Holmes had done the college entitled him to be indulged. The port circulated again and the young man, James Doughty, began his story.

"Peter's family," he said, "the Alderbrooks, have a place not far from here, on the edge of Otmoor. As it happens, I know the area rather well. I sometimes spend a day walking around there when I need to clear my mind. The Alderbrook family go back to the Conqueror, soldiers and squires mostly, but a hundred or so years ago there was one of them, Sir Thomas Alderbrook, who developed into a person of some cultivation. He dabbled in poetry, played the flute, collected pictures. Above all, he was a great traveller in his youth, Egypt, India, the Far East. And as he travelled, instead of simply despatching antiques and statuary back to the ancestral home, he took to sending animals— a tapir here, a pair of porcupines there—it must have driven his steward to distraction. Eventually Sir Thomas arrived home with a somewhat diminished fortune, a dose of recurrent fever that would plague him for the rest of his life, and a large and amiable orang outang which—Sir Thomas being by all accounts something of a republican—he called by the name of George, after the king. And, for the next twenty years or so, man and ape lived in perfect contentment.

"At some point, Sir Thomas conceived an enthusiasm for astronomy, had a stone tower built, and mounted a telescope. Now, this is where we come to the point of the story. The orang outang George took delight in scrambling up and down the outside of this tower. The creature would go roving about its business in the woods all night while its master was watching the stars, but every morning as the sun was rising, it would shin up the outside of the tower and join him in his observatory at the top. Then they'd breakfast together on dishes of China tea and oranges. For years it went on like this until, sadly, one day when Sir Thomas was quite an elderly man, poor George caught a cold in his hairy chest and died. This sad event happened around this time of year, on the day before midsummer. Sir Thomas wrote an epitaph in iambic pentameters—you can see it here in our library:

> *My rufous friend whose frank and kindly gaze*
> *Has watched with me Aurora's earliest rays*
> *These many years—*

Somebody coughed a protest. The narrator smiled and went on in prose.

"And he had him buried at the base of the tower he loved to climb. The night after, midsummer eve, there was Sir Thomas consoling himself by looking at the stars. One of his keepers, watching out for poachers, happened to be near the base of the tower just before sunrise. Well, I daresay you can imagine the rest."

"Go on, if you please. The reports of a witness are always preferable to imagination."

I glanced at Holmes as he spoke, wondering if he could be mocking the young scholar, but he seemed as alert and interested as if this were a proper case rather than after-dinner nonsense.

"Well, there at the base of the tower, something long and white rose silently into the air. The man—obeying the instinct of all keepers confronted with something strange—immediately let fly at it with his shotgun, and swore he must have hit it in the region of the heart. But with no effect. The pellets passed harmlessly through it and on the long white thing went, straight up the outside of the tower, just as it did in life, to keep its breakfast appointment with its master. The keeper remained convinced to the end of his life that what he'd seen was the ghost of the late orang outang."

"And Sir Thomas?" Holmes asked.

"Later in the day, it occurred to the old man's household that he hadn't been seen since the night before. So the butler and the housekeeper went to the tower, climbed the steps to the observation room at the top, and found their employer stone dead, with two cold and untasted bowls of China tea poured beside him."

"With an expression of unutterable horror on his face?" one of the dons asked sarcastically, probably resenting the attention the young man was getting.

"By no means. Perfectly tranquil and at peace. The doctors said his heart had finally given out. He was an old man, after all, and the fever had been weakening him for years. He was buried with due honours in the family vault, and as far as can be established, has never gone in for haunting or anything else unbecoming a deceased English country gentleman."

"But the orang outang?" Holmes asked.

"Indeed, the orang outang. If you go to the village of Nether Alderbrook, anyone there will tell you that every midsummer morning as the sun comes up, George the orang outang rises from his grave and climbs the tower, just as he's done for more than a century past."

"But would you encounter anybody who has actually witnessed the phenomenon?" somebody asked.

The sporting-looking don remarked that if a man bought enough beer in a country pub he'd find witnesses for herds of flying purple hippopotami if he wanted them. There was laughter, and the party broke up without further discussion on the subject.

NEXT MORNING, AS the Principal was showing us round the fellows' garden before our return to London on the midday train, he said, "I must apologise for Peter Alderbrook's discourtesy last night. I fear there is some lack of amicability between him and James Doughty."

Normally, I believe, the Principal would not have talked about college affairs to outsiders, but high office is a lonely business, and he had good reason to know he could rely on Holmes's discretion.

"It is always a difficult situation," he went on. "Fellowships at St. Simeon's are greatly coveted, and owing to the propensity of our fellows to live to a prosperous old age, vacancies seldom occur. When they do, there is naturally much competition for them among the best of the younger men. It is our custom to narrow the list to two, after much enquiry and discussion, and invite those two candidates to spend a term with us so that we can make a final decision as to their suitability."

"Does that decision depend on their intellectual attainments or their temperaments?" Holmes asked.

The Principal laughed. "You're thinking that in that case things would go hard with young Alderbrook on last night's evidence? Well, I won't deny that compatibility comes into it. After all, we shall be dining in the company of the man we choose several days a week for the rest of our lives. But you saw young Alderbrook at his worst. At best, he is an entertaining and unassuming companion. And James Doughty, although admittedly a lively conversationalist, may be a little over-boisterous at times, as you also saw last night. Intellectually he's very sound. He has a great interest in Nordic languages and has already published papers on ancient Icelandic quite remarkable in a man so young."

"And Alderbrook?"

"Mathematics. I confess that as a classicist I am ill-equipped to understand his subject, but those who do, tell me that he has one of the best brains of his generation."

Holmes stopped to smell a rose.

"I wonder if the tension between the two young men might be increased because one has had an easier route to St. Simeon's high table than the other. Young Alderbrook comes from an Oxfordshire landed family, whereas Doughty . . ."

The Principal smiled. "Ah, you caught the traces of a Midlands accent. But if I may say so, your deduction, for once, is too hasty. James Doughty does indeed come from the manufacturing classes, but his path has been a relatively smooth one. His father owns several pottery factories and combines a very satisfactory fortune with a reverence for learning. It was always his dearest wish that his only son should enjoy the university education denied to the father, so young Doughty has had nothing but encouragement in his studies."

"Whereas Alderbrook?"

"Quite the reverse. Although the family was once wealthy, its fortunes have decayed. His father died some time ago and what's left of the estate is in the hands of a half brother considerably older than he is, with nothing but scorn for higher mathematics or anything else that can't be hunted or eaten. Alderbrook had to pay his way through university by teaching pupils at a crammer. I suspect that may account for some of the friction between the two of them."

ONCE WE WERE back in our rooms in Baker Street, a development in an important case kept Holmes occupied. St. Simeon's and the story of the ghostly orang outang faded from my mind, until one day Holmes surprised me by suggesting a visit to the zoological gardens in Regent's Park, only a short stroll from Baker Street. I was more than ready for the fresh air, but the proposal surprised me because he'd never been an enthusiast for aimless excursions. And there was, indeed, nothing aimless about the way he strode past day-trippers and perambulators to the cages that housed the larger primates.

"Here's our orang outang."

He was looking into a cage that contained just one long, thin ape that had a gentle face creased like an anxious old man's and a covering of fine chestnut hair. The animal's expression combined intelligence and melancholy in a way that was disconcertingly close to human. It looked at us, then stretched out a long arm and swung itself to the top of its cage with an effortless flowing motion.

"Would he be capable, I wonder, of climbing a tower, or are his arms adapted rather for swinging from branch to branch?" Holmes asked. "With your systematic knowledge of anatomy, you should know, Watson."

"We didn't study apes at medical school."

I spoke shortly, rather displeased with him. The ghost story had seemed amusing enough for passing the time over port, but I couldn't understand why it was still in his mind. He laughed.

"You believe I'm wasting our time. Nevertheless, I have a suspicion that we haven't heard the last of our spectral ape."

These suspicions were confirmed two days later when a telegram was brought to Holmes while we were at breakfast. It was from the Principal of St. Simeon's, whose natural courtesy managed to defeat the terseness of the telegraph office: *Please accept apologies for inconvenience but should be very obliged if you were able to visit as matter of some urgency to favour us with your opinion on most unhappy event.*

"What shall you do?" I asked.

"We have no very pressing case on hand, so I shall obey his summons. You're free to accompany me, I hope?"

We took a cab to Paddington Station, caught the Oxford train, and not long after midday we were sitting in the Principal's study, a gracious room lined with bookcases and cabinets displaying objects of art and antiquity. The two small pieces of jewellery on the table in front of us—a wedding ring and a locket—stood out because they seemed cheap and commonplace in such a setting.

"The police allowed me to borrow them and show you," the Principal explained.

Holmes picked up the ring first and looked at it through his pocket lens.

"So a plump and hardworking young woman appears to have been unfortunate in her choice of partner."

The Principal raised his eyebrows.

"The circumference is too small for a man's finger," Holmes explained, "but quite large for a woman; therefore her fingers are certainly not slim. It is quite new; therefore she is probably young, but it has many small scratches likely to be caused by hard domestic work. It is brass; therefore her partner could not or would not buy gold; and although poverty is not necessarily a bar to a happy union, the fact that it has come into the possession of the police suggests her recent history has not been a fortunate one."

"Indeed not," the Principal said in a low voice. "The unfortunate young woman is deeply unconscious from a head injury and may not survive." Holmes put down the ring and picked up the other object on the table, a locket on a chain, equally brassy and cheap. He opened it and showed me a photograph and a lock of dark hair inside. The photograph was of a man's face and had been trimmed to a small oval to fit the locket. Although not of very good quality, it was clearly our talkative young acquaintance of the high table, James Doughty. We sat down, and the Principal told us sadly what he had gathered from the police.

"The young woman's name is Sally Nebbs. She is employed as a dairymaid on the Alderbrook estate at Nether Alderbrook, the very place that we were discussing the other night. She lives out with her aunt in the village. Two days ago her aunt went to wake Sally and found her absent and her bed not slept in. A search party discovered her lying unconscious at the base of the old observatory tower in the grounds."

Holmes was leaning forward intently. "What is the police theory?"

"They believe—with some cogency—that the unfortunate young woman spent the night at the top of the tower, and at daylight attempted to take her own life by throwing herself down to the flagstones beneath."

"Why should a healthy young person try to kill herself?"

The Principal looked down at the carpet and seemed to find some difficulty in speaking.

"When the doctor examined her, it became clear to him that she was in . . . a certain condition. He believes she is four or five months gone and her situation must very soon have become obvious to everybody."

"No record of any marriage, I take it?"

"None. Her aunt—who has no great fondness for the girl—has told the police she believes she was 'carrying on with somebody,' as she puts it. She bases that supposition on the fact that Sally often stayed out late in the evenings and seemed to have money to spare, to spend on ribbons and trinkets."

"And what does Mr. Doughty say about this? I remember that he mentioned he sometimes took walks in the area."

"Indeed. But he denies totally and categorically ever having met the young woman, let alone carrying on any intrigue with her."

"What does he say about his picture in her locket?"

"That he can offer no explanation for it whatsoever. He is angry and distressed that suspicion has fallen on him, but quite resolute in maintaining his innocence of any wrong doing."

"And do you believe him?"

"I have to say that I am very tempted to do so. But there is the evidence." He nodded his head toward the locket and the ring.

"Perhaps you would like to speak to him yourself. He is still in college, although I have asked him to avoid embarrassment by not mingling with the fellows."

"No," Holmes said. "I shall not speak to him at this point. I doubt whether Watson and I would achieve any more by questioning than you who know him better. But if you would be kind enough to ask the porter to call a cab, I think we shall pay a visit to Nether Alderbrook."

Later, as the Principal was waiting with us at the porter's lodge for a cab, Holmes asked him one more question.

"The young woman's injuries—were they only to the head or was there damage elsewhere?'

"None, I gather. The harm was caused by what I think medical men refer to as a depressed skull fracture."

THE CAB TOOK us through the sprawl of the Oxford suburbs, up Headington Hill, and from there onto country lanes winding through the fields and copses south of Otmoor. It was a warm day so we rode with the window down, and the scents of honeysuckle, cow parsley, and freshly cut hay were a holiday for the lungs after the soot of London. Holmes seemed unmoved by the pleasures of the countryside and stared straight ahead, deep in his own thoughts. Our driver was not familiar with the country, and stopped to ask a farm labourer the way to Nether Alderbrook.

"You be nearly there, sir. First left and you'll come to the manor house. But if you're wanting to see Squire Alderbrook you're unlucky on account of he's gone over to Wiltshire to buy weaners."

Since the lane indicated was too narrow to admit a cab, Holmes told the driver to wait for us and we proceeded on foot. We soon found ourselves alongside a stone wall that might have been imposing once, but was now broken down and neglected. Holmes led the way through a gap where the stones had fallen away.

"I don't think we need trouble anybody at the manor house. That must be the observatory tower over there."

The top of it was just visible on the far side of some trees. We walked towards it, keeping close to the wall to avoid attracting the curiosity of estate workers, but there was nobody in sight. The parkland, like the wall, had a neglected air, the coppice tangled and overgrown, as if it hadn't felt a forester's hand for years. On the far side of the trees we came to the foot of a little hillock with the tower on the top of it, like a small lighthouse in shape. A curving stone-flagged path, much overgrown, led us up the hillock to an iron-studded door of weathered oak planks set in the base of the tower. Holmes put his hand on the latch, and it swung open easily and soundlessly.

"Freshly oiled," he remarked.

The air inside was musty with the damp that never completely goes from stone buildings in England, even at the height of summer. It would have been a depressing interior, even without the thought of the poor young woman. The light was dim with only narrow shafts of sunlight slanting in through narrow windows high up, the floor scattered with the jumble of abandoned things that collect in unused buildings: feeding troughs, an old chaff cutter, various crates and cases. As our eyes became used to the dimness, the inside of the building revealed itself as no more than an empty cone with a wooden staircase spiralling round the walls to a platform that closed off the top of the tower.

We mounted the staircase cautiously, but though it creaked under our weight old Sir Thomas must have supervised his builders well because it held firm. A square trapdoor on the underside of the platform opened as easily as the door downstairs, and we found ourselves in the sudden light of the old observatory chamber. It was surrounded with high sash windows, the glass in them mildewy and cracked. Sir Thomas's telescope had been removed long since, but the platform for it was still there, with the head of a pulley beside it, similar to the arrangements in stables for drawing bags of feed into lofts.

"That must have been the way Sir Thomas had his telescope brought up," Holmes said.

I thought of the old man sitting there a hundred years ago watching the sunrise and waiting for his orang outang; but that whimsical memory was overlaid by the thought of the poor young woman of only a few days before dragging her shame and grief up the same stairs we had just mounted and nerving herself for the final act. Holmes, unaffected as usual, simply pushed up one of the sash windows and went outside onto a projecting stone balcony. It was a perilous, unrailed space, just wide enough for two people. The view was magnificent: to the north the marshy fields of Otmoor with its little brooks glinting in the sun, then the rise of the Cotswold Hills, and to the south the towers and domes of the great university city. Holmes looked down to the flagstones.

"Watson, have you examined many suicides that occurred from a height?"

"From time to time, as a student. Suicides provided a constant supply of corpses for dissection."

"Did any of them have injuries only to the head?"

I thought for a moment.

"No. Invariably multiple injuries, fractures to limbs, ribs, and spine, and damage to internal organs."

"Exactly. But this young woman seems to have managed the unusual feat of landing on her head. How would she have achieved that?"

In an instant he'd stepped to the edge and drawn his tall body upright on tiptoe with arms stretched above his head like a diver.

"Holmes!" I cried. For a moment I feared he was going to carry his experiment to the ultimate. But he only laughed at my alarm, lowered his arms, and stepped back.

"It would take, I think, a great deal of nerve and resolution to plunge down headfirst. More nerve and resolution than one might expect from a young woman fond and foolish enough to have got herself into such a predicament."

He stood looking down for a while, then we made our way back down the stairs. Before we left he spent some time poking around amongst the rubbish.

"Do you smell something, Watson? Not the usual smells—something fresh."

We sniffed. There *was* something, though I couldn't identify it at once.

"Hemp," he said. "New hemp rope. Can you find any new rope here, Watson?"

We searched, but could find nothing but a few ancient scraps, far too damp and mildewy to have given off the fresh smell. Then Holmes, rooting in a corner near the door, gave a shout of satisfaction.

"What have we here, Watson? Help me get it out to the light."

It turned out to be a large lead weight with a ring on the top of it. A quarter of a hundredweight, the kind of thing that might be used by a wholesale grocer bagging up his wares.

"Quite new and shiny," Holmes said. "It hasn't been in there long."

He seemed remarkably satisfied with it.

"If I intended to bludgeon somebody about the head with a weight, I think I'd choose something easier to handle than two stone," I said.

"Very likely."

"Aren't you going to examine it for bloodstains?" I suggested.

He did so, though I had the impression that it was only to humour me, but without result. We walked back to where our cab was waiting and were at St. Simeon's in time for tea in the fellows' garden. The Principal couldn't hide his anxiety.

"Have you come to any conclusion, Mr. Holmes?"

"Yes indeed. In fact, I believe the case is as good as solved. But there is still a small experiment which I must perform before I am entirely satisfied. I can promise you an explanation by this time tomorrow, but between now and then I hope you will indulge me in small diversion."

"Anything. Anything at all that we can offer."

"Tomorrow is midsummer morning. I propose a visit to the late orang outang."

It took all the Principal's gratitude and courtesy to save him from being offended. "Surely, Mr. Holmes, you don't take this ghost story seriously?"

"On the contrary, Principal, I take it very seriously. So seriously that I ask you to join my friend Watson near the observatory before sunrise tomorrow as a witness. I suggest that you take Mr. Doughty with you and, since we shall be trespassing on his ancestral land, Mr. Alderbrook."

Rather stiffly, the Principal agreed. He added that since we should be staying another night he looked forward to seeing us at high table again.

"I'm sure Watson will be delighted. I am afraid my duties must take me elsewhere, but we shall meet at dawn tomorrow at Sir Thomas's tower. How is the young woman, by the way?"

"Unchanged. Her life hangs in the balance."

Holmes acknowledged this with a nod and left soon afterwards, having condemned me to a dinner among the dons on my own. It was a much more subdued occasion than on our earlier visit—the news of the cloud over young Doughty had obviously spread in spite of the Principal's efforts. Feeling that an outsider's presence was unwanted at such a time, I went to my room as soon as I decently could after coffee was served, and snatched a few hours sleep. At two in the morning a college scout knocked softly at my door to deliver the Principal's compliments and the news that a cab was waiting at the gate.

AN AWKWARD LITTLE procession filed along the lane towards the estate of Nether Alderbrook in the thin darkness before sunrise, I leading the way with a lantern, with the Principal behind me, then James Doughty, with Peter Alderbrook bringing up the rear. It had been a miserable cab journey from Oxford—the Principal nervous, Doughty quite silent but moving like a man full of pent-up anger, Alderbrook hardly more forthcoming. Alderbrook had given his consent to our invasion of the estate, but was clearly annoyed that Holmes should take seriously what he regarded as a ridiculous family story. We took up our positions as I had been instructed at the base of the hillock with a good view of the east side of the observatory tower. There was no sign of Holmes. The sky faded to the delicate white that precedes sunrise, and the first birds started singing. I heard a slight movement behind us and turned to find Holmes there, but there was no telling what direction he had appeared from. The Principal turned and started asking him a question, but Holmes held up his hand.

"Observe."

The orange rim of the sun was just visible now. We all stared at the tower. In the silence, I was aware of the thumping of my heart and that quivering of doubt that all but the most sceptical of us must feel when brushed by even the possibility of the supernatural. Then, when the sun was a hemisphere balancing on the horizon, it happened. A white shape rose from the earth at the base of the tower. Long and thin, its spindly arms reached imploringly upwards. Doughty gasped and tried to move forward, but Holmes put a hand on his arm to restrain him. For a moment the white figure seemed to hesitate, outlined in the half-light against the grey wall. It began to ascend the tower, hesitantly at first, then gathering speed and flowing rather than climbing up, so like the ape at the zoo that my heart came into my mouth, and for that moment I believed we were seeing Sir Thomas's pet of a hundred years ago. When it disappeared a collective gasp came from us. I'm not ashamed to admit that I was shaking, and as for the Principal, his knees gave way so that he might have fallen if I hadn't supported him. Young Doughty spoke first, openly angry now.

"What foolery is this?"

Holmes was the only unperturbed one among us.

"Foolery indeed, and I must acknowledge it as my own. If you would be kind enough to wait on the other side of those trees until Dr. Watson comes for you, it will be my pleasure to demonstrate how the trick was done. Would you be kind enough to assist me, Watson?"

I followed him inside the tower, leaving a puzzled and, I think, resentful group behind us. I shared their surprise that my friend should have used his undoubted powers—and incidentally deprived us of a good night's sleep—for such an end. But once we were inside, his manner changed to a nervous energy that made it clear this was something other than a diversion. He bent to pick up something off the floor, and I recognised the lead weight, now attached to a long hemp rope leading upwards in the dim light until it disappeared through the trap-door to the platform.

"Watson, would you oblige me by going up into the observation chamber and pulling the weight all the way up until it's level with the pulley. Then throw the slack end of the rope and the thing fastened to it down to me outside."

I climbed the staircase to the upper chamber, now bright with the sun streaming through its many windows, and did as instructed. When I'd made the rope fast I looked out of the window to see Holmes waiting on the flagstones below.

"Have you got it, Watson?"

"Yes."

"Excellent. Now throw our phantom friend down to me."

I unhitched the free end of the rope. There was something attached to it, a huge and floppy puppet made of wire and old sheeting. I recognised the ghostly orang outang, and felt ashamed of my moment of fear. However, I threw the thing through an open window and watched the rope snake out to where Holmes was waiting at the base of the tower. He went out of sight for a while, and I couldn't see what he was doing. After a few minutes he reappeared.

"All secure, Watson. We're ready for our audience. Bring them inside."

The rope now stretched tightly from the weight on the pulley down to the ground, where Holmes must have secured it in some way. I fetched the others and brought them to join Holmes inside the tower. He seemed pleased with himself, rubbing his hands, which I noticed were covered in earth.

"Now, for my little experiment I want to position you gentlemen carefully, so that you may observe what happens. Mr. Doughty, against the wall over there. Principal, by the door, if you please, Watson beside you. Mr. Alderbrook, if you would please stand here, exactly in the centre." Grudgingly, the others did as instructed.

"Excellent. I believe we have about one minute to wait. I must ask you to maintain exactly the positions in which I have placed you and not stir an inch. Is that clear?"

They murmured their agreement, but the tension was rising. The Principal coughed from the dust, Doughty jingled change in his pocket, Alderbrook opened his mouth and closed it again.

"It will be clear to gentlemen of your intelligence," Holmes went on, "that the trick employs a pulley system to drag our ghost up the tower. As long as the rope is securely held down on the outside, the orang outang cannot begin his climb, and remains in his shallow grave, lightly covered with earth. Once that tension is released, the counterpoise will descend and the ghost will climb the wall. For the ascent you witnessed, I attached the end of the rope to a thinner cord and pegged it down in the ground."

He looked round at the four of us and smiled.

"It was perfectly secure apart from one small consideration. My thin cord was in fact a length of slow match. Once I had set it smouldering—calculating the time as carefully as possible to coincide with the sunrise—I could stroll to join the rest of you and observe the event which I had set in motion. Is that clear to you, gentlemen?"

He took out his watch. It could be heard ticking in the silence.

"Forty seconds to go," Holmes said softly.

Beside me, the Principal put a hand to his forehead but stayed in his place.

"Twenty seconds."

By the wall, Doughty seemed about to move but restrained himself.

"Ten seconds."

"You monster!" A shout broke the silence. Peter Alderbrook leapt sideways, then flung himself towards the door.

"Stop him, Watson!"

The young man was completely unnerved, so it was no great matter to knock him to the ground where he lay writhing in a litter of straw and leaves, murmuring over and over again, "Oh, you monster. You cruel monster."

Holmes walked over to where Alderbrook had been standing under the poised weight.

"Peter Alderbrook, you are under arrest for the attempted murder of Miss Sally Nebbs. It is useless to resist. There are police officers stationed within call."

"Holmes," I shouted, "for God's sake stand aside."

He looked at me.

"The slow match, the weight! Any second now it will—"

He smiled. "I appreciate your concern for my welfare, Watson, but it is unnecessary. On this occasion, the slow match was unlit. Mr.

Alderbrook, had he known, could have stood there from now to next midsummer sunrise quite unharmed."

The profanities that arose from Alderbrook when he heard this might have been regarded as tribute to the breadth of an Oxford education, although the Principal didn't seem to think so.

LATER, AS WE stood by the road watching the receding back of the police wagon carrying Peter Alderbrook back to Oxford, although to harsher lodgings than St. Simeon's, the Principal broke his silence.

"I understand the mechanics of the crime, but how in the world did he induce the poor young woman to stand exactly where the weight would descend on her head?"

"By much the same method, I would suggest, as I employed in his own case. She is a simple country girl, remember, and one who would have known Peter Alderbrook from childhood as her master's younger brother. If he told her that the ghost was the subject of gossip and requested her help in a joke at the expense of some of his Oxford colleagues, she would have done as he instructed. Once she'd been felled by the weight, he carried her outside to make it appear that she'd leapt from the tower. He must have thought that she was dead, and was perhaps too squeamish to observe closely."

"But in that case, wouldn't it have been in his interest to propagate the ghost story rather than resist it?" the Principal asked. "You saw for yourself that he was angry when Mr. Doughty mentioned it."

Holmes smiled. "You will have observed, I'm sure, that the best way to make sure a story spreads is to appear eager that it should not. Alderbrook had only to plant the seed by telling Mr. Doughty about his family history, and rely on personal rivalry and gossip to do the rest."

James Doughty looked ashamed.

"Yes, I'll admit we didn't care for each other and I shouldn't have made fun of his family. But that hardly compares with what he did. To try to kill an innocent girl I'd never met just to make out I was secretly engaged to her . . ." His voice trailed away.

"I believe the stakes were higher than that—" Holmes said. But the Principal had begun speaking at the same time so he courteously waited to listen.

"How did she come by the locket with Mr. Doughty's photograph?"

"Alderbrook brought it with him. When Watson and I were your guests, I happened to notice a line of photographs of college rowing eights in the corridor leading to the senior common room. An unfaded patch of wallpaper suggested one had recently been moved. I saw no particular significance in it at the time, but I think if you investigate, it will prove to have been a photograph that included Mr. Doughty. He is innocent of anything except tactlessness. But on the more essential point of what Alderbrook had to gain—"

But again he was interrupted, this time by the arrival at a run of a man neither of us had set eyes on before. His face was reddened by wind and quite probably drink, he wore a tweed jacket and breeches, and his voice, audible from some distance away, was unmistakably of the hunting and shooting class.

"Who did this to my girl? Who did this to my poor Sally?"

He came to a halt by our little group like a bull against a fence and went on repeating the question.

"You refer to Miss Sally Nebbs?" Holmes asked calmly. "May I ask who you are, sir, and what is your relationship to her?"

"I'm John Alderbrook and I own the ground you're standing on. As for my relationship, as you call it, I don't know what damned business it is of yours, sir, but she's my intended wife. I go off to Wiltshire, meaning to get the parson to do the business as soon as I get back, and I come home and find the poor girl at death's door. So what I want to know is—"

Holmes took him aside and explained, I believe, quite kindly. As it turned out, poor Sally came through her crisis that Midsummer Day and, so I'm assured, opened her eyes to find her bluff beloved standing over her, weeping tears of joy on learning not only that she would live but her unborn baby was still safe in spite of all. The parson did his business and made the dairymaid Sally Nebbs into Squire Alderbrook's wife just as soon as she was able to walk to church. But that was still in the future as the Principal and Doughty travelled back with us to Oxford in the cab and Holmes finished his explanation.

"On the more essential point of what Alderbrook had to gain from his crime, it seemed unlikely that a fellowship at St. Simeon's, however coveted, would provoke such a cold-blooded and elaborate crime. The inheritance of a family estate—even an impoverished one—was another matter. Peter Alderbrook must have held quite reasonable hopes that his unmarried elder brother would drink himself to death or break his neck in the hunting field before he produced an heir. When he heard not only that he'd got one of his servants with child but actually intended to marry her, the temptation to remove two obstacles to his future with one stroke proved irresistible. My only difficulty was finding a way to make him confess, in case the poor girl never recovered consciousness, so for that purpose I summoned up the ghost of the late orang outang. Now, if you would very kindly drop us at the station we'll take the train back to town."

So it was chops at Baker Street that evening instead of a feast at St. Simeon's high table. I doubt if my friend noticed the difference.

A *Scandal* in Drury Lane, or The *Vampire* Trap

Carolyn Wheat

PROLOGUE   1809

IT WAS NOT *the* Great Fire of London, but it was *a* great fire of London. Stories would be told of it years later, but none more oft repeated than this:

The theatre caught fire, who knows how? For in those days, my children, the stage was lighted, not by electric lights such as we have now, no, nor even by gaslight, which some said was the most romantic lighting of all, but by oil and candle, oil and candle.

Oh, the dreadful fires we had then! Shouting "fire" in a crowded theatre meant something *then*, I can tell you! (A fire in Brooklyn, across the water, struck fear into the hearts of actors around the world. All the bodies laid out in rows, covered with blankets, an entire city block, the newspaper said. There wasn't a theatrical anywhere in the world but didn't shudder at the thought.) We put on our greasepaint and donned our costumes and trod the boards, our faces lit by candle footlights, but we always knew that every performance could be our last. All it took was a tiny gust of wind, a bit of draught; a candle listed toward the velvet curtain, caught a loose thread, and the rest was history.

History visited the Drury Lane Theatre in London on February 28, 1809. Well, let us give the place its true and full name: Theatre Royal, Drury Lane.

Why Theatre Royal, you ask, child?

Ah, there's a tale. Once upon a time—as we both know, this is how true tales must begin and no other way will do—some evil men took charge of the land and banned all plays. Wicked men, they were, and not a humourous bone in their bodies. This is a pun, which you will no doubt discover sometime in your life, but no matter now.

"Now is the winter of our discontent made glorious summer by this sun of York"—you've heard Grandpapa say those words many times, haven't you, dear? Well, the winter of our discontent—the actors' discontent—was made summer by that glorious son of Stuart, King Charles II. He brought the theatre back to London and established playhouses under his own domain. We were respectable again, and the Theatre Royal, Drury Lane, was the most respectable theatre of them all.

Ah, the plays we performed in those days, child—Shakespeare, of course, but you know my forte is comedy, so it was Goldsmith I loved, and Sheridan. Your Grandpapa and Grandmama had their proudest moments in the Theatre Royal, Drury Lane, playing what became known as Restoration Comedy. Witty dialogue, powdered wigs, silk trousers, and beauty patches. Today's theatergoers would laugh themselves sick, but I tell you, child, we had London at our feet.

Time passed, and so did all of us. Sheridan stopped writing and did what all theatre people secretly hope to do, but seldom accomplish: he bought the Drury Lane. Anyone with sense could have told him it was a bad bargain, but when has anyone in the theatre been surrounded by persons of good sense?

It was in the days of mad King George. The Prince Regent was a great man for the theatre—so many of his, er, lady friends were theatricals themselves—and he loved his evenings in his Royal Box. He had Royal Boxes in every single theatre in London, but the one he loved best was the plush velvet enclosure in the Drury Lane. He even came when Sheridan—old, decrepit, facing the fact of his own mortality—decided against all odds to restage his greatest triumph, *The School for Scandal.*

It was a period piece, and therefore a gamble. How could modern audiences be expected to enjoy the spectacle of bewigged old caricatures exchanging exhaustingly witty banter? Cuckolded husbands hiding behind screens; ambitious, scheming brothers; country wives seduced by the city's vices—the old comedy creaked more loudly than the boards of the ancient theatre.

Yet audiences came—and laughed. Somehow the old magic returned; the exhilaration of a city so long theatre-deprived seeing itself mocked on the stage came alive again in Sheridan's revival of his old masterpiece. The Prince Regent guffawed loudly in his box and that was all it took. The Drury Lane was packed.

Old Sheridan might have died a contented man instead of the shell he became after that fateful night. I promised you a fire, child, and so you shall have one. A great conflagration that consumed every board and stick of the old, wooden Drury Lane Theatre.

Oh, the crackling and the ash! The sky over the West End was lurid with smoke and flame. It was like a snowstorm writ in orange and black. The eyes stung and the nose ran and the spectacle drew such an audience as Sheridan would have dearly loved, could he have charged the price of a ticket. It was as if the very bowels of hell had risen into London's skies—all right, child, Grandpapa will stop now and get to the point of his tale.

Sheridan was a drinker. Yes, dear, many of us are, and what's the harm? But on this night he carried a bottle of wine, very carefully, as if it were a babe in arms, to the curb in front of his theatre. He sat himself down on a chair someone brought from somewhere—the lobby, perhaps?—and watched his life's dream, his life's savings, going up in smoke. He lifted a glass to his lips from time to time—he had not sunk so low as to drink without a glass, no, not yet, not yet—and it was in this attitude that a watchman came upon him.

Yes, dear, I said a watchman, for there were no proper policemen in those days. The watchman asked Sheridan what he was doing, and the old playwright lifted watery blue eyes, gazed at the watchman with a pure innocence that only very good drink can produce, and said, "May a man not take a glass of wine by his own fireside?"

* * *

1896

"YES, OF COURSE I recall the case, Watson," Holmes remarked, although I had only just opened my mouth to remind him of it.

I had grown used to his little feats of mind reading, but in this case there was no mystery about his deduction. The day's newspapers all carried headlines wreathed in black announcing the passing of Sir Augustus Harris, dubbed "Druriolanus" by the *Telegraph* for his vigorous and successful management of The Theatre Royal, Drury Lane. I had spent many a happy evening at the theatre partaking of Harris's entertainments and I regretted the death of one who had made so many people happy.

A smile came and went in the flash of an eye. "I am not accustomed to using a Turkish bath as a consulting office," Holmes said, "but in Sir Augustus's case it seemed prudent to make an exception."

"He was not Sir Augustus then," I commented.

I fell into a dreamy reverie as I remembered that blustery November afternoon. Holmes and I, rosy and flushed from our steaming, sat at our ease in the deep plush armchairs, cigars in hand, enjoying the splendor of the décor surrounding us. Dark wood paneling, tall windows with stained glass at the top casting faint pastel shadows, and—in the center of the room—a fountain made of faience from the Doulton pottery works, all combined to produce an atmosphere of luxury suited to a Turkish pasha, and therefore most welcome to two ordinarily austere gentlemen of London.

A third gentleman, flushed of face and excitable of temperament, came up the stairs into the room, taking them two at a time. He wore a morning coat and striped trousers, and his large stomach pressed most uncomfortably against a fawn waistcoat. His round pate loomed even larger due to a conspicuous lack of hair above the brow and his beard was neatly trimmed. He approached us and burst out, "Mr. Holmes, your landlady kindly informed me that I should find you here. I am at my wits' end, and I beg you to forgive my unpardonable intrusion and listen to my tale."

It was only by a slight narrowing of the lips that I perceived my friend to be put out by the appearance of this importunate client. I suspected Mrs. Hudson would be in for a mild reproof for having sent the man to us during our hour of rest, but Holmes only said in a tone designed to calm our visitor, "Pray take a seat, Mr. Harris, and tell me the whole story from the beginning."

I sighed with satisfaction and relief. I'd recognized Harris at once and hoped Holmes, in spite of his studied indifference to popular theatre, might do the same. It was inevitable that the leading actor-manager of the Drury Lane Theatre should consult Holmes about the mysterious happenings that had robbed him of his leading lady, much to the dismay of the theatregoing public.

"Mr. Holmes," Harris said, pacing about the room, clearly too agitated to sit. "My theatre has been half empty for three long nights; I cannot bear to think of three more. I posted a closed notice for tonight and I might as well close until the Christmas pantomime."

"What is the difficulty?" Holmes inquired. "Watson here has been kind enough to read me all the reviews of your latest production and it seems to be another triumph for you and your company."

"My leading lady, God help me, is the most superstitious woman in England," the harried theatre owner said. "I have had to put up with hysterics because she lost her lucky piece of cloth from the costume of her first success; she pinned it to her corset every night and would not perform without it. As it turned out, a new stagehand found it in the wings after a performance and tossed it into the dustbin."

The florid-faced man took a deep, shuddering breath and said, "That was nothing compared to the evening a black cat walked across the stage during the second act. All the lady's training deserted her and she screamed as if the hounds of hell were upon her for a solid five minutes by my own watch."

His lips pursed. "Let anyone enter her dressing room with the left foot instead of the right and he will be ordered to leave the room and perform a silly ritual of turning round three times and repeating a nonsense rhyme. Let a stagehand whistle and she will demand his immediate termination from the production. Let a hat land on the daybed in her dressing room—she will not go on that night."

"Is she," Holmes enquired, his fingers steepled underneath his chin, "so very valuable to the success of your play?"

Mr. Harris was no less appalled by this question than I myself. Had Holmes been in Timbuktu for the past five years the question might have been permissible, but surely no one else in London could have asked it.

"My dear Mr. Holmes," the actor-manager said after a moment's shocked pause, "this is Dorcas Glendenning of whom we speak. Let your modern audiences prefer Ellen Terry and Mrs. Patrick Campbell. The older playgoers know true quality when they see it, and they see it in Miss Glendenning. I have attempted to continue the production with her understudy, with the result that my box-office receipts are down by 40 to 50 percent. Yes," he said as if in response to a question neither Holmes nor I had asked, "yes, I can sell some tickets at half price to people of low taste who know no different, but what does it profit a manager to fill his gallery if he has to paper his stalls?"

"Apparently your production weathered all these storms of superstition, if I may call them that," Holmes remarked, "so why have you closed for tonight?"

"Miss Glendenning is convinced," the manager replied, running fingers through hair that was no longer there, "that the theatre is haunted. She will not go on until the ghost is removed."

Holmes raised a single eyebrow.

Harris sighed deeply and took a chair at last. "The old Drury Lane burned to the ground in 1809, Mr. Holmes," he explained. "Sheridan owned it then. Before the fire, he'd staged a revival of his famous play *The School for Scandal.*" He gave a wry smile and said, "He'd have done better to stage *The Rivals,* for that was the situation between his two leading juvenile actors. One was Lawrence Routley—yes, the very Routley who was knighted several years ago—and the other a man named Allen. Routley played Joseph Surface while Allen took the role of Charles Surface. If you recall the play, you remember that these two brothers vied for the hand of Maria, the ingénue."

To my surprise, Holmes nodded. I hadn't expected him to know *any* English play, since his taste ran much more to Italian and

German opera. He surprised me even more by saying, "I have heard the legend. It was said that Routley killed his rival, who indeed disappeared and was never seen again after the fire."

"It is the shade of Allen that appears to walk in my theatre," Harris continued. "He is dressed in grey, wearing the breeches and wig of the period in which *Scandal* is set. He wears a long grey cloak and his face, they say, is grey as well."

Holmes shrugged. "Anyone may wear a costume of grey. Anyone may put on stage makeup and create a ghostly effect with phosphorus and smoke."

Harris drew himself up to his full height and wrapped around himself some of that aura that allowed him to command the stage. "I am a man of the theatre, Mr. Holmes. I have created earthquakes on a nightly basis, replicated shipwrecks, and produced ghosts on command. There isn't a trap or pulley or mirror illusion that I don't know about. I've considered the matter from all angles, and I cannot see for the life of me how this trick was done—if it is a trick, which I firmly believe it to be."

"You speak in riddles, Mr. Harris. Pray explain what you mean by 'this trick'."

"This ghost does not just walk, Mr. Holmes. It disappears into thin air."

"Impossible," Holmes and I said at once, almost in unison.

"That may be so, Mr. Holmes. Indeed, I believe and hope that it is. But until I can convince my company that this chimera is a figment of their imaginations, I shall have no players and no crew to continue my production."

"Very well," Holmes said. He rose briskly from his chair. "Watson and I will be at the theatre within the hour." He gave his quirk of a smile. "I shall endeavour to bring Science to bear on the profoundly unscientific mind of your leading lady."

Holmes might not have been as familiar as I with the theatrical West End, but the streets surrounding the Theatre Royal, Drury Lane, were not unknown to him in his professional capacity. Running parallel to Drury Lane itself was Bow Street, home of the Bow Street Magistrate's Court, and at the end of Bow Street was the turning into the Strand, where Holmes often dined at Simpson's after searching public records at Somerset House. As our hansom cab passed the lovely Lyceum Theatre, with its Corinthian columns, I could not help but think of my first wife Mary, nee Morstan. During the case in which I made her acquaintance and which I later recorded as "The Sign of the Four," Mary, Holmes, and I met a mysterious man at the third pillar from the left. Consequently, the theatre has always maintained a special place in my memory.

I had been inside the magnificent Theatre Royal, Drury Lane, on many an occasion and I felt comfortably at home as we walked through the lobby past its twin staircases. My sense of feeling at home ended when Harris led us down a rear passage that took us backstage. Instead of plush velvet seats and polished mahogany fittings, all here was unfinished, raw, in a state of being built or torn down. Instead of well-placed electric lights, the dim bulbs backstage cast long, ominous shadows. Where a theatre audience would see fancifully painted scenery lit to resemble a real setting, from this vantage point the paint seemed garish and unreal. Overhead beams and wires seemed about to tumble onto our heads, and under our feet old boards creaked and groaned.

Harris had assembled and introduced those members of his company who had witnessed the ghost's appearance. We took them one by one, sitting on stools in that part of the stage actors call "the wings."

" 'E's all in grey, Mr. 'Olmes," a young wardrobe assistant said in a breathy cockney accent. "Not wearing proper trousers, but them breeches and stockings what they wore in the old days. Wears one of them powdered wigs."

"What did this apparition do?" Holmes enquired with utmost gravity.

"Do? 'E flung 'is cloak over 'is shoulder and looked ever so dashing. Then 'e disappeared. All at once. 'E was there and then 'e wasn't there. It gave me such a turn, you can't imagine!"

She held her hand over her heart in the manner of a melodramatic actress. "I came all over faint."

"How long would you say this singular vision lasted, Miss Dorkins?"

"Oooh, let me think now. It couldn't have been more than a minute or two 'cause I was just fetching Mrs. Amberley's costume for act two and she started shriekin' like a banshee and I had to get a move on, sir, grey man or no grey man."

Our second witness, a young ingénue fresh from the provinces, showed far less presence of mind than the wardrobe assistant. "I fainted dead away, Mr. Holmes. I can tell you I've never been so frightened in my whole life, not even the first night I went on in a play where I had lines to speak. My friend that was with me screamed and I did too and the next thing I knew I was on the floor and she was waving smelling salts under my nose." She gazed up at Holmes with eyes as large and brown as a doe's. "Oh, I wish now I'd never come to London! We had no ghosts in Sussex, I can assure you."

A beefy man with a farmer's face and a Yorkshire brogue stepped into the room. His overalls and thick fingers marked him as a carpenter-stagehand.

"So you think you've seen a ghost, do you?" Holmes barked out the question in a challenging tone, as if daring the man to repeat his allegation.

"I seen a man disappear before me very eyes," he said with equal belligerence. "If you can show me a man of flesh and blood what can do that, I'll say nowt about ghosts."

"Describe this vision," Holmes commanded.

The stagehand's description matched that of the wardrobe mistress. The disappearance he had witnessed was even more startling than the one the girl had described. "It wasn't really all at once," the stagehand explained. "It was more like he crumpled up and then vanished. He swung that cape, and then he shriveled, like, and when I looked back, he was gone."

Holmes pounced on that last statement, as I knew he must. "When you looked back," he repeated. His eyes gazed intently into the bovine eyes opposite his. "Why had you looked away?"

The man shrugged massive shoulders. "Some fool behind me dropped a plank. I guess the ghost frightened him."

"You are certain this was not a stage illusion?"

"Mr. Holmes," the stagehand said with palpable condescension,

"I've thought about it a million times, and I'll be blowed if I can come up with an explanation. One second it was there, walking big as life, and the next it curled up in a whiff of smoke and vanished into thin air. Thin air, Mr. Holmes."

Holmes did his best to look suitably impressed. "The alleged ghost could not have slipped down a trap door or been covered by a curtain?"

"That it could not, sir. The man shriveled up like a dried banana peel before my very eyes and disappeared. If I could explain it, I'd do it, but I can't. I'm with you, sir; I don't hold with these apparitions and such; I believe in what I can see and taste and feel and smell—but I did see this and I can't for the life of me explain how it was done if it was a trick."

"Be honest, Mr. Cubbins. Wasn't this ghostly apparition somewhere near one of your trapdoors?"

"Mr. Holmes," the man replied. "This entire stage is built upon traps. You can't take a step without walking over one. I'll show you all of them if you like, from the

Vampire to the *Corsican,* but I'd stake my life on it that a trap alone could not cause such a disappearance."

I was quite looking forward to seeing these exotically named traps—named, I learned, after the plays in which they were first used—when the air was rent by a bloodcurdling scream. Holmes hastened toward the sound and I, my hand on my revolver, followed close behind.

"Peacock feathers! Who dared bring me peacock feathers?" The voice was one that had thrilled a million theatergoers, but now it was raised in stark, sheer terror.

Holmes reached the door first. As he opened it, Harris strode down the hallway, his usually ruddy face purple. "Oh, Lord, not again. I'll sack whoever is responsible for this!"

"Are peacocks so very unlucky, then?" Holmes enquired mildly.

The showman grimaced. "The late Sir Henry Irving referred to one as 'that miserable bird of malignant fate'," he replied. "Everyone in the theatre knows that they are not permitted within our precincts."

"It would appear that someone is determined to contravene all of Miss Glendenning's superstitions," Holmes remarked.

This was a new idea; I stopped short and considered that the parade of black cats, lost lucky pieces, whistling, and now peacock feathers might not have been coincidental. The open door revealed the most beautiful woman I have ever seen. From a distance—say, from a seat in the dress circle to centre stage—Dorcas Glendenning was magnificent. Up close, she was even more than that. Dignified, with glossy chestnut hair and a flawless complexion, she burned from within like an incandescent bulb. I moved to step into the room, but Harris held me back with his arm. "Right foot first," he reminded me.

Harris moved at once toward his leading lady, removed the offending feathers from her hands, and proceeded to soothe her with gentle words. "I have brought Mr. Holmes in to investigate this matter," he said. "I'm sure you are familiar with his reputation as a detective. It is just one sign, my dear, of the lengths to which I am prepared to go for your peace of mind."

Holmes gave a slight bow, but Miss Glendenning looked far from impressed.

"Are you familiar with Professor Sidgwick's excellent work, *Phantasms of the Living*?" The actress regarded Holmes through a lorgnette, as if studying a rare and poisonous butterfly. "Or perhaps you have read *The Occult World* by Alfred P. Sinnet?"

Holmes astonished me with his answer. "Indeed, I have, Miss Glendenning. Both are indispensable if one is to understand the workings of the World Beyond the Veil."

"Ah, so you are not fully a skeptic," the lady said, her tone warming.

"Madam," Holmes replied with a slight bow, "I am a skeptic in all matters, whether large or small. How could I fail to be skeptical concerning the greatest mystery of them all?"

"Glad as I am," the actress replied, "to know that you are not completely ignorant of The Other Side, I have nevertheless taken it upon myself to hire my own consultant in this matter." She turned toward the Chinese screen in the corner of the room and made a beckoning gesture. A large woman in a purple plush walking suit stepped from behind it. A broad purple hat with lavender-dyed ostrich plumes completed the lady's ensemble.

"Allow me," Dorcas Glendenning said, "to introduce Cassandra Trelawney, of the Society for Psychical Research."

Miss Trelawney gazed around the dressing room with large, myopic eyes. She fixed upon Harris and said in a dreamy voice, "The vibrations in this theatre are almost overwhelming to one such as I. We Seers are often cursed with an overabundance of feeling and are like tuning forks in our response to the presence of the Spirits."

It was with great difficulty that Harris refrained from rolling his eyes. He gave a stiff bow and said, "Please, Madam, avail yourself of every resource I can offer. I will go to any lengths to rid my theatre of this apparition and return to business as usual."

"Pray show me where the Spirit appeared," the lady replied. As Holmes and I had been about to investigate the same spot, we led Miss Trelawney back to the wings, where the stagehand awaited us.

There were indeed trap doors all over the stage. I tested one myself, stepping onto a small moving platform and being gently lowered to the area directly below, where a labyrinth of pillars and posts, winding staircases, pulleys and winches awaited me. One by one our party descended to this netherworld. The last to arrive, Miss Trelawney, stepped off her platform and placed her hand over her forehead.

"I feel strong vibrations," she said in response to Miss Glendenning's expression of concern. "I am convinced we are close to the Spirit we seek."

Dorcas Glendenning looked both pleased and apprehensive; Harris, clearly unimpressed, said nothing.

"The emanations are particularly strong here," the woman in purple said as she glided toward the wall at the back of the stage. "I feel the vibrations so powerfully that there can be no doubt: someone died in this place, died by violence."

Her voice was low and thrilling, and I thought for a moment that she must have trained as an actress herself. How better to work her magic on the gullible souls she mesmerized into speaking with ghosts than to use all the arts of the place in which we stood?

"You must open this space," Miss Trelawney commanded, pointing toward a wall at the back of the stage. "The Spirit is restless and demands to be liberated."

"Open the—" Harris gazed from one woman's implacable face to the other's. "I can't—it makes—Dorcas, you must see that—"

It was clear from the adamantine gaze of his leading lady that nothing would do but to open the wall and prove, once and for all, that there was nothing in this ridiculous claim that a dead man haunted his theatre. He nodded to the stagehands, who went in search of axes and crowbars.

I could scarcely believe that Holmes was permitting himself to be a party to this folly. What earthly good could be served by tearing down the walls of this grand old theatre to root out a chimera? It occurred to me at last that Holmes was merely giving his purple-wearing adversary enough rope with which to hang herself. The louder she insisted upon the presence of a ghost, the sillier she would look when the wall came down to reveal a dusty, ancient broom closet.

The axe whacked its way into the dry wood with a loud barking crack. Three or four hard swings were all it took to make a hole the size of a paving stone in the wall. All in the room save Miss Trelawney stepped forward to peer through the opening. She stood apart, her eyes gazing straight ahead without focus, as if she had no need to confirm her belief by seeing the actual contents of the closet.

" 'Strewth," one of the workmen said with feeling.

I nudged him out of the way and had my own look. It was with great difficulty that I, a medical man, kept my composure. I found myself staring into the huge hollow eyes of a skull. The skull was connected to a skeleton, out of the chest of which protruded a large broadsword.

On the floor lay several playing cards of an exceedingly old-fashioned design, along with golden guineas, the whole under a thick layer of dust. But it was the sword that held my gaze.

" 'Is this a dagger which I see before me?' " I quoted without thinking. Behind me came a banshee's shrill cry. "He did it! He quoted from—" here the voice grew deep and ominous—"*that play*!"

I turned to see Dorcas Glendenning imitating the shade of Allen and crumpling into a heap on the floor. Beside me, someone whispered, " 'Fair thoughts and happy hours attend upon you.' "

I attended upon Miss Glendenning, who had merely fainted. I blushed as I remembered the most widespread theatrical superstition of them all: that one must never quote *Macbeth* or even call the play by its name.

The wardrobe assistant led the actress to her dressing room, where she was revived with tea and biscuits.

"Has this man been walled up in this theatre for eighty years?" Holmes murmured.

"He has, Mr. Holmes. He has," the lady in purple pronounced. "He has walked these corridors hoping to be seen, hoping to be rescued from his obscure grave."

"So this is Allen," Holmes said. "The man Sir Lawrence Routley allegedly murdered."

"There is no 'allegedly' about it, Mr. Holmes," Cassandra Trelawney pronounced. "The ghost of William Allen returned to accuse his murderer."

"I simply cannot, will not, believe in a ghost," Augustus Harris said firmly. "I must believe in this deceased individual, because I see the skeleton with my own eyes. I cannot think, however, that the illusion of the ghost is anything but a man-made effect."

"Then how was it done?" the lady in purple challenged. Harris shrugged. She turned her large, accusing eyes on Holmes.

"I cannot say at this time," my friend replied. "I must think. I must analyse. I must dissect this apparition. It seems to me impossible to explain, yet explain it I must or be consigned to the pathetic role of a believer in the spirit world. I can hear Lestrade now," he said, with a wry smile on his face, " 'Oh, what a noble mind is here o'erthrown!' "

I ventured to suggest that Lestrade had never heard those words in his life, but it did not matter.

"I know the words," proclaimed Holmes, "and if he does not say them of me, then I will say them of myself."

It was quite a three-pipe problem. I know this because I was obliged to inhale the acrid and vile smoke from all three pipes. I am not averse to tobacco, but I do prefer a more gentlemanly blend than that which my friend imbibed when embarked upon a mental quest of great import and difficulty. He always said that shag stimulated his mental faculty almost as well as that "seven percent" solution that he *would* use in spite of my medical advice.

I slept and rose; he did neither. He huffed and he puffed, wreathed in smoke like the image of a Red Indian with a peace pipe—yet I discerned no peace in his hawk-like countenance. At last he jumped from his chair as if it had been electrified, shouted, "I see it! There is only one way it could be done! Ingenious, Watson, most ingenious! I must go to the Egyptian to verify my hypothesis."

I had no idea what the Egyptian Rooms at the British Museum had to offer in the way of enlightenment, but I saw him no more than day, and then was summoned by telegram to appear at the Drury Lane theatre at four o'clock that afternoon.

I was not the only person so summoned. Harris met me in the lobby, accompanied by Dorcas Glendenning, Cassandra Trelawney, and the stagehands that had opened the makeshift tomb.

"Mr. Holmes wishes us to meet him backstage," Harris said, leading the way through the public section to the private area of the theatre.

When we arrived, Holmes was nowhere to be seen. We waited and talked, but the delay became awkward and I found myself glancing at my watch, wondering what had delayed my friend. Miss Glendenning proclaimed herself affronted by this ill treatment and declared that she would return to her dressing room.

I felt it before I saw it: a sudden blast of cold air struck me from behind. I turned and saw a tall man wearing a curled and powdered wig, dressed in breeches and stockings, with a long grey cloak around him. I gasped.

Miss Glendenning screamed. The stagehand pointed and said, "Yes, that's what I saw!"

The ghost—for I could not call it by any other name, although I dearly longed to do so—seemed to float above the theatre floor, gliding as if on wheels instead of human legs. It glowed ever so slightly, not so much as to call to mind a theatrical effect, but just enough to tell me it was not of this world. It wore the powdered wig and breeches of a past century, and a long cloak wrapped around it as if to ward off a chill so cold it defied mortal imagination. All of a sudden the figure stopped swinging his cane and undid the cloak, only to fling it over its shoulder with a flourish.

Then it was gone. It shriveled like ash from the fire, dwindled into a memory, and curled it into nothingness.

It could not have happened. I could not have seen it. Yet my eyes beheld the sight the witnesses had described, and I was as baffled and amazed as the lowliest, least educated of them. A human being had appeared and disappeared before my eyes and I had no idea how—unless, of course, he was truly made of ectoplasm instead of solid flesh.

This could not be. There were no such things as ghosts, yet I saw what I saw.

I stole a glance at the lady in purple. To my amazement, the look on Cassandra Trelawney's face was not one of sublime satisfaction at seeing her thesis proved. Nor was it one of awe at the workings of Those Beyond the Shade. Instead, the medium's face wore a look of mingled surprise and anger.

Why anger? The answer soon became clear as the gentleman in grey stepped from behind the wings and presented himself with a slight bow. It was Holmes, who smiled and said, "I can never resist a touch of the dramatic."

"But how—" I began, all amazement at his feat. For not only had Holmes deduced how the trick had been done, he had reproduced it to perfection.

"How, Watson?" he said, his face alight with mischief. "It was the easiest thing in the world, once I disabused myself of the idea that the costume and the person had to disappear at the same time."

I must have looked blank, because Holmes chuckled. "It is a most ingenious illusion," he added, admiration in his tone. "It has the advantage of seeming so impossible that the observer doesn't even begin to ask how it was done, but simply accepts that he has witnessed a miracle of sorts. The solid flesh of a human being appears to shrivel and curl into nothingness, vanishing in a puff of smoke. Yet, we know, as scientific men, that such things cannot happen."

"How was it done?" Augustus Harris demanded. "I have been in the theatre for above forty years and I have never heard of such a thing."

"You have been in the legitimate theatre, Mr. Harris," Holmes replied. "To see this illusion performed, you would have to attend The Egyptian Theatre and witness the performance of a master magician like Devant or Maskeleyne."

"No magician could have spirited himself away in such a manner," Dorcas Glendenning said with scorn in her beautifully modulated voice.

"I did not say the ghost spirited himself away," Holmes said tartly. "I said he appeared to do so. Illusion is the key to the art of the magician. Truth is supplanted in the eye of the beholder by misdirection and misleading evidence. In this case, there were two distinct elements of the disappearance: the vanishing of a corporeal human being, and the disappearance of a suit of clothing."

"But the person posing as the ghost wore the clothing," I burst out. "Surely they both disappeared at the same time."

"That," Holmes replied, "is what the magician intended you to see. The human eye sees a man in a suit and cloak; a man in a suit and cloak disappears; therefore, they disappeared at the same time and in the same way. But did they?"

"But how could—" I began, but broke off as the head stagehand nodded and gave Holmes a wide smile.

"Then it was the *Vampire* trap," he said. "Only the 'ghost' didn't just jump into it like he'd do on a stage, with his costume on. He left his cloak standing there, empty."

"Empty and hanging by hooks he'd pulled down when he raised his arms to toss the cloak around his shoulders in that dramatic manner. He slipped out of the cloak and slid down the trap. A split second later, the costume, sans corporeal flesh, began to shrivel and curl."

"All by itself, Mr. Holmes?" Dorcas Glendenning demanded, her face brick red and her eyes blazing. "This is a ridiculous attempt to explain the mysteries beyond our material world. Not only do you have a naked ghost slipping down a trap, but you have a costume that dwindles into a puff of smoke all by itself."

"Hardly without human agency, madam," Holmes said with a slight bow. "Behind the costume, a long pipe was inserted through a hole in the wall behind the ghost. Someone sucked the costume, which was made of thinnest gauze in spite of its solid appearance, into the tube, creating the shriveling effect. Add phosphorous and a touch of theatrical fog and you have an illusion for the ages. As the witnesses stare in fascination, a seemingly solid creature disintegrates like ash blown on the wind."

"But who produced this trick?" Harris cried. "And why?"

"The illusion requires five participants," Holmes said. "One portrays the ghost, as I did just now. Another," he added, gazing up at the fly gallery, "dangles the hooked wires that catch the cloak. A third works the trap from below and a fourth pulls the costume through the tube."

"That makes four," I said. "What does the fifth participant do?"

"In each case, the witness to the ghost reported a sound. This sound not only covered the noise of the trap opening and closing, it diverted attention from the illusion for a brief moment. In one case, the sound was a call from a dressing room; in another it was a dropped board. In a third case it was a scream. All carefully timed to coincide with the trap."

"My theatre," Harris said grimly, "is filled with conspirators, it seems."

Holmes nodded. "The conspiracy began with a carefully planned campaign against Miss Glendenning. Every possible opportunity was taken to create an atmosphere of bad luck into which the ghost fit perfectly."

"But why?" Harris cried. "Was there so much animus against my theatre?"

"As to that, Mr. Harris," Holmes replied, "I suggest you ask Miss Trelawney."

The woman in purple shook her head and laughed scornfully. "I see you will stop at nothing to deny the existence of the Spirit World.

Why should I be called to answer for a ghost that was seen before I ever entered this theatre?"

"You are not unfamiliar with the theatre, are you, Miss Trelawney?" Holmes asked in his silkiest voice. "I do not mean as a spectator, but as a performer. You not only possess a theatrically trained voice, but you knew the correct words to say when Watson quoted from the Scottish play."

My eyes widened. I had thought the words I'd heard after my gaffe odd. " 'Fair thoughts attend' upon something," I murmured.

Harris and Miss Glendenning said, almost in unison, " 'Fair thoughts and happy hours attend upon you.' " For the first time, I saw the full force of Dorcas Glendenning's smile as she shared the moment with her fellow actor.

"It is a line from *The Merchant of Venice*," Harris explained. "It is the counter-jinx to ward off the evil."

"The entire point of the ghostly apparition, which was the culmination of the unlucky events surrounding this play," Holmes declared, "was to cause Miss Glendenning to bring Miss Trelawney to the theatre so that she could point to the place where the skeleton would be found."

"But why?" Harris asked plaintively.

"Why does anyone want a body found?" Holmes replied.

"To expose a crime," I replied. "Perhaps to right a wrong."

"That is no excuse," Miss Glendenning said, glaring daggers at the purple-clad medium. "Those feathers! That cat! I suffered agonies, and all so that a filthy pile of bones might be uncovered."

"That 'filthy pile of bones' was my grandfather, William Allen," Cassandra Trelawney said, her tones as tragedy-laden as any leading lady's. "He died at the hands of a murderer who went on to the fame and fortune that should by rights have been his. It was only right that he be brought to the light of day and given a Christian burial at long last."

"But why now, madam?" Harris asked. "If your grandfather has occupied his hidden resting place for eighty years, why now? Why did you wait?"

"She did not wait," Holmes replied. "She did not know where her grandfather lay until quite recently. That is the only explanation that makes sense."

"It was Routley's own words that gave me the clue," Miss Trelawney said. Her large eyes were considerably less ethereal as she spoke. "He recently published a book of memoirs in which he mentioned playing cards in the lower levels of the Drury Lane Theatre during the run of *School for Scandal*. He didn't have the nerve to mention my grandfather by name, but he did accuse an unnamed fellow actor of cheating at cards. My mother remembered that her father was quite fond of a game of cards and made the connection between her father's disappearance and the prop room where the actors gambled between acts. I knew Mr. Harris would never consent to open the walls on such a thin speculation, so I used Miss Glendenning's rather notorious reputation for superstition to gain entry here."

"Superstition?" The actress gave each syllable its full value. "Do you mean you have no belief in the spirit world at all? You are a complete and utter mountebank?"

Cassandra Trelawney gave a small smile. "On the contrary, madam, I am a fellow professional. I, too, tread the boards, albeit a rather different set of boards."

Miss Trelawney drew herself up to her full height, which was not more than five feet, and said with dignity, "We Allens were a theatrical family of note until that man killed my grandfather. Since his death, we were driven off the legitimate stage and into music halls and magic shows. Such a comedown! My mother should have been a Duse or a Bernhardt, and instead she allowed my father to throw knives at her."

I glanced at Dorcas Glendenning. With another turn of her mercurial temperament, she seemed to have forgotten her anger and now stood transfixed by the medium's passionate confession. For a moment, I wondered if I would someday hear the same thrilling notes and see the same gestures replicated onstage. And then I realized with a quiet, internal smile that of course I would. Such was the nature of the art.

"We do, it is true," Miss Trelawney continued, "reign supreme as illusionists at the Egyptian Theatre—you must come and see my brothers' act sometime, gentlemen—but if matters had been different I would have been stunning in the Scottish play."

"I would never play that horrid role," Dorcas Glendenning said with a tiny shudder. "Not only is the play unlucky, but I could never portray a woman with such strange notions of hospitality."

That was my last moment with the great actress. Holmes and I said our farewells and returned to the other side of the footlights. I enjoyed many more performances at the Drury Lane Theatre and many more after-theatre suppers at Gatti's in the Strand.

"I HEAR THERE is a new play at The Egyptian Theatre that might interest you," Holmes said, tossing the newspaper with Harris's obituary into the fire. "It is called *The Mascot Moth* and it features an ingenious illusion that all London will soon be talking about. An actress dressed as a moth makes a singular disappearance before the eyes of an astounded audience. No one can figure out how it was done." His eyes twinkled.

"If we attend," I said with a smile, "shall we spoil our fellow spectators' fun with the explanation, or permit them to enjoy their wonderment?"

"My dear Watson," Holmes replied with mock severity. "I made a solemn vow to the Allen-Trelawney family to keep their secrets. A magician never explains an illusion."

Sherlock Holmes and the Mummy's Curse

H. Paul Jeffers

I N THE THREE years following my introduction to Sherlock Holmes in the chemistry lab of St. Bart's hospital by our mutual friend Stamford—resulting in Holmes and me sharing lodgings in Baker Street—I had grown accustomed to Holmes's investigations beginning with the arrival of a telegram or letter, our landlady announcing an unexpected caller, or the plodding footsteps of a Scotland Yard detective ascending the stairs with a grudging appeal for assistance. On one or two instances I happened to be the instrument that launched Holmes upon what he commonly called "a problem." Such was the occasion on a warm April evening in 1883. We had barely settled into our chairs in the sitting room of 221B Baker Street on the second evening following our return from the Surrey home of the villainous Dr. Grimesby Roylot when Holmes bolted from his chair and declared, "Watson, our exertions in this singular episode at Stoke Moran have earned us the reward of a superb dinner."

Half an hour later, we were seated in Simpson's-in-the Strand. As always when Holmes patronized that venerable establishment, our table in the upstairs dining room was next to a large window overlooking the busy thoroughfare. "In this passing parade of humanity," he had said in explanation on a previous occasion, "and in a city of four million inhabitants, all jostling one another, there is no telling what convergence of events or trifling happenstance might unloose a chain of events resulting in a calamity, or simply one of those incidents that seem whimsical on the surface, but are rife with dire consequences for those involved."

While Holmes alternately peered down to study the constantly changing street tableau, he picked at the roast beef that had been carved from one of the immense silver trolleys, known as "dining wagons," which had been the hallmark of Simpson's since it opened its doors in 1848. I was enjoying a steak, kidney, and mushroom pudding for which the restaurant was equally and justifiably renowned. As I glanced around the crowded, festive room, I was astonished to see a comrade from my army service striding boldly towards our table.

A burly figure in the uniform of my former regiment, the Fifth Northumberland Fusiliers, and with a shock of unruly red hair that had among his fellow officers earned him the nickname "Rusty," Major James McAndrew would have been an arresting figure anywhere, but making his way across the large dining room he was especially noticeable because of a bandage encircling his head like a laurel wreath. As he drew near our table, he flung out his powerful arms and bellowed, "By Jove, it really is you, Watson!"

"Rusty, my dear friend," said I, rising to grip his large hand. "This is a surprise. I had no idea you were England. How good it is to see you. May I present my friend, Sherlock—"

"No introduction is required, John. It's an honour to meet you, Mr. Holmes. As a devoted reader of Watson's accounts of your investigations in *The Strand* magazine, I assume that your keen eyes have taken my measure and your detective's mind has deduced my entire life story."

"I wouldn't go so far as to say that I know everything about your life, Major," Holmes replied as they shook hands, "but the tattoo of a ship below a cross on your left wrist and one of a mermaid on the right are evidence that you went to sea as a very young man. They are in the unmistakable style of a particular practitioner of body adornment who worked the Portsmouth docks three decades ago."

"Right you are!"

"How long it has been since you gave up seafaring for the army is impossible to state."

"Because my father had been a captain in the navy and thought I had the makings of an officer, I shipped out in 1845 at the age of thirteen, but after five years, I decided that I'd rather be in the Army. Earning the rank of Major took another twenty. What else have you observed?"

"You are a man of exceptional ability, courage, loyalty, and patriotism. All of these virtues are evidenced by your lifetime of service to your country. You are also adventurous and impetuous. I deduce from these traits that you switched to the army because you craved more excitement."

"It was at the time of the Great Mutiny. My blood was boiling to punish the Mughals and Muslims for their perfidy, after all that we had done for the good of India. This is fascinating, Mr. Holmes. Please continue."

"Although the ring finger of your left hand indicates that you are not married," said Holmes, "I'm certain that a man of your dashing countenance and demeanor has not lacked opportunities to engage in affairs of the heart. You felt strongly enough about one woman called Elizabeth to have her name placed under the tattoo of the mermaid."

"That is true, sir, but I decided early on that the hard life of a sailor and later of the army on the northwest frontier of India in the aftermath of the Mutiny was not one that a gentleman should impose on the gentle sex."

"Beyond these observations, Major, I note only that you have been quite lucky in your life in that you have returned to England from the wars of the East with your body evidently intact and your spirit unbroken, undoubtedly because of a deeply religious nature that is indicated by the tattoo of the cross, and may I say, because of the strengthening of your faith by your participation in the rites and rituals of Freemasonry?"

"I see how you reached your conclusions concerning my naval and military life—it's quite simple, really. But on what basis can you state with such conviction that I am a Mason?"

"You revealed it yourself."

"Really! I don't recall—"

"I know that Watson is a Master Mason. You and he greeted one another with the unique handshake of those who have attained the third degree of Masonry, therefore you are also a Master. What I cannot state with conviction is whether you joined the fraternity before or after you entered into the army. As Watson will attest, I never guess."

"I was accepted as Entered Apprentice in a military lodge when I arrived in Bombay in 1873 and raised to Fellowcraft a year later in Calcutta. I received the apron of the Master Mason in 1879 in the lodge of the Fifth Fusiliers at the time of the Second Afghan War. I am proud to say that Watson presided over the induction ceremony as Most Worshipful Master."

Recalling that moment with pleasure and pride, I interjected. "I was honored to do so."

"When you were transferred to service with the Berkshires, I lost track of you. I later heard through the grapevine that you had been wounded and were sent home. The next thing I knew, you had become an associate and chronicler of the world's most illustrious private detective. It's wonderful to see you again, John, and to observe that you seem to have fully recovered from your wound. I must say, you look smashingly well."

"Now and then I feel a twinge in my leg to remind of that bloody day."

"You've had quite an injury yourself, Major," Holmes observed.

Raising a hand to the bandage and gingerly touching it, McAndrew replied, "Receiving this bump was nothing as romantic as the Jezail bullet that felled John at Maiwand."

"How did your injury happen?"

"I was struck a glancing blow by a tile that had become dislodged and fell from the roof of my quarters in Pimlico Road near the Chelsea Barracks."

"You're a fortunate fellow," I said. "You could have been killed."

"Indeed so. In my case, the mummy's curse does appear to have gone amiss, but perhaps only because I was a minor member of the expedition that disturbed the old gent's bones. I am not a believer in the occult, but this incident has almost made me one."

Leaning forwards with a look of astonishment, Holmes exclaimed, "Such an extraordinary statement requires elucidation, Major."

"Yes, I suppose it does, but I'm afraid that I've kept you from enjoying your meal long enough. Another time, perhaps."

"Really, Major," said Holmes insistently, "I cannot allow you to refer to your injury as the result of a mummy's curse, then go off and leave Dr. Watson and me to simply go on eating as if nothing were more important than our next course. Draw up that chair and tell us everything from the beginning."

"I am not one of our countrymen who take an interest in the so-called supernatural," said McAndrew as he seated himself, "but, as you observed, Mr. Holmes, I am a man of faith. You cannot be a Freemason and not believe in a Supreme Architect of the Universe."

"Quite so," said I. "It's the cornerstone of the Craft."

"Because I am a Christian," McAndrew continued, "I made my way homeward from my service in Afghanistan by way of the Holy Land. I naturally visited the biblical city of Ur and the rivers of Mesopotamia. After a few days in Baghdad, I continued to Jerusalem. I wished to see the Jewish Temple Mount, now claimed by the Mohammedans as their third most holy shrine, and to visit the Church of the Holy Sepulcher. Because I am an amateur archaeologist, I was also interested in exploring the discoveries of Edward Robinson, Charles Warren, and, of course, General Charles Gordon. As you know, he has located a skull-shaped hill and a nearby garden that he has identified as the true location of Calvary and Our Lord's burial place, rather than the tomb in the Church of Holy Sepulcher, as the Roman Catholics believe. After my explorations of the Holy City, I journeyed to Cairo to have a look at the pyramids of the Giza Plateau and the Sphinx. During my stay at the Mena House, a very fine old hostelry in the shadow of the Great Pyramid of Cheops, I chanced to meet Basil Porter. He is a nephew of Lord Porter, under whose auspices a dig had been organised. He graciously invited me to join them. The expedition was led by

Professor Felix Broadmoor of Cambridge University. Perhaps you've heard of it."

"The newspapers were full of it, and rightly so," I said emphatically. "I expect that Her Majesty will presently recognize its achievements with the appropriate honours."

"As well she should," said McAndrew. "However, Lord Porter has been subjected to a firestorm of criticism from some quarters for not consigning the expedition's finds to the nation by turning everything over to the British Museum."

"I'm certain that will eventually be sorted out," said Holmes. "Please go on with your story and the matter of the mummy's curse."

"The expedition was hoping to locate tombs from the period of the Sixth Dynasty king named Raneferef. We did not find a royal sarcophagus, but located the burial place of a minor official called Sarenput. It was a discovery of breathtaking riches. Believe me, gentlemen, nothing I had seen of the wealth of Indian maharajahs matched the treasures that we unearthed. The mummy itself was in an excellent state of preservation in a tomb that had escaped the grave robbers that through the millennia have looted so many burial chambers, perhaps because of the curse that had been carved into the door of the main chamber. It was so chilling that it is etched in my memory so indelibly that I can recite it exactly: 'The priest of Hathor will punish any of you who enters this sacred tomb or does harm to it. The gods will confront him because I am honoured by his Lord. Anyone who desecrates my tomb will drown, burn, be beaten, and be destroyed by the crocodile, hippopotamus, and lion. The scorpion and the cobra will strike him. Stones will crush the trespasser.' "

"Ah, at last," Holmes exclaimed "Now, we're getting somewhere. You have associated the stones of the curse with your unfortunate encounter with the falling tile."

"I am not a superstitious man, but my injury, occurring after some peculiar and tragic events since the conclusion of the Porter-Broadmoor expedition, has caused me to wonder if there might be something to this curse business."

"Your story becomes even more compelling," said Holmes. "What were these peculiar events, as you so colourfully put it?"

"The first was the collapse of a tunnel at the tomb site. No one was injured or killed at that time, but we had to work very rapidly to shore up the walls in order extricate the diggers."

"The next incident?"

"One of the ships carrying several larger artefacts from the dig to England was lost in a Mediterranean storm. Again, there was no loss of life or injury, but the artifacts are now lying at a depth that leaves them unrecoverable."

"When did someone die?"

McAndrew smiled appreciatively. "I can see that Dr. Watson in his writings has not exaggerated your facility at deduction, Mr. Holmes. Several weeks ago, an expert in Egyptian hieroglyphics who translated the curse, Anthony Fulmer, was killed in a train wreck in Kent."

Recalling reading in the newspapers that several persons had died, I muttered, "A terrible accident, indeed."

"What happened next?" asked Holmes.

"Last week Felix Broadmoor was waylaid in the night by a robber on a street near his home in Cambridge. He was so badly beaten that he died without recovering. The police have attributed the incident to a gang of toughs who have been plaguing the area. As far as I know, there have been no arrests."

"How many individuals participated in the expedition? "

"Including diggers, carters, and others that we hired from the local population, there were about two hundred. Those who came out from England were Lord Porter, as financial backer; his nephew Basil; an exceptional Egyptologist from the BM named Geoffrey Desmond, who is still in Cairo; Mr. Broadmoor; and Mr. Fulmer."

"Six men," I said, "two of whom are dead and yourself injured. If one were inclined to believe in the occult, your mummy's curse would seem to have taken quite a toll."

With a sigh, McAndrew replied, "I'm certain all of this is pure coincidence, but it does provide me with a good barracks yarn. I only wish I possessed the Watson talent for spinning a riveting tale. When will I have the pleasure of reading your next story in *The Strand*?"

"You will find it especially interesting, as it involves the deadliest snake in India."

McAndrew shuddered. "The swamp adder?"

"Exactly, along with a whistle, a saucer of milk, a ventilator, and a bell pull."

"Fascinating. I'm eager to read your account of the case."

With a cautioning look at me, Holmes said, "There were aspects of the affair, involving the young woman who brought the matter to my attention, that I do not believe would serve any useful purpose if they were made public at this time. Don't you agree, Watson?"

"Quite so, Holmes."

With that, Major McAndrew repeated his concern that he was keeping Holmes and me from our dinner, voiced a hope that he and I might meet again soon to reminisce about army days, and excused himself.

"Your friend has suddenly whetted my appetite for all things Egyptian," Holmes said as the sergeant returned to his table. "This interesting encounter has provided me reason for us to call upon a remarkable man I have been wanting to meet. When we return to Baker Street you can look him up in the Index under *P*."

A set of commonplace books, the Index was an alphabetized conglomeration of facts, snippets of data, numerous press clippings, notations by Holmes on scraps of paper, and trivia that Holmes had accumulated over a period of decades that were as astonishing in scope as his ability to recall the exact volume in which they were to be found.

"The name you seek," said Holmes, "is William Matthew Flinders Petrie."

On a biographical article torn from a two-month-old edition of the *Times*, the item noted that Petrie was the author of *Stonehenge: Plans, Description, and Theories*, published in 1880, followed recently by *Pyramids and Temples of Gizah*. "The son and namesake of a civil engineer and professional surveyor, and the maternal grandson of the famous navigator and explorer of the coasts of Australia, Professor Flinders Petrie is a remarkable man in his own right," declared the writer of the article. "As with many great men, he had little formal education, yet he has become a respected mathematician and highly esteemed in the emerging field of Egyptology as the father of modern archaeology."

Seated pensively in his favourite armchair and lighting a long pipe as I continued to read, Holmes said, "I do not in the least exaggerate when I state that Flinders Petrie's methodology of precisely recording and preserving data has raised the excavation of ancient sites from rooting around aimlessly in the earth with a pick and shovel to a science. You have often quoted me on the importance of trifles. Well, this fellow leaves me in the dust, so to speak. What I observe in the importance of cuffs of sleeves, thumbnails, and the great issues that hang from a boot lace, this man discerns in a shard of five-thousand-year-old Egyptian pottery. As I can reconstruct a crime and deduce the identity of a criminal from a cigar ash or an ink smudge on a sheet of stationery, Flinders Petrie divines the structure of an entire civilization."

Returning the "Index" to the shelf, I asked, "Where do we locate this paradigm?"

"Where else but the British Museum? If you have nothing to occupy you in the morning, I hope you will accompany me to Bloomsbury. Following our consultation with Flinders Petrie on the subject of mummy's curses, I shall treat you to a fine midday meal at a nearby public house, the Alpha Inn. I understand it is under new ownership, so I doubt anyone will remember me, although I spent many hours there after mornings in the Museum's Great Reading Room when I resided around the corner in Montague Street."

At eleven o'clock the next morning, as our hansom cab rattled along Marylebone Road to the Euston Road then turned down Gower Street, I allowed my mind to imagine Holmes during the time he had dwelt in Bloomsbury. Wondering to what mysteries to solve he might have directed his unique powers of observation and the art of deductive reasoning in the years before I had met him, and whether he would ever reveal them to me, I looked at him out of the corner of my eye and found a figure that had become familiar, yet always retained an air of mystery. His body was next to me, but his mind was far away. As we rode in the utter silence that I had learned to expect on such occasions, he sat to my left with his head turned slightly. He gazed through the window with a blank expression that I knew masked a brain that was alert to everything around him, but racing ahead in time in anticipation of what he expected to learn from Flinders Petrie on the subject of curses inscribed on the walls of tombs.

When the cab slowed to turn into Great Russell Street, my companion stirred, sighed, and muttered, "This was where the wine merchant Vamberry had his shop. Poor fellow. He was such a fool, wouldn't you agree, Watson?"

"How would I know? I have never heard the name."

"No, of course not. Before your time. Here we are! The good old BM."

Leaping from the hansom, he dashed through the iron gate, across the stone plaza, up the steps, and under the portico of imposing pillars so quickly that I lagged behind. As I caught up, a uniformed attendant was saying. "It's been a long time, Mr. Holmes. What game is afoot today? Blackmail? Robbery? A nice murder?"

"Perhaps, Mr. Dobbs. Perhaps," Holmes replied. "Call it the adventure of the mummy's curse. Which way to the office of Professor Flinders Petrie?"

"Up the stairs, past the Etruscan gallery, and straight ahead. Last door on the right."

"Think of it, Watson," said Holmes as we hurried up the steps and down a long corridor. "Within these magnificent walls reposes the tangible history of mankind, with its glories and tragedies catalogued and preserved, gathered from the four corners of the globe in what is the greatest gift to the world of the long reach of the British Empire!"

"Indeed?" I said, breathlessly. 'What about parliamentary government?"

"Said like a true and loyal British citizen, Watson!" Stopping before a plain door with a sign that announced DEPT. OF EGYPTOLOGY, he exclaimed, "Here we are! The domain of Flinders Petrie, unquestionably."

Three swift raps on the door produced from within the room the reply, "It's open."

Entering the office, Holmes and I found a slight figure with a neatly trimmed brown beard and moustache. Wearing a white laboratory coat, he bent over a coal-black, mummified corpse. Stepping boldly across the room, Holmes said, "Professor Flinders Petrie, I presume."

Peering intently down at the mummy, the professor replied, "You arrive at an auspicious moment, gentlemen. This man is unquestionably of the Third Dynasty."

"Forgive the intrusion, Professor," said Holmes. "I am Sherlock Holmes. This is my friend and associate, Dr. John H. Watson. If our call upon you is an inconvenience, we can return at a more opportune time."

"This chap has kept his secrets for nearly four millennia, sir," replied Flinders Petrie, looking up. "A few more minutes is of no consequence, Mr. Holmes. How may I be of service?"

"You are very kind, sir. What can you tell us about the Porter-Broadmoor expedition?"

The question was greeted with a puzzled expression. "Before answering, Mr. Holmes, I must inquire as to whom you represent. Are you here on behalf of Lord Porter?"

"We represent only ourselves."

Stepping away from the mummy to a sink at the far side of the room to wash his hands, the professor said, "That is a disappointment. I was hoping that Lord Porter had sent you. If you are not his agent, why are you interested in seeing me?"

"We are here because you are universally recognised as the preeminent authority in the emerging field of Egyptology."

"Emerging is the right word. Anyone who claims to be the preeminent authority on the study of Egyptology is treading on shaky ground. We have only begun to scratch the surface of the subject, gentlemen."

Finished cleansing his hands, Flinders Petrie invited us to continue our conversation in a small, comfortable office adjacent to his laboratory that was a jumble of Egyptian artefacts. "Are you aware, Professor," said Holmes, "of a series of unfortunate events concerning the recent Porter-Broadmoor expedition that some people have attributed to a curse that was found in the tomb? I refer to the collapse of a tunnel during the excavation, the sinking of a ship carrying artefacts, and the deaths of two of the expedition members."

"Surely, Mr. Holmes, you of all people cannot lend credence to the fantastic stories that these unfortunate events were the result of a curse. Regardless of what you may have read in newspapers about promises of death and doom for members of that expedition, those incidents were coincidence, pure and simple."

"Do you doubt," asked I, "that the expedition found a curse in the mummy's tomb?"

"I would have been surprised had they not. Curses of some kind have been found in every tomb in Egypt. They are as common as quotations from the Holy Bible on the gravestones of Christians in England. For as long as history has been written there have been tales of spells and curses. Read Plato's *Republic* and you will find he noted that if anyone in his time wished to injure an enemy, for a small fee one could hire a sorcerer to bring harm to an individual through an incantation, sign, or effigy to bind the gods to serve the purpose. All of this nonsense about curses in Egyptian tombs began in the imagination of a writer of horror stories named Jane Loudon Webb. After visiting a bizarre theatrical show in Piccadilly Circus in 1821, in which several mummies were unwrapped, this woman penned a science-fiction novel entitled *The Mummy*. Set in the twenty-second century, it featured a vengeful mummy that came to life and threatened to strangle the book's hero. This fantastic tome was followed in 1828 by publication of an anonymous children's book, *The Fruits of Enterprize*, in which mummies were set ablaze to illuminate the interior of an Egyptian tomb. The understandably irate mummies went on a rampage.

"The latest of these flights of imagination was the handiwork of a quite distinguished American author. In 1868, Louisa May Alcott published a short story, 'Lost in a Pyramid, or The Mummy's Curse.' In this grotesque fantasy, an explorer used a flaming mummy to light his way into the interior chamber of a tomb, where he found a golden box containing three seeds that were taken back to America and planted. They produced flowers which his fiancée wore at her wedding. When she inhaled the perfume, she lapsed into a coma and was transformed into a living mummy. It is a pitiful comment on our age, gentlemen, that people do actually believe in all this rot.

Now we find the shelves of our bookstores and our libraries filled with novels about monsters assembled from body parts and brought to life by mad scientists, and tales of werewolves and vampires. Even one of our country's promising new writers of stories, Arthur Conan Doyle, has dabbled in tales of the occult and supernatural, much of it apparently inspired by the American scribbler and lunatic, Mr. Edgar Allan Poe."

"You are obviously a man with strong opinions," said Holmes.

"If you seek an explanation for the unhappy events associated with the Porter-Broadmoor expedition, you would do well to look beyond the mummy's curse to the obvious explanation. It is human imagination that has discerned horror in happenstance. I refer you to a recent inventive newspaper article that appeared following the unfortunate murder of Professor Broadmoor. The item drew upon an interview in which the nephew of the financier of the expedition referred to the curse that had been found in the tomb. Suddenly, a murderous attack upon Broadmoor was in the mind of a reporter for a sensation-seeking newspaper the latest in a sequence of mysterious occurrences ominously linked to a mummy's curse. What a comment that is on the gullibility of the English people."

"You inquired as to whether Dr. Watson and I were sent to see you by Lord Porter. May I ask why you thought so?"

"I called upon him and his nephew several weeks ago in an attempt to persuade him that he bore an obligation to share his findings with the entire world by turning over the results of his expedition to the British Museum. My argument was along the line that he must choose between the transitory pleasures of personal wealth and the lasting glory of knowing that his name could forever be honoured by the naming of a wing of the museum for him. I left his home feeling quite encouraged that he would come round to my position on the matter. A few days later, to my great delight, he sent me a letter stating that I would presently be hearing from his solicitor, the Honourable Dudley Walsingham, concerning creation of just such a permanent exhibition. When you appeared, my hope was that you were his agents. I'm afraid now that my expectation that his remarkable collection might take the form of an exhibition for the Museum is groundless. What a great loss that is, gentlemen."

Leaving Flinders Petrie to resume his examination of the mummy, Holmes asked, "Well, Watson, what do you make of our professor of Egyptology?"

"A remarkable man! I found his lecture on the subject of curses fascinating. I share his belief that the proper place for the repose of the artefacts of the Porter-Broadmoor expedition is within the British museum. He is also spot-on about the deplorable state of the press. Its only interest seems to be in drumming up a fresh sensation in order to sell more newspapers."

"Quite so, my friend," said Holmes as we crossed Great Russell Street in the direction of the Alpha Inn on the opposite corner, "but the press can be valuable, if you know how to use it."

Although the next morning provided the kind of cold and foggy climate that invited one to remain indoors, Holmes was not present as I entered the sitting room and pulled the bell cord to signal Mrs. Hudson that I was ready for one of her bracing breakfasts. When I went to the pipe rack I kept on the mantle to choose my first briar of the day, I found a note from Holmes stating that he would return at noon.

Promptly at that hour, as I was reviewing my notes on the affair at Stoke Moran, Holmes entered the room, dropped two envelopes onto my desk, and said, "These items are for you."

Until that moment, I had accepted without comment his habit of examining the missives and parcels addressed to me and delivered by postmen, telegram delivery boys, and messengers. Not an item for me passed into my hands without first being examined and commented upon. But on this grey and depressing morning, perhaps because of my review of the horror that had recently occupied us at Stoke Moran, or as a result of the damp weather exacerbating the wound I had suffered at Maiwand, I said in exasperation, "Must you always examine my mail?"

"Why, Watson," Holmes responded in a wounded tone as he fixed me with an expression of shock and bewilderment, "I had no idea you could become upset over such a trifling matter."

I thereupon was subjected to a typical Holmesian explanation of his conduct to the effect that nothing was more instructive to a criminal investigator than handwriting, postmarks, and inks. "Have you no concept," he asked, "of all that may be detected about senders of items in the manner in which they address their correspondence? Was it written in a hurry? And what of the stationery? Volumes of information may be unearthed from a letter without opening it."

Only partly assuaged, I grumbled sarcastically, "I have no doubt that one day you will sit down and write a monograph on the subject."

Taking a pipe from his pocket, he replied, "I shall indeed. To date I have catalogued no fewer than fourteen kinds of ink used by the Royal Mail in its postmarks and very nearly one hundred watermarks of British paper manufacturers, as well as more than a score from the United States. For example, in the past year you have received eight letters of paper made in San Francisco. This has led me to deduce that a very close relative of yours is a resident of that city, and, I am sorry to observe, may recently have suffered a serious setback, probably in relation to his health." He paused to light the pipe. "Am I correct in deducing that your correspondence is regarding your brother's illness?"

"Yes, but how—"

"The writing on the first five envelopes was masculine. They were addressed to 'John Watson.' The lack of a 'Mister' or 'Dr. John H. Watson' suggests a familiarity connoting there is a family connection. The latter missives were from the same city, but written by a woman whose form of address included your title. Because a sister would write to 'John,' this indicates that she is probably your brother's wife."

"Probably? There's a word that I have never heard cross your lips."

"I am correct in stating that your brother is not well?"

"He suffers from a nervous disorder that leaves him increasingly palsied."

"When do you plan to sail to America?"

"Why do you assume that I'm contemplating such a trip?"

"Really, Watson! The second envelope you have received is a bulky one bearing the name of the Cunard Steamship Company. Its dimension can only mean it contains a schedule of Atlantic crossings."

"I have not yet made a decision."

"When you do, I shall provide whatever assistance you may require."

"Thank you. Where were you off to this morning?"

"Here and there."

With that, he settled into his chair, filled his pipe, struck a match, and lapsed into one of his long, contemplative silences that were as impenetrable as the swirling fog of Baker Street.

Gone again throughout the afternoon without explanation, he burst into the sitting room at a quarter to four, flung one of the city's sensational newspapers into my lap, and exclaimed, "Look at the Stop Press on page one."

Locating the small item, I read:

LATEST VICTIM OF THE MUMMY'S CURSE?

Our correspondent in Kent reports what appears to be another example of the curse that has befallen the recent expedition to investigate ancient tombs in Egypt. The financier of the ill-fated party, Lord Porter, was found dead early this morning in the bedroom of his estate in Kent. Although Chief Inspector William Crawford of the local constabulary stated that the elderly Lord Porter's death appears to have been of natural causes, we are reminded of the deaths of two members of the expedition, and other misfortunes that occurred since the discovery of a curse within the tomb when it was unearthed several months ago.

"Deaths of two leading participants in this expedition into the sands of Egypt may be dismissed as coincidence," said Holmes. "Three require an enquiry. There is an express train that we can catch if we hurry. I have sent a wire to Inspector Crawford asking him to rendezvous with us at the railway station at seven o'clock."

Less than a week had passed since Holmes and I had boarded another train at Waterloo Station to travel to Leatherhead, and onwards by a trap hired at the station inn to Stoke Moran. As on that occasion, it was a delightful day of fleecy clouds and bright sun, although we now passed through the spring countryside at a later hour. When the train arrived at our destination, I peered from my window at a short, rotund, middle-aged man in a brown suit and tan derby pacing the platform. Turning to Homes, I stated, "That must be our Inspector Crawford."

"Yes," Holmes replied, looking over my shoulder. "Heavy, black shoes. One can usually spot a policeman by his choice of sturdy, comfortable footwear."

After an exchange of greetings, Holmes asked Crawford, "Has anything been disturbed in the room in which Lord Porter's body was found?"

"Except for removal of the corpse to the mortuary round nine o'clock last evening, the bedroom is just as it was," replied Crawford excitedly. "I instructed the household staff that no one was to enter the bedroom until the coroner has ascertained the cause of death."

"Excellent work, Inspector!"

Riding in a carriage driven by a uniformed constable, we arrived at the estate of Lord Porter and passed through a gateway flanked by large stone figures with human heads and the bodies of lions. At the end of a long, curving driveway bounded by tall oak trees stood an old mansion whose doorway was guarded by a pair of stone rams. Holmes's loud rap on the door was answered by the butler. As we entered a spacious foyer decorated with Egyptian artefacts, Holmes asked him, "What is your name?"

"Bradley, sir."

"How long have you been Lord Porter's butler?"

"Nearly ten years."

"Had Lord Porter seemed out of sorts lately? Was he a nervous man? Did he at any time express fear that his life was in jeopardy?"

"Not to me, sir."

"Did he ever speak to you about his recent expedition to Egypt?"

"Not about the expedition itself, sir. But lately he expressed concern about stories in the newspapers concerning allegations that he was more interested in the profits to be garnered from that adventure than in the scientific aspects and advancement of knowledge."

"Who was present in the house when Lord Porter died?"

"Only the staff, sir."

"Had there been recent visitors?"

"Lord Porter's solicitor was here on Monday."

"That would be the Honourable Dudley Walsingham?"

"Yes, sir."

"Anyone else?"

"A Major McAndrew called. He had been invited to luncheon with Lord Porter. I believe he was a member of the expedition. Last evening, Lord Porter's nephew came to dinner. Soon after they ate, Lord Porter went to bed and Mr. Basil returned to his home in London."

"I sent the nephew a telegram last evening informing him of the death," said the Inspector, "but have received no reply."

"Bradley," said Holmes, "please show us to Lord Porter's bedroom."

Located to our right at the top of a curving stairway, the bedroom was a large chamber that had the aspects of a museum.

"Please remain in the corridor, gentlemen," said Holmes brusquely, "while I have a look round the room."

What followed in the next few minutes was a scene quite familiar to me, but a matter of wonder and puzzlement to Inspector Crawford. "What is he looking for, Doctor?" he asked of me in a whisper as Holmes moved carefully through the room, examining the area around the bed, kneeling briefly to peer at the carpet, and going to the room's two large windows.

Abruptly returning to the doorway, Holmes asked the butler, "Did Lord Porter smoke?"

"Until his physician ordered him to give up tobacco two years ago, he enjoyed a pipe."

"Was he an active man?"

"Prior to the Egyptian expedition, yes."

"But not since?"

"I'm afraid the journey and the time he spent in the desert took its toll on his vitality. He spent most days either at his desk in his study or in bed."

"Thank you, Bradley. That will be all."

"Very good, sir."

"Now, Inspector," said Holmes, "take us to the mortuary."

In a small room adjacent to the office of the constabulary, the sheet-shrouded body of Lord Porter lay on a large table. Drawing back the covering, Holmes proceeded to examine the corpse from head to toe. Presently, he declared, "Interesting. Have a look, Watson. I call your attention to a slight discoloration of the skin around what seems to be a puncture just below the hairline on the right side of the back of Lord Porter's neck."

Examining a small, reddish welt, I said, "It could be an insect bite. To state exactly what it is would require examination of the tissue under a microscope."

"Inspector, " said Holmes, "I'll be interested in knowing as soon as possible to what your coroner attributes it."

"Certainly, Mr. Holmes. Is there anything else I can do?"

"Not at the moment, but you may be hearing from me quite soon."

Although I was fairly bursting with curiosity as Holmes and I returned to Baker Street, I had learned that he would illuminate me when he deemed it appropriate to do so. He had said to me on several occasions that I possessed the grand gift of silence and that this had made me quite invaluable as a companion. Consequently, when he left our lodging in the morning and did not return until late in the afternoon, I was resolved to make no enquiries as to his purpose or whereabouts. It was that evening during dinner that he looked up suddenly from a platter of Mrs. Hudson's incomparable broiled trout and muttered, "These are murky waters, Watson. Whether I prove to be correct will be known only when we hear again from Inspector Crawford."

The message he awaited arrived the next afternoon. A telegram from Crawford was the briefest Holmes had ever received:

COBRA VENOM

Waving the wire as if it were a flag, Holmes said exultantly, "That is the penultimate stone in this intricate construction, Watson. All that is left is to send to Inspector Crawford a telegram in which I shall propose a question to be put to the butler, along with my advice to Crawford that if the butler's reply is in the affirmative a charge of murder be brought against Basil Porter."

Crawford's reply arrived later that day in another brief telegram:

HE HAS GIVEN A COMPLETE CONFESSION.

DETAILS TO FOLLOW.

As I read the message, I exclaimed, "This is amazing, Holmes. You have solved this case without having met and questioned the person you suspected!"

"There was no need, Watson. I had an accumulation of facts that pointed to Basil Porter. This nefarious nephew possess one of the most brilliant and devious minds to ever challenge my powers. You'll recall that I said after our meeting with Flinders Petrie that the press can be a valuable instrument if you know how to use it. This man seized upon the seemingly mysterious events of the tunnel collapse, the sinking of the ship, the accidental death of Anthony Fulmer, and the murder of Professor Broadmoor to plant in the mind of a newspaper reporter the idea that these events were the effects of the mummy's curse. In an attempt to lend further credibility to this explanation, he attempted to murder your old comrade in arms, Major McAndrew. Had we not encountered the Major that evening in Simpson's in the Strand, Basil Porter's crimes might have gone undetected and unpunished."

"What caused you to suspect him?"

"Among the numerous puzzling facets of this case, I found it curious that on notification of his uncle's death that Basil Porter did not rush back from London. When I found what seemed to be an insect bite in the back of Lord Porter's neck, but could have been a scratch made by a pin a hypodermic needle, I suspected that Lord Porter had been injected with a poison. When I received confirmation that it was cobra venom, I saw no explanation that was logical, except that it had been administered by the nephew. To be certain, I had to eliminate the only other visitor to Lord Porter that day, your friend McAndrew. I had to know if the two men had been alone at any time on that day."

"That was the question you asked Crawford to pose to the butler."

"In my examination of the rug in Lord Porter's bedroom, I found not only traces of cigar ash, but evidence that someone had paced up and down in a state of extreme excitement. You know my methods. What does that tell you?"

"There had been a heated argument."

"Precisely, but concerning what? Among my excursions following our sojourn to the domain of Inspector Crawford was a call upon Lord Porter's solicitor, the Honourable Dudley Walsingham. My purpose was to inquire as to the beneficiary of Lord Porter's will. It was quite a formidable estate, even before the spectacular treasures brought back from Egypt. My enquiries directed toward knowledgeable men in the financial circles and bankers in the City resulted in evidence that Basil Porter has been on the brink of bankruptcy for quite some time."

"You therefore surmised that Basil expected to be rescued from his dilemma by killing his uncle and inheriting an estate which had been substantially increased in wealth as a result of the treasures brought back from Egypt."

"But this prospect was suddenly jeopardised," said Holmes, "when Lord Porter appeared to accede to Professor Flinders Petrie's appeal to donate the expedition's finds to the BM. It was then that Basil devised a plan for murder that he had hoped would appear to be the result of the curse found in the tomb. To lay the foundation for this fantastic proposition, he killed Professor Broadmoor and in an exceedingly clever use of the press, he called attention to the coincidental incidents of the tunnel collapse, the ship bearing expedition artefacts that sank, and the death of Fulmer in the train accident. Of course, I had no proof of any of this. Each of these occurrences could be readily explained as happenstance. The only occurrence that I was able to investigate was the curious incident of the roof tile that injured Major McAndrew. This meant a visit to his quarters in Chelsea. In examining the rooftop, I found not only that the tile had been pried loose, but footprints of the person who flung them down on McAndrew. If this attack had been done by a magically animated mummy that had been wondrously transported to Chelsea, he had taken time to be fitted for a pair of shoes. We are left with no other explanation but this extraordinary drama had to be the work of Basil Porter. At that point, I had to be certain he was the only person on that day who had the opportunity."

"But what if Major McAndrew had also been alone with Lord Porter that day?"

"Motive, Watson! What motive could McAndrew possibly have had to kill Lord Porter?"

"Well done, Holmes!"

Although Basil Porter had admitted to the murders of his uncle and Felix Broadmoor, he presented to jury and judge at his trial the fantastic explanation that his deeds were the result of a brain fever that developed into insanity, which he brazenly blamed on the mummy's curse. This astonishing device proved unavailing. Convicted of two murders, he was sentenced to death and hanged for his crimes. Meanwhile, because Lord Porter had no other heirs, the treasures of the Egyptian expedition were declared the property of the Crown and consigned by a judge of the probate court to the British Museum, there to be under the supervision of Flinders Petrie. That distinguished scholar continued his work as an archaeologist, for which he would presently be knighted and named Professor of Egyptology at University College of London in 1892. The Egyptian Research Council that he established in 1894 eventually became The British School of Archaeology and, ultimately, the Petrie Museum of Egyptian Archaeology in Malet Place.

As I was reviewing my notes on this extraordinary affair a few days after Holmes's solution to a case that I had decided to record under the title "The Mummy's Curse," I gazed across our sitting room at Holmes and interrupted his repose with a thought that had suddenly occurred to me. "You have proved that Basil Porter devised a murderous scheme to inherit vast wealth," I said, "but has it ever entered your mind that none of this has proved that all of these unfortunate events were not the result of the mummy's curse?"

Holmes leapt from his chair. "What are you saying?"

"It could be interpreted," said I, with a smile and arching eyebrows, "that Basil Porter was simply the instrument by which the mummy's curse was, in fact, fulfilled!"

"Good old Watson," said Holmes with a puff of smoke from his favorite briar. "Your romanticism is as permanent a fixture as the pyramids of Giza. And just as mysterious!"

DEATH IN THE EAST END

Colin Bruce

MY DEAR FELLOW, this is a most pleasant surprise! Pray come in."
I was entirely sincere. It is always flattering when the former student returns to consult the teacher. Irving Greyshott had come to my practice fresh from an internship at Guy's, and I had enjoyed showing him how to cope with the disorderly rush of life which is general practice. He had been kind enough to tell me how vital my practical advice was, after the rather theoretical nature of his training in the ivory towers of that great hospital. In due course, as was proper, he had decided to strike out on his own in the east of the city, and from what I had heard he was doing quite well.

Today, however, his manner seemed rather tense, and he downed the single finger of whiskey I poured for him with the air of one who wished it had been more. This was evidently more than a social call.

"So, how fares the East End?" I asked.

He grimaced. "Different. I wish now that I had been more appreciative of the comforts of a practice in a prosperous area like this one. It is a good class of patients that you get here, sir."

"I am hardly one of Harley Street's famous," I said. "As you know, my patients are more often shopkeepers and artisans than they are bankers and lawyers. Every class of person comes to a general practitioner. And for goodness' sake call me Watson. You have a practice of your own now, and I am no longer your senior."

My former colleague seemed to relax a little, and settled back in his chair.

"Well, I grant that you must expect all kinds of patient, wherever you set up. But in some neighbourhoods of the East End, it is really like going back in time a hundred years or more, compared to these parts. You are dealing with people who come to a doctor only when they are truly at death's door. People who are born, grow up, grow old, and die within a few hundred yards of the same spot, without ever travelling beyond their local warren of streets. It gives them a strange and limited perspective on life, a fatalistic viewpoint that can seem quite eerie to an outsider.

"Home visits can be disconcerting. The very first of those I had to make was to an old lady living on her own. There are a lot of these, Watson, for their husbands, if they ever had one, tend to work in rough conditions and die in middle age. I came into the tiny bed-sitting room where the lady lived, and was puzzled at what she was sewing: she was joining sheets together, yet making something too large to be a bolster case. I walked further into the room, and nearly fell into a pine box on the floor, a box so small and cheaply made that it took me a moment to realise I had almost fallen into her coffin. She was sewing a shroud for herself!"

I could not help blinking. "Perhaps she was anxious not to give her children trouble and cost, expenses extra to the funeral," I said.

Greyshott shook his head. "It is more than that. Family ties are not necessarily to be depended on in these parts: it is more that the old people have a mortal fear of not being properly buried at all. It is partly bound up with pride, and partly with a kind of superstition that you may not get to heaven unless you arrive respectably parcelled up, so to speak. I now know that the practice is very common; some old ladies keep a coffin in their room for years, actually sleeping in it every night, wrapped in a shroud instead of sheets in anticipation of the final journey they know they will make sooner or later."

He tried to smile. "It is all a little discouraging for the well-meaning doctor paying a house call, and trying to act bright and cheery. But some visits are more worrying. To be frank with you, it is such a connection that brings me here tonight." He looked expectant. "I do not suppose that, just by chance, your colleague Holmes might be about?"

My mood dampened, rather. "He is away in Edinburgh," I said shortly. "But really, you know, despite his many talents, he lays claim to no medical knowledge. If you think that I will not be—"

Greyshott waved his hands hastily. "That is not my meaning at all, Watson. It is to yourself before any other that I would turn for practical medical advice. But, you see, this particular case involves a patient who is not merely ill, but now seems to have altogether dropped out of sight. I thought if we could cover both possible angles to the case, so much the better. Let me describe the circumstances to you."

How would Holmes handle this? I hesitated only for a moment— I was feeling less than fully well myself that day, with just a touch of stomach cramp—before rising and taking my hat and coat from the stand.

"I shall come and see for myself," I said. "Let us hail a hansom. You can explain as we drive."

I STARTED TO regret my kind impulse as soon as Greyshott leant forward to shout our destination to the cabbie.

"Thirty-three Old Chapel Street, off Roman Road," he bellowed. Then he looked at me. I must have gone pale, for he added immediately, "I say, Watson, I know it is a rough area, but doctors have pretty well-respected immunity in the eyes of the local gangs. I assure you we shall be in no danger."

I shook my head, angry that he should think me such a coward as to be afraid of ordinary street ruffians. But there was no way Greyshott could know the sinister associations that particular area had for me, and I was not about to enlighten him. The cab rattled forward over the rough cobbles, and I could not help wincing as my stomach pain shot up my left side. Fortunately, the streets were remarkably clear of traffic, and in no time we had gone the full length of the Euston Road and were leaving the central gaslit streets behind.

"Now, tell me about this troubling case," I said.

Greyshott sighed. "It concerns a large family," he said. "Family arrangements in the poor parts of the East End are never quite conventional. Yet here and there you find a woman who, seemingly by strength of character alone, manages to bring up a large family. One such is—or was—Margaret May. She looks after a dozen children, only three of whom are her own by her now-deceased husband. The others are presumably nieces and nephews born out of wedlock, or other such 'orphans': one learns not to ask too many questions. It is hardly our Victorian ideal of a family. The older children are very wise in the ways of the street, and I very much doubt that the sources of the family income would stand close scrutiny. Yet the children are fed and clothed, protected from worse fates the world has to offer, and I am neither policeman nor judge.

"One day two of the older children came and begged me to come: their mother was ill with a high fever and delirium. When I say 'begged,' in fact they brought with them a purse, and held out an absurdly large sum of money before me. Their street wisdom did not prevent them having an exaggerated idea of a doctor's modest income! I declined the money, and went with them."

The darkness had closed in about us as he spoke. Now our way was illuminated only by the burning torch carried by our cabbie, and its occasional mate above the doorway of a rough-looking inn. With the bright lights made possible by modern science out of sight, there was little to show we were still in the London of the nineteenth century. But now a brightly moonlit field showed on our right: a football pitch was marked out on it, with rough goal-posts at either end. Greyshott noticed my look towards it, and misunderstood.

"What a blessing it is that London has such open spaces, Watson. The authorities do little to feed and clothe the poor and the orphans, but we must give them some credit for preserving good open spaces for healthy outdoor play. The value of such land must be huge, nowadays, yet the councils somehow resist all temptations from property developers, whether offered overtly or dishonestly."

"That is no altruism!" I said, and wished I had bitten my tongue instead.

"Why, what on earth do you mean?"

There was no option now but to go on. "Have you heard of the plague pits of London?" I asked.

"Of course. The mass graves where victims of the Great Plague were buried, back in the seventeenth century. Even today, it is forbidden to dig in those areas, and the penalty is death by hanging, for the fear is that the plague may still be alive down there and break loose once more. But I am not sure how effective this penalty is in practice, for the location of the pits is secret."

I smiled, although it was hardly a matter for humour. "They are more extensive than you suppose. The reason London retains its great green parks, the reason aldermen resist all bribes from those who would build houses on those areas, is that they are the regions of the Pits. Trying to dig foundations anywhere would earn the perpetrator death."

Greyshott looked at me openmouthed. "Why, I never heard that. How is it that you know so much about this?"

This was the last question I wanted to answer. "Tell me more about this Margaret May and her family," I said hastily.

"Well," he resumed, "I went to see her, and she did indeed have a high fever, with much difficulty in breathing. I did the appropriate things, but was not overly concerned. She seemed to be a woman robust in constitution, as well as personality. But with so many people depending on her, I made a point of calling again the following day, only to be told that she was better and did not need to see me.

"I was told this by a group of the older children at the door; several were in earshot. I went on my way, for I had other patients to attend to, but I was puzzled, for her recovery must have been remarkably swift. I went back again the following morning, and was once again denied entry. By this time, the children had wrongly concluded that the reason for my return was that I wanted paying. Again, two of the eldest stood in the door, and one produced both coins and notes from his pocket: 'Mother told us to pay you for her. She is quite well, but busy; in fact, she has gone out.' "

"I did not believe that for a moment. 'I do not want payment,' I said. 'But I must see her for myself.' And with that I tried to push my way past them.

"But they blocked my way with quite substantial force. 'We know that you are a doctor,' said the eldest quickly. 'But you may not come in. We have private things lying about.'

"I had no option but to desist. Often such households do indeed have 'private' things lying about, such as ill-gotten goods. Yet I remained concerned. Margaret May was a rich woman, by local standards. Doubtless, there was considerable wealth hidden about the house, for such people do not use banks. The awful thought came to me that her incapacitation with fever might have left the older children with the opportunity to plan some dark deed. Some instinct told me, just from the way the children clustered about and looked at me, that something in that household was terribly wrong."

At this point our cab halted suddenly. We were at the entrance to Old Chapel Street itself, but the way was blocked on one side by a makeshift bonfire, and on the other by an overturned costermonger's barrow. Several youths lounged about, and in front of us, blocking the narrow passage that remained, stood an older, ferret-faced man. The arrangement was familiar to me. The fact that much of the East End is controlled by gangs, each defending access to its little kingdom in degrees that vary, is hardly a secret. My companion leaned forward and half stood.

"We are Doctors Greyshott and Watson, on our way to attend a patient," he said loudly.

The man nodded and made to stand aside: it is indeed true that doctors largely have immunity from these checkpoints. But then something seemed to strike him.

"Did you say *Doctor Watson?*" he asked slowly. Then, stepping up onto the running-board of the hansom, he held up his lantern and peered closely at me. I deliberately did not meet his eye, but could not help wincing from his breath, foul and smelling of garlic. "That is a name to conjure with in these parts," he smiled grimly. "We are very indebted to your granddad, to be sure."

I kept my voice steady. "He was not my grandfather, but two generations further back than that. Are you willing to be held responsible for all the sins of your forefathers?"

He stepped down and back from the cab. "That was not my meaning at all. I am sure we are indebted to your ancestor, Doctor.

Firm but fair, no doubt, firm but fair!" And with a cackle of laughter he waved the cabbie forward. As we passed, he tipped his hat to us ironically. Greyshott turned to me.

"Watson, your manner has really been quite strange ever since I told you the address we are going to. I asked your help to clear up one mystery, not create another. Tell me frankly, man, what is all this about!"

I swallowed painfully. But I did owe my colleague an explanation, and really, there seemed no alternative. I have always been a truthful man, and I decided to make a clean breast of it.

"We were talking of the Plague which struck London in the seventeenth century, decimating the population," I said thickly.

"We were. But that was two hundred years ago. The Plague ended with the Great Fire of London, in 1666."

I shook my head. "That is the simplified story: that the Fire effectively sterilised the city, as we would now think of it. But the reality is less tidy. In fact lesser outbreaks continued well into the eighteenth century, although they were contained, probably by gradually improving sanitation as much as by other efforts. The last was exactly one hundred years ago. Its epicentre was here in the East End, in the very oldest part of London, which dates back to well before the Romans came.

"At the time of the outbreak, my ancestor was Surgeon-General to the city, in charge of public health matters. There was much speculation why this particular area seemed vulnerable to outbreaks—it was not the first time it had been implicated—and suspicion attached to the catacombs.

"Underneath modern London, of course, we have a maze of tunnels accommodating sewers and now even underground railway lines. But in those days, the largest such network of tunnels was the ancient catacombs, a maze whose full extent had never been fully explored, and which had served London instead of a graveyard for countless centuries. The catacombs of Rome and other continental cities are more famous, but not necessarily more extensive, than those of London. The catacombs were home to others than the dead and the rats. There was at that time a large population of poor people who worked or begged on the streets by day, but made their homes in the catacombs at nights. Europe was still coming out of the period known as the Little Ice Age, and despite their atrocious features, the catacombs provided shelter far below the reach of the weather. There grew a suspicion that the plague originated in the catacombs, and that it was the poor dwellers there who were responsible for bringing it up to the London above and spreading it.

"The city fathers asked my great-great-grandfather for his advice. They were horrified by his reply, but he was evidently a persuasive man as well as a cold-hearted and ruthless one, and his orders were put into effect. The following night a team of stonemasons, themselves under threat of death if they refused or breathed any word of what was planned, went into action. The entrances to the catacombs were sealed up without warning, with the living inhabitants still inside. It is said that their cries and pleas could be heard through chinks in the stonework the following day, and many after it. But my ancestor would not permit any pity. The entombing was merely made more complete, and eventually the voices were heard no more."

Greyshott shivered. "A grim tale, indeed. But I can see your progenitor's viewpoint. The good of the many must be placed ahead of that of the few. Doctors have to make harsh decisions of this kind, more often than we ever tell the world about."

I shook my head. "Perhaps so. Yet they could at least have made some effort to evacuate the children."

"Surely that would have been impracticable without spreading the plague?"

"Perhaps. But what worries me most is the possibility that my ancestor was not merely acting for the best in a rational way, in uncanny anticipation of our modern theory of germs, but bowing to, or perhaps even believing himself, a far less worthy hypothesis."

I lowered my voice so that the cabby should not hear us. "There were rumours at that time that the plague was spread not by living people coming forth from the catacombs, but others far more sinister. Blackened, wizened things, animated in a way no one understood, stepping out under cover of the night. You have heard the old superstitious saying, *The dead cry out for company.*' In the London of a hundred years ago, this was suspected to be literally true: corpses from the catacombs were supposedly creeping up to infect the living above, animated by a terrible jealousy. The likelihood that my ancestor condemned a thousand children to die for fear of that absurd superstition is what makes me truly ashamed."

My colleague sighed. "A horrible notion indeed. But you do not know that for sure. And as you just implied to that street ruffian, we could none of us stand to be judged for the deeds of all our ancestors. Anyway, let us put such speculations aside, for we are here."

As he spoke, the cab rumbled to a halt before a frontage of brick visibly eroded by its years of exposure to the acrid East London fogs. Greyshott's knock at the door was answered not, as he had led me to anticipate, by an eruption of urchins, but by a single shy-looking boy who could not have been more then ten or eleven years old, barefoot and peering at us from under a mop of hair so fair it was almost white.

My colleague addressed him in a kind but no-nonsense tone. "Hello, Timmy. Where are all the others?"

"They are all out blagging, Doctor. They will not be back till tomorrow."

Greyshott refrained from asking him what 'blagging' was, no doubt wisely. "May we come in?" he asked.

The boy shook his head unhappily but firmly. " 'Arry said I was not to let in you in, sir, no matter wot you said."

I bent down to talk to the lad on a more equal basis. "And what about me?" I asked. "My name is John Watson. I promise you, I only want to help, and not cause you any troubles."

The boy pondered this. It was evident that he knew it was against the spirit of the orders the older boys had given him, yet he was obviously keen for company in that large, lonely house. Eventually he stood to one side.

I looked at Greyshott. "Do not wait," I said, knowing that he must have other patients to see. "I will call on you tomorrow."

I followed the boy into the house and sat down gingerly on an old horsehair sofa which was bursting at the seams to such an extent that it was rather like sitting on a hassock.

"Tell me, Timmy, how is your mother?" I asked.

He sat quite expressionless. After a few seconds, a small tear rolled down one cheek.

"Timmy, she is dead, isn't she?" I said very gently. He gave the faintest nod.

"What happened? Did Harry or somebody else hurt your ma?"

He shook his head. "No, it were just the fever. We tried our best, Mister, honest."

"Well then, there is no use pretending it hasn't happened. We must find other adults to look after you all, and, you know, your mother must be buried."

He looked down at his feet.

"But Mister, Harry and the others wanted to magic her. They say sometimes magic can make people better. Even—even dead people. They thought if they tried very hard, they might do it. They have even been reading in books."

I looked at the boy with great sadness. It is well known that sometimes a mother will refuse to admit her baby has died, and carry it around and even attempt to feed it for many days, so strong is the maternal instinct. Rarer, but nevertheless known to doctors, are those cases where children will refuse to accept the death of a mother on whom they have been dependent, clutching at the most desperate straws of alternatives.

"Timmy, I am very sorry, but magic does not work. Certainly it cannot bring back the dead," I said.

He looked me in the eye. "Yes, it can," he said defiantly.

I sighed. "Timmy, I really wish it could. But—"

"You don't understand, Mister. *It did work.* Yesterday, she spoke to me. She told me she would come up to my room and visit me tonight."

I strove to keep my expression neutral as I stood up.

"Take me to her, Timmy," I said.

"Promise you won't take her away? Harry said Doc Greyshott would take her away and put her in a box in the ground, and the magic couldn't work then."

"Timmy, I promise that I will not take her away tonight, and not at all unless I am quite, quite certain that nothing can be done for her." I was telling the truth, for the wild hope had occurred to me that Margaret might merely have been deeply unconscious. Harry and his brothers were hardly professional diagnosticians, after all.

Timmy led me down a corridor and into a small windowless room. A ring of bright candles guttered around a chair. My hopes were instantly dashed. Indeed, hardened medical professional though I nowadays am, it was all I could do to restrain a gasp of horror. The thing in the chair was not merely dead, but wizened and blackened, its features almost unrecognisable. Once, in the tropics, I had seen a man who died of jungle fever reduced to such a state, but never before in this country. Thankfully, someone had cast a veil over it, but it was a sight to give an adult nightmares, never mind a sensitive child.

"Timmy, I am very sorry—"

His voice rose to a scream. "She spoke to me, sir! Last night she spoke to me! She was bad, but she's getting better. She said she'd come to me tonight. Spoke and moved, she did. You're not taking her away, sir! You promised!"

I looked at him. He seemed utterly sincere. Clearly, he had been having dreams so vivid that he was genuinely convinced of their reality. Elaborately, although feeling a fool, I went through the motions of examining the corpse for signs of life. The body was freezing cold, of course, and *rigor mortis* well advanced. As I proceeded, I made a decision. I could not possibly leave the boy alone in the house with the corpse of his mother, and all other considerations apart, there was no question of getting an undertaker at this time of night. There was only one thing to be done.

"Timmy, I am going to stay here tonight, and keep an eye on—on your mother. I will stay right here in this room." I meant it, for I was not risking having the boy slip past me into that grisly company. "If she were somehow to—to speak, or to move, I could not possibly miss noticing it. Is that a fair offer to make?"

He nodded, apparently delighted and relieved, a thing which caused my stomach to churn.

"And if she does move, and come up from her chair, you will admit that you doctors are wrong, and she may stay with us?" he asked solemnly.

"If such a thing should happen, I will admit the wrongs of the medical profession throughout history, and may the punishment for them all be on me!" I smiled.

I took the boy up to his bedroom, tucked him in as best I could, and returned downstairs for a night to which I did not look forward. Nevertheless, I rummaged around until I found some old newspapers, and then returned to the inner parlour which was at least brightly lit, for whatever obscure occult purpose the ring of candles had originally been intended.

I got a considerable start when I entered. My imagination was playing tricks on me, for I could have sworn that the corpse *had changed position.* Just as a man sitting in a chair feels the need to shift a little now and then for comfort, so the corpse's limbs seemed to be at just slightly different angles than before. Cursing myself for a fool, I nevertheless could not bear to look at the remains. I arranged a chair with its back to the corpse, and facing the wall. I was comforted by the thought of Sherlock Holmes's maxim: 'The real world is quite enough for us! If there is an afterlife filled with ghosts, maybe they talk to other ghosts, and for all I know torment them, but they can hardly have access to the world of the living, or surely there would never be a murderer not haunted by his deeds.' And as Holmes has shown me, there are only too many evil men who can, and do, live at peace with themselves even after such a crime.

Presently I settled down enough to read, but the stomach pains I had been sensing grew until I felt a tight band across the left side of my chest. Eventually I was forced to drop the newspapers and pass the time by examining the cracks in the wall in front of me. The thin plaster clearly showed the pattern of the stonework beneath: an archway blocked with large lumps of stone, not neatly placed together as in a drystone wall, but clumsily arranged with great gobs of cement in between, as if the work had been done in extreme haste.

Then it was that realisation dawned: I was, in all likelihood, looking at one of the entrances to the catacombs my ancestor had sealed up. He might have stood or sat in the very position I now occupied, urging the masons on in their horrific work, directing them to ignore the pleas of the doomed trapped behind this permanent barrier to the light above. Distantly, in the street outside, I heard a cart rumbling by, and a man's voice shouting. I could not make out the words, but it sounded almost like a chant. Could it possibly be *'Bring out your dead! Bring out your dead!'*—the cry of the poor wretches forced to carry the corpses of those who had died to the mass burial pits, almost certainly contracting the plague themselves ere long. I remembered the grim stories I had heard of doctors refusing to come to visit those suspected of the affliction, preferring to pronounce them doomed than risk their own health. Thus they had fanned the flames of natural fear until it grew into the unreasoning terror which had led families to flee their own homes, leaving behind any member suspected of exposure—sometimes even small children pleading to know why their parents were looking at them so strangely, why they were being abandoned.

The words I had spoken in my promise to the boy came back to me. What strange influence had possessed me to say *'I will admit the wrongs of the medical profession throughout history, and may the punishment for them all be on me!'*

I sat still for a length of time I have no way to estimate, feeling a deepening chill spread over my whole body as the night fell altogether silent. But then, quite suddenly, and very nearby, there came a loud creaking noise. I tried to convince myself that its location was uncertain, but I knew better: the sound was coming from behind and to my right, from the chair where the dead woman sat. And I knew with dreadful certainty that I had heard that timbre before: no one who was once a medical student training on cadavers will ever forget the sound that a joint stiff with rigor mortis makes when it is bent. I made a desperate effort to stand up—and found myself still absolutely motionless. My body was no longer mine to command. It was then that I recalled the increasing frequency of the pains in my left side which I had been putting down to indigestion, and the notorious capacity of doctors for ignoring their own health until it is too late. And I suddenly realised the awful fallacy of my confidence that I would never have anything to fear from ghosts, just because they had no ability to touch the *living*. I, a doctor, had failed

to notice the moment of my own death, even though my consciousness somehow continued.

In utter paralysis, I saw the veiled and wizened figure move slowly
into my field of view, and past me. I was inexpressibly relieved that
its back was to me. How I hoped, hoped desperately, that it would
not turn round, that I would not have to look into that shrivelled
and distorted face so terribly reanimated. And, in fact, the figure
turned towards the door, and stretched out its blackened hands to
open it wider. But before it could pass through, there came a patter
of feet outside and a high-pitched cry.

"Mam, mam, is that you?"

The figure spoke in a hoarse, croaking voice.

"Yes, Timmy, I am coming for you."

"Mam, mam, please don't speak like that, it scares me! Mam, I
have been so lonely. I'm afraid the others are not just blagging, but
have left me."

"No, Timmy, they will be back. Don't be lonesome. I am here."

Very slowly the door swung open to reveal Timmy's white face.
But he kept his eyes averted, too scared to look directly at the
dreadful thing that was facing him.

"Oh, mam, they will be so pleased when I tell them you are
walking again!"

"You must not tell them, Timmy, not yet. I must have my rest
during the day."

"Oh, but I must tell them. I will explain that you still need your
rest, like when you had the fever, till you are quite better. But they
must know. Think how angry they would be with me if I kept the
good news from them."

"If you tell them, terrible things will happen. Now you must help me."

"Mam, they would be able to tell something was up, and have it
out of me anyway. I will do anything I can, but I am not able to keep
secrets from Harry and the rest."

The figure's voice rose to a menacing hiss.

"Timmy, this is what will happen if you tell. You will become dead
as I was."

"Oh, no, mam, please, please! But I would rather you were alive, and still loving me even though I was dead, than the other way around."

"Timmy, I would forget you, that is how it works. We would lay you in a box, and the lid would be nailed down. Then the box would be placed deep in the earth, and we would all forget you, and never come to visit ever, and you will be lonesome, so lonesome, forever and ever!"

By this point, the boy was keening like an animal, in an agony of terror. It was intolerable that this should continue, and as my pity for the child became stronger even than my own fear for myself, the impossible happened. I became able to move! I stood, and as I did so, the veiled woman turned her face to me. That was the thing I had most dreaded, yet it was not I who screamed first, but she. She fell instantly into a heap on the floor. At that moment there came a tremendous hammering on the front door of the house. The boy ran frantically away. Seconds later I heard the noise of bolts being drawn open, and then a confusion of voices. The child was safe in the hands of the living, where he belonged. My job was done, and it was with a sense of relief that I felt the darkness take me.

AN INDEFINITE TIME later, I became aware of a dim reddish glow. Slowly the realisation came: I was seeing strong light through closed eyelids. With an effort I opened my eyes. I was lying on my back in a bright room—everywhere sunlight on white walls and ceiling. There were noises very close by. I turned my head and beheld neither an autopsy room, nor heaven, but Mrs. Hudson placing a bowl of steaming soup on my bedside table. She smiled at me.

"I will fetch Mr. Holmes; he wanted to be told the minute you awoke."

A moment later I was looking into my friend's face. He was smiling, but a little quizzically. He spoke before I could say anything.

"I must thank you for leading me to a most curious case, Watson, when I set out in pursuit of you. One unique in my annals.

"Suppose that a woman, rich by local standards, has died. And her very evil sister, who has a backdoor key to her house, not to mention a talent for creeping silently about, conceives a truly ingenious plan, a plan made possible by local ignorance and superstition. What if by gradual subterfuge, moving the corpse about at some times and impersonating it at others, she can convince the youngest and most gullible member of her sister's family that she is his mother come back to partial life? I am afraid your unexpected appearance gave her a nasty shock, Watson!"

I was speechless for some time. Then, "So my paralysis was merely due to cramp, and my own imagination, and a touch of indigestion," I said wonderingly. "Holmes, I really thought that I had died." I shivered, despite the warmth of the sunlight. "And I still cannot entirely rid myself of the idea that the past and the dead came very close to me last night. The experience seemed so real, so absolute." An extraordinary thought came to me. "Holmes, is it conceivably the case that it really was a heart attack, that I *did* die? And that, because my desire to be able to move again stemmed from compassion, from my wish to help another, *someone* or *something* decided to give me a second chance? The terrible actions of my ancestor could not be forgiven, but—"

Holmes held up his hand to stop me. "We are not responsible for the actions of our forefathers, Watson. Yet we must indeed beware of traits which we may inherit from them. You undoubtedly have a compassion which your great-great-grandfather lacked. But you must be ever wary of a certain tendency to believe in superstition!

"Presently, you will see Timmy's dreadful aunt in her normal and all too mundane guise, when you appear as a witness at her trial for conspiring to conceal a death. Now, drink your soup. A new case has arrived this morning, and I need the help of an assistant sound in mind and body."

Author's Note: *The history and urban culture on which this story is based is real. However the horrific incident of the catacombs occurred in Edinburgh rather than London, and the plague pits of London are situated not under the well-known parks, but beneath other land kept in public ownership, whose present-day use would surprise many people.*

THE ADVENTURE OF
THE DOG IN THE NIGHTTIME

Paula Cohen

I HAVE MENTIONED once or twice, in writing up the remarkable cases of my friend, Sherlock Holmes, that he frequently refused his help to the powerful and the wealthy if their problems made no appeal to his sympathies, but that he would devote weeks of the most intense application to the affairs of some humble client whose case presented those strange and dramatic qualities that appealed to his imagination and challenged his ingenuity.

Holmes's natural kindliness, in fact, would often lead him to investigate even the most obvious problems for clients who had no other avenue of assistance; and, in reviewing my notes for the year 1890, I have come across a case that, while seeming at the outset to be one of the most mundane ever brought to him, had one of the most inexplicable endings that I have been privileged to record. Indeed, its memory still returns to haunt me on those autumn evenings when the fog rolls in, dank and impenetrable, and all London taps its way along the lightless streets.

We were seated, Holmes and I, on either side of a hospitable fire in his Baker Street lodgings, immersed in our papers. My wife had gone to Dorset for a fortnight, in aid of an ailing childhood friend, and I had elected to pass my enforced bachelorhood in my old familiar quarters. On this November night the rooms seemed especially pleasant, as one of the densest fogs in many a year, yellow, acrid and cold, had settled upon London two nights before, and beyond the windows sight and sound had ceased to exist. Only Holmes, always indifferent to the weather, chafed at being within and devoid of any problem with which to occupy his mind.

"I am sadly disappointed," he said, tossing aside his newspaper in disgust. "For a man with a larcenous bent, Watson, such a fog was made in heaven. Where is the enterprise of the London criminal class, that they let a small matter of weather keep them indoors?"

This particular "small matter" had emptied the streets, and London was now a spirit world where vague forms appeared and disappeared in the mist. Only those in direst need would risk an excursion on the all but invisible pavements.

"But one must be able to see in order to commit mayhem," I replied. "And consider how much more vigorous your foes will be for their few days of rest."

Holmes flung himself back into his chair with an exasperated sound and a baleful look at me. Just then the doorbell clanged, followed a moment later by a loud female voice in the hall below and the sound of footsteps rushing up the stairs. Holmes rose with a delighted smile and had the door open before our visitor reached the landing.

She was a stout, plainly dressed woman, somewhat above middle age, with a round and kindly countenance that now wore a look of wild distress. The hair beneath her bonnet was disordered, her face was flushed with running, and her whole person shone with the damp through which she had passed. She paused in the doorway, gasping, with her hand at her throat, looking as though she would faint. Holmes drew her swiftly to the fire.

As she fell into the waiting chair, still struggling for breath, I took her wrist. Her pulse was dangerously high. We helped her off with her bonnet, cloak, and gloves, and Holmes pressed a glass of brandy into her hand to steady her.

"There's no time!" she cried, pushing it aside, her frantic eyes darting from one of us to the other. "My lamb is gone! First my boy and now she. Am I to lose them both in the space of a fortnight? Which of you is Mr. Holmes? You must help me find them!"

Holmes's voice was soothing. "I am Sherlock Holmes, and I will do all I can to assist you. But first you must tell me what has happened. And to do that you must compose yourself."

He urged the glass on her again, and this time she obeyed. I kept my fingers on her wrist as she sipped the brandy, and her laboured breathing slowed. All the while Holmes's keen eyes minutely examined her person.

"Do you not find it troublesome," he said, seating himself across from her, "to keep such a very large dog?"

She started so violently that the glass nearly fell from her hand. "But how on earth do you know about Robby?" she cried. "No one could have told you about me, for no one knew I was coming here. I rushed from the house without telling a soul."

"And you ran all the way. But surely a cab would have been better. St. John's Wood is no very great distance, but on such a night as this it is far indeed."

"Aye," she said, "and I would have run twice the distance, if need be. But there were no cabs to be had, for love or money, and I had to get here as fast . . ." She stopped, staring, as his words sunk in, and her reply was a whisper. "How do you know where I live?"

"There is a smudge upon your right shoulder," said Holmes. "The neatness of your attire, otherwise, tells me that you did indeed rush from your house, or else you would have seen it and brushed it away. By its shape I can determine that it was made by a dog, and by its size and location on your shoulder I conclude that the dog that placed it there is very large, possibly a mastiff or a wolfhound. And while dogs abound in London, dogs of that size fare better where they can exercise freely. St. John's Wood provides both proximity to a park and the nearness to Baker Street to allow for your arrival on foot.

"There, you see?" he said, smiling at the dawning comprehension on her face. "It is my business to see things that other people do not. Why else have you come to me?"

"And I thank heaven for your vision, Mr. Holmes, for I'm as helpless now as my lamb, who's been blind since she was a child. And now she's disappeared, not two weeks after her brother, and I'm almost dead with fear for the both of them. I'm not a rich woman, Mr. Holmes, but I will give you everything I own if you can find them for me and bring them home safe."

"You say your boy has been missing for two weeks. How long has the girl been gone?"

"She walked out this afternoon, just after tea, to post some letters for me, and take Robby for a turn in the park. She never returned. The dog came back without her not an hour ago, whimpering and scratching at the door, and I left straightaway to come here."

"She went for a walk in this fog?" I exclaimed.

The woman turned, startled, as if she had forgotten my presence. "She hates being shut indoors, Mister . . . ?" she answered.

"This is Dr. Watson," Holmes said, "who has often assisted me with my cases."

Our guest nodded. "She's out in all weathers. She always has been, from the time she was a child. And then, what's a fog, no matter how deep, to a lass that's blind? Robby is her eyes and her protector, and she never sets foot out of the house without him." She turned back to Holmes with a look of anguish. "I'm near out of my mind, Mr. Holmes. I should have come to you sooner, when Gregory didn't come home. How can this have happened? Who would want to harm them? Why would anyone want to harm them?"

"We don't know yet that they have come to harm," Holmes said. "What are their names and ages?"

"Ellen and Gregory McCadden." Her hands twisted as she spoke. "Ellen turned seventeen in June. Gregory is twenty-two, and a sailor."

Holmes leaned back in his chair, his long legs extended, his steepled fingers touching his chin. "And your name?"

She blinked then, suddenly realising that she had not yet introduced herself. "You must forgive me, gentlemen," she said more quietly. "I am greatly afflicted just now, and my manners are not what they should be. My name is Hilda Blakey . . . Miss Hilda Blakey."

"These are not your children, then?" Holmes said.

"Nay, my sister's. But Maggie lived only a week after being delivered of my lamb, and Gregory was but five years old when his mother died. I moved into the house to help their father; what would a clerk know of raising two bairns? A month later he left the house—to get some tobacco, he said—and never came back. A neighbour saw him boarding a train at Euston Station, and that's the last we heard of him. And so the children became mine, and I am their mother as sure as if I bore them both. Their father left them nothing but the house and a pile of bills when he vanished, and I took in laundry to put food on the table. Aye, and I've been a washerwoman seventeen years, now. And I would do it all again and more," she said, "for they are my beating heart, and all I care for in this world."

Holmes nodded his encouragement, and our visitor continued.

"It was my neighbour, Mr. Farrington, who told me of you, Mr. Holmes—him whose reputation you saved by finding that manuscript he was accused of stealing. He gave me your name a fortnight ago, when Gregory didn't come home and I couldn't find out what happened to him. I should have come to you then, but Gregory's shipmate turned up on our doorstep two or three days later, and after that I wouldn't leave my lamb, not with him around."

"Gregory's shipmate?"

"Aye, Edwin Prentice, and may his soul . . ." She stopped herself, bit her lip, then took a breath and continued. "He came to pay court to Ellen. He said he had been a mate of Gregory's, and that Gregory had told him of Ellen and her gentleness and beauty, and that is what Gregory would say, right enough. And I liked Mr. Prentice, at first, for was he not the friend of my boy? But soon enough I grew to mistrust him—and to fear him, as well, for I saw what Ellen could not . . . how his eyes searched about him when he thought I was not looking, as if seeking something. And once, when Ellen and I had both left the room and I came back sudden-like to get something, I found him tapping the floorboards with his heel. He laughed when I asked him what he was doing, and said that his foot had gone to sleep."

She snorted. "He must think me a fool. But my Ellen only smiles when I complain of him, saying that I would object to anyone who might court her—aye, and she's right enough about that, Mr. Holmes, and that's the truth of it, for no one is good enough for my lamb—but I keep close watch on them, nevertheless, never letting her be too long with him, and never out of my sight."

Holmes nodded. "In my experience, Miss Blakey, a woman's intuition is greatly to be trusted. What else made you suspicious of Mr. Prentice?"

"He said he was Gregory's shipmate a year ago, when they sailed to the Argentine. But there have been sailors in my family for generations, Mr. Holmes, and all that I've known were honest, blunt-speaking, plain men, better with their hands than their words, and that includes my Gregory. This one, though, is smooth as glass . . . his words, his looks . . . aye, even his hands."

Holmes smiled quickly, and gazed upon our visitor with increased interest. "What of his hands? Can you describe them?"

In reply she showed us her own, which were coarse and cracked and of a boiled red color from years of immersion in caustic soap and hot water. "They were softer and whiter than these, that's for certain, with nary a crack or a callus. If his hands have done a day's rough work, then I'm Her Majesty at Windsor."

"Did you see them closely?"

"Aye, I did. I had him make himself useful, as he was spending so much time with us, and hold out his hands so that I could wind yarn into a ball. What sailor ever had hands like that, I ask you?"

"Did you ask him about them?"

"Not about his hands, nay. But I asked about Gregory, and his ship, and his answers were all proper . . . meaning that I could find no outright fault in them; and he knew Gregory right enough, down to the scar on his back from cutting himself deep as he ducked under a fence when he was a little boy."

"And yet you were not satisfied."

"Nay, I was not."

Holmes nodded again. "You have told us that Ellen is blind, but that she was not born that way?"

"Aye, sir. She could see perfectly well until she was seven. And the bonniest, brightest blue eyes she had, too. And so she still does. To look at her you'd think she sees as well as you or me. But she was thrown from a wagon when she was seven. The horse shied and bolted as she was jumping down, and she hit her head on the mounting block. She lay like the dead for three days and when she woke at last she was stone blind."

Miss Blakey's own eyes filled with tears. "That was hard, Mr. Holmes; that was cruel hard. A lively, high-spirited child she was, and loved nothing better than to run after her brother and his friends, and I let her, knowing that Gregory would look after her and see that she came to no harm. And he did, watching over her always, keeping her safe—until the accident. He blamed himself, of course, but it wasn't his fault. He was holding the horse's head to steady it, but a cat ran between its legs just then, and the beast reared. Gregory's never forgiven himself. It was he who brought Robby home, to watch over Ellen when he was at sea."

"How long ago was that?"

"Four years back, when Gregory turned eighteen and signed up for his first voyage. Robby was but a pup then, a starveling from the streets. I never thought he could grow so big, but Gregory knew, which is why he chose him. The dog lives for Gregory and his sister. Aye, and he would kill for them, if need be."

"And what do you think has happened to Gregory?"

"And that's a question, too, that's been tearing at me. He was due home two weeks back, but he's not come. His ship came back all right, with him on it, and I know this because I enquired, and even heard from his captain. Gregory collected his pay and bid his mates farewell, telling them that he was heading home . . . and that's the last anyone knows of him. Between Portsmouth and London he vanished into the air."

"You've heard nothing from him?"

"Nothing at all."

"Could he have stopped with a friend," asked Holmes, "or has he a sweetheart who might have delayed him?"

"He has many friends," Miss Blakey said, "but he'd been gone six months this time, to Ceylon and back with stops along the way, and he'd never stop with friends before coming home to his sister and me. And even if he had, he would have gotten word to us, knowing how we'd fret. As for a sweetheart, Gregory's a handsome lad as could have his pick of the girls, but there's no one special lass, I'm sure of it."

"So Gregory is expected and does not return, and Mr. Prentice appears on your doorstep instead."

"Aye, that was the way of it."

"Do you have any explanation for this coincidence?"

"If you're asking me, Mr. Holmes, whether I think that my boy's vanishing and Edwin Prentice showing up are somehow bound, I'll tell you yes. But I don't know why, nor what's become of him. And now Ellen . . . ah, God, what'll I do?" She wept quietly.

"Only a few more questions," Holmes said. "Have either or both of your children recently come into an inheritance?"

"Oh, no, sir. We've no relations but one another."

"Have you or Gregory any money put aside, then?"

"Aye, nigh on twenty pounds. I put by what I can, and Gregory's been working at odd jobs since he was just a lad to help us make ends meet. What wasn't needed for our upkeep was always put aside in a special place. It's all for Ellen, and not to be touched under any circumstances. Gregory has hopes that one day there'll be a doctor who can help her see again."

"Has she been examined by an ocular specialist?" I said.

" "Nay, sir, not yet. Twenty pounds is a goodly sum, but we fear it will take more. And we'd not wish to take her to a doctor and perhaps raise the lamb's hopes only to tell her that we can do nothing for her because we lack the money."

"And the twenty pounds is all?" said Holmes.

"All?" Miss Blakey said, sniffing and drawing herself up. "Our Gregory has been working since he was twelve to put together that sum. He took on a man's burdens long before his time so that he could right the wrong he felt he had done to his sister by his carelessness. Every penny of that twenty pounds signifies a day's heavy toil. No one can know how much it has meant to him . . . to all of us!"

"I meant no disrespect," Holmes said, with that gentleness so often evident in his dealings with women. "But in my experience, twenty pounds, while indeed a goodly sum, as you say, is usually not a sufficient a motive for kidnapping." He reached up a long hand for his index of biographies, carefully culled from various sources over the years. "Let us see what information I might find about our soft-handed sailor, Edwin Prentice."

The index, however, failed to produce an entry for anyone with the name he sought. Loath to waste any time, and eager to put his restless energy to use, he requested both Miss Blakey's latchkey and permission to search her cottage for clues. She acquiesced eagerly and rose from her chair to set out with him, but I forbade her to leave.

"Your pulse is still too rapid for safety," I said, taking her wrist again. "I cannot, in all good conscience, allow you to return home tonight, by foot and through this fog. You must think of your own health, for the sake of your children."

"But it is the children I'm thinking of," she pleaded. "I must be home, gentlemen. What if Ellen returns and finds me gone? In all her life she's never known me not to be there for her. What if she's back already?"

"In which case," Holmes said, "speed is of the essence, and despite your impatience to return home, your presence would slow us down. I give you my word. If Ellen is there we will let you know as quickly as possible." He turned to me. "I said 'we.' The night is foul, Watson, but you have braved worse than this. Would you care to accompany me?"

"I would have been insulted had you not asked me," I replied. "It will be like old times."

"Excellent," he replied, clapping me on the shoulder. "You will find your service revolver in the drawer where you left it. I have kept it cleaned and oiled, in the anticipation that you would someday need it again, and tonight seems an appropriate occasion."

Ten minutes later we were ready to start out, and Miss Blakey was being made comfortable by Mrs. Hudson, who had agreed happily to take her in for the night.

"There is one thing more with which I need your help," Holmes said to Miss Blakey, as we bade her farewell, "and that is your dog. If you left him unconfined in your house it would be best not to intrude upon him uninvited, at least not without some idea of how to mollify him. Is there a way?"

"Aye, there is," she said. "I sometimes leave Ellen alone with

Robby for a bit while I deliver a load of laundry, and the tradesmen who come by need a way to make themselves known so they can be admitted safely. Can you whistle, Mr. Holmes? Then only whistle the refrain from 'Scots We Hae,' and Robby will greet you like a great lamb."

Moments later we were trudging in the direction of St. John's Wood along the near-deserted streets, our way made only faintly visible by the bull's-eye lamps we carried. The swirling brown air distorted all sense of direction, and I felt as a blind man must, feeling for obstacles before me with hands and feet, and grateful for the dim flare of the streetlamps that glimmered like apparitions in the murk.

"Unless I am very much mistaken," Holmes said, "it is something very much more than twenty pounds that Mr. Prentice is seeking." His voice, deadened by the fog, sounded strange and flat and did not carry more than a few inches, so that he spoke close to my ear. "But we will find out soon enough, for I believe that a thorough search of Miss Blakey's house will yield us much and point us in the right direction."

At a brisk pace on a sunny afternoon, our walk would have lasted no more than twenty minutes. Now it took us better than four times that to traverse Park Road, then up Wellington Road to Cochrane Street, and still another ten minutes to find Miss Blakey's cottage, tucked away behind a narrow lane of carriage houses and stables.

The light of our lanterns playing on the door revealed it gaping on its hinges. There was no sign of force upon the door handle or the locks. Beyond the door, an eerie picture met our eyes. Miss Blakey had rushed out leaving the lamps still burning and the fire blazing in the grate, but both lamps and fire had burned low since her flight. The cold mist, now pouring through the wide-flung door, made the dying flames dim and smoky, so that the tiny entrance hall and the parlour beyond it wavered like rooms in some feverish dream. We stopped at the parlour door and stared within.

Pictures ripped from the walls lay where they had been flung amidst the contents of drawers that had been emptied onto the floor; smashed crockery and slashed pillows lay everywhere, covered by a blizzard of feathers. A dark trail of blood ran from a doorway at the far side of the parlour to a black pool that seeped from beneath a fringed shawl. We crossed the room, stepping over piles of debris, fearing the worst.

Beneath the shawl lay the dog, Robby, eyes glazed in death, fangs bared. The great beast had been shot repeatedly. An empty revolver had been flung into the corner near the body.

Holmes straightened up from his examination of the corpse, wiping his hands upon the shawl. "He is still quite warm," he said, "and rigour has not even begun. See for yourself. He cannot have been dead for more than an hour or two."

He busied himself then, with a minute scrutiny of the tiny house, which consisted of but two rooms upstairs and two rooms down. I remained below in the parlour, poring over the destruction, searching for I knew not what that might reveal what the intruder had been seeking. Holmes, however, vanished upstairs, and only a few minutes later I heard his triumphant shout. He appeared soon after, holding something out to me in the palm of his hand. It was a small key, of the kind that fitted into boxes used to hold valuables.

"The person who did this," he said, gesturing round, "is shrewd, but not subtle. It does not occur to him that those accustomed to dealing with the blind will make things evident to the faculty of touch, not sight. For a blind girl to quickly locate an item as small as this key, it needed to be where she could feel for it easily, but where it would not be readily seen by anyone else."

"Where was it?" I asked.

"In her room. A heavy bureau stands against the wall, and this was hanging from a nail in a small recess that had been hollowed out at the back of the bureau's leg. The drawers have been emptied and searched, but it never occurred to our intruder to overturn the bureau itself, or to examine the back of it."

"And what is the key for?"

"Clearly something of great value, or else our friend Edwin Prentice would not have gone to the trouble to kidnap Gregory McCadden, spend weeks wooing his sister, and then tear this place apart in his frustration when he was unable to find what he sought."

"You think they are still alive?"

"I think the chances are good, but they diminish every minute. Prentice would not kill the boy until he had the secret he needed. That he was unable to obtain it is evidenced by the kidnapping of his sister. That neither of them divulged the secret is evident from the key in my hand. Now, in his anger, he may kill one or both."

He picked up his lantern, turned, and followed the trail of blood to the rear of the house, through the small dining room and even smaller kitchen, and then into the scullery, which had been built out from the main cottage and outfitted with deep coppers and a mangle for the washing of laundry. The scullery was the most devastated room of all, lying knee-deep in debris and shattered glass.

"If you wished to hide something in a place this size, Watson, where a sightless young woman could find it with ease, where would you put it?"

I gazed around me. "The treasure was here?" I said.

"*Is* here," he replied, "unless I am greatly mistaken. This, you see, is where the death struggle began. Mr. Prentice appears to have entered the house without difficulty, probably because of his regular visits here these past two weeks. Ellen McCadden, at some point, had doubtless told him the secret of the whistled tune that would allow him to pass unmolested. He proceeded to ransack the upstairs rooms, then came down and did the same to the parlour and dining room."

"But the dog did not attack him?"

"Not yet. Mr. Prentice, after all, had both the key to the front door—you noticed, of course, that the lock was intact—and the secret whistle. The dog may have felt there was something wrong, but his training would have prevented him from attacking, at least until the intruder approached this spot." Holmes stepped up to a small, slightly raised alcove in the scullery. Two tin basins, crushed and dented, lay nearby, and he picked them up and stood them in the alcove, pushing them back against the wall.

"One held the dog's water and the other his scraps," Holmes said. And indeed, amidst the shards of glass, cutlery, crockery and sodden cloth that littered the floor were bits of bread and meat. Removing the basins once more, he squatted before the alcove and began to pry among the bricks with his long fingers. "Gregory McCadden was clever in his choice of hiding place. Not many would contemplate looking here with such a Cerberus on guard. It would be a rare burglar indeed," he said, "or an overconfident one, who would attempt something so foolhardy."

He gave a small grunt of satisfaction as one of the bricks yielded to his fingers, and he drew it out of the wall. The brick next to it shifted as he did so, and after removing it, too, he bent and shone the beam of his lantern into the resulting hole.

"*Et voila!*" he said, and reaching within with the air of a magician pulling a bouquet from a hat, he slid out a shallow, hinged iron box. I leaned nearer as Holmes inserted the small key he had found into its lock, turned it, and raised the lid.

The banknotes were in two piles, each about three inches thick. We counted them, each taking a pile. Gregory McCadden's twenty pounds had multiplied fifty times.

"A thousand pounds will more than pay for surgery to restore Ellen McCadden's sight," said Holmes, placing the notes back inside the box. "And what remains will ensure a comfortable old age for the woman who sacrificed herself for two children she did not even bear."

"Where did McCadden get it?" I asked, as he closed the lid and returned the box to its place, fitting the bricks in as he had found them.

"On one of his voyages, no doubt. Perhaps the voyage to the Argentine, a year ago, that Edwin Prentice claimed to be on. But now that we know what it was that Mr. Prentice sought, it is time to find him."

"How?" I protested. "He could be anywhere. We know nothing of Edwin Prentice."

"We know that he was injured," Holmes said. "Robby did not die without leaving his mark on his killer. Look!"

He pointed to the trail of blood. "The dog attacked Prentice here, in the scullery," Holmes said, walking us back through the kitchen and dining room, "and the two wrestled their way here, to the parlour. Only look at the room, and you will see that I am right. Much of the destruction—the overturned drawers, the slashed pillows—was committed before Prentice entered the scullery. Look there, and here, and here. See where the blood lies upon the surface of the furniture and scattered debris, and not beneath it? Prentice was already badly wounded before the struggle reached this room. It was here, however, that he was finally able to draw his revolver and subdue his adversary."

"Is it possible," I said, looking at the devastation around me, "that no one heard? Would not the noise of such a struggle—not to mention the report of gunshots—have roused the neighbourhood?"

"Miss Blakey's cottage stands a good distance from her nearest neighbours, Watson. Add to that the fog, which deadens all sound, and I think it highly improbable that anyone could have heard what transpired here."

We left the house, playing our lanterns along the smears and spatters of blood that Edwin Prentice had left in his wake. Twice, Holmes thought he had lost the trail, only to find it again after what seemed like an eternity of doubling back and searching. The fog stung my eyes and tore at my throat, still so thick that we seemed, for all our walking, to be continuously in the same place. Even my hardened nerves could not withstand that seemingly endless journey through the swirling void. Nothing whatever was visible, save for the foot or two of pavement ahead that was illuminated by our lanterns, and I became fanciful, wondering whether time itself had stopped, and absolutely certain that something walked behind us in the mist.

"Over there," said Holmes in my ear.

"What is it?" I said, straining my eyes to where he looked, but seeing nothing.

"Battlebridge Basin," he replied.

We had reached that part of Regent's Canal between York Way and the Caledonian Road. Around us in the blackness were wharves and mills and deep, silent water.

"Shutter your lantern," Holmes said.

We permitted ourselves only a pencil-thin beam of light, but still it was sufficient to show us the trail of drops as it veered and wobbled.

Our quarry had grown unsteady on his legs from loss of blood, but the path led eventually, with many swerves and stumbles, to a low metal door in the side of a building.

"Do you recognise it, Watson?" Holmes said. "This is Gatti's Ice House."

The great brick edifice, where ice from Norway's fjords was stored for London's summer use, was only some thirty years old, but already had an ominous reputation. Two great wells yawned in its floor, cold and deep, where immense blocks of ice were stored until wanted. During the construction of the second well a workman had fallen to his death, and his fate added to the sense of menace that surrounded the place even in broad daylight. On this night, with both sight and sound impaired, it seemed unspeakably sinister as it loomed before us.

The heavy door, having swung to behind Prentice, had not shut completely. Playing his lantern across it, Holmes picked out a bloody palm print and a long, thick smear.

"See, Watson," he said. "His right arm has been badly mauled. He has been holding it with his left hand, and here is where he thrust open the door with his shoulder."

We crossed the threshold; and, despite the blackness within, I found myself able to breathe freely for the first time since we left Baker Street. The fog curled in with us as we entered, but the air beyond in the great, cavernous space, was cold and almost thunderously clear. Our first footfalls on the stone floor rang out like clarions, and thereafter we advanced on tiptoe, hearing a murmur of voices ahead until, suddenly, a woman shrieked.

"No!" she screamed. "Leave him! I will tell you! I will tell—I swear I will!"

"Too late." It was a man's voice, and with it came the sound of a heavy weight being dragged. "He has had his chance, and you have had yours."

The woman shrieked again, and suddenly there was the sound of a violent struggle.

"Come, Watson!" shouted Holmes, throwing open the shutter of his lantern. "And take care for the ice pit!" He rushed forward.

In the full beam of light two figures grappled at the rim of a gaping chasm that smoked, not with fog, but with cold. The man was of medium height and heavily built, and his right arm swung useless at his side. Clinging to him, her clawed hands groping for his eyes, was a slender young woman, her yellow hair long out of its combs and spilling down her back. A still, crumpled figure lay on the floor near them, perilously close to the edge and to a final drop into eternity.

Neither the man nor the woman uttered another word, nor were they aware of our approach. Panting and scuffling, they swayed back and forth, locked in a violent dance. They were better matched than they appeared at first glance. The blind girl, well used to darkness, fought madly against her one-armed enemy, and every lurch and stumble brought them nearer to the pit.

I had my revolver in my hand by now, but there was no chance for a clear shot. Holmes and I stood helpless, watching that deadly struggle, and it was then that I heard the sound.

It was low at first, then louder, and it came from everywhere and nowhere, a sound like boulders moving or a rumble from the belly of some great beast. The brick walls threw the sound back and back at us until the vast chamber seemed to throb. Even the two combatants heard, and paused in their battle. Ellen McCadden lifted her head and turned, her wide, sightless eyes looking beyond us.

"Robby!" she shouted, twisting from Prentice's grip. "To me, Robby! To me!"

She dropped to her hands and knees, hugging the stone floor, not knowing in her blindness how near she was to the edge. Prentice swayed openmouthed, his face white, his bloody arm dripping in the light of our lanterns, and a huge shadow came hurtling towards him out of the blackness behind us. I saw the arc of its spring as it sailed overhead, saw the last look of terror in Prentice's eyes as he turned to flee and stepped into empty air, heard his dying shriek and the sound of his body striking the bottom.

Holmes and I rushed to the girl, who still clung to the floor on her hands and knees, sobbing. "Don't be alarmed," I said, as we reached her side. "We are here to bring you and your brother to safety."

Raising her to her feet, we walked her a safe distance away from the pit and sat her down on a wooden pallet. Holmes remained with her while I went back to see to her brother. The young man was unconscious, his head and face bleeding and covered with bruises. He had been beaten severely, and from his gaunt, unshaven state, I knew that he had been held with little or no food since his disappearance two weeks before. None of his wounds, however, was fatal, and with rest and care he would make a full recovery. As I pulled him away from the edge of the pit, he groaned and began to stir.

"Lie still," I told him. "I am a doctor, and other help will soon be on the way. Your sister is safe," I said, as his eyes tried frantically to search the recesses of the chamber, and he nodded then, closed his eyes again and almost smiled.

Before I went to rejoin Holmes and the girl, I shone my lantern down into the ice pit. The summer had been warm, and ice had been in great demand. Edwin Prentice's body lay forty feet below, sprawled like a rag doll on a tumbled hill of ice, a dark, gleaming stain spreading beneath him.

"What is it?" Holmes said, as I reached his side. "You look as if you had seen a ghost." Ellen McCadden sat huddled beside him, her face buried in her hands.

"Edwin Prentice lies dead on the ice," I said.

"The ice wells are deep," he replied. "And hard."

"He lies alone."

Holmes looked at me strangely. "Who else would be with him?"

"Did you not see the dog? But you heard it, surely. The girl heard it, she called to it. Did you not see it spring at Prentice?"

"Shadows from the lantern light thrown against the mist."

"Prentice saw it, Holmes. He turned to flee."

"Watson," he said quietly. "The dog is dead. It lies in Hilda Blakey's cottage, shot to death. We both examined its corpse."

"And the sound? My God, that sound!"

"Ice shifting and falling in the well. It moves beneath its own weight, as glaciers do. Hark!" he said.

And the sound came again, this time, as he had said, from the ice well itself, a curious, deep, growling sound that echoed from the walls and distant ceiling. I listened, a cold sweat making me shiver.

Ellen McCadden lifted her head. "Robby," she whispered, and wept.

Holmes shook his head as the noise died away once more. "You know what I believe. When you have eliminated the impossible, whatever remains—however improbable—must be the truth. The dog is dead, Watson, as is the man who killed it. But Hilda Blakey's children are alive, and that is all that really matters. I will leave you with them while I summon the police."

And with that, he picked up his lantern and strode out into the fog. I remained behind, and brought Ellen McCadden to where her brother lay. She knelt beside him and lifted his head into her lap, stroking his hair until Holmes returned.

The fog lifted the next day, and two days later my wife returned from Dorset. I returned to my happy domestic routine and my practice, and did my best to forget about my nocturnal walk through the fog, and the icehouse, and the dog that I could not have seen.

Two months later, in late January, Gregory McCadden called at Baker Street to thank Sherlock Holmes for saving his life and the life of his sister, and to pay him handsomely. I had dropped in on Holmes between my medical rounds, and had the good fortune to be there when the young man arrived. A handsome, hardy youth with a robust constitution, he was already largely recovered from his ordeal.

"Edwin Prentice was a business agent for the line on which I sailed," he explained. "In eighty-eight he was on my ship, bound for Argentina. He was only a few years older than many of us aboard, including me, but he had been everywhere and knew the world. Above all, he loved gaming. He would wager on anything—how many storms we would run into, how much the cargo would fetch when we unloaded at Buenos Aires—it didn't matter.

"I've always been careful with my money, Mr. Holmes, spending as little as I could and never wasting a penny; and so I largely avoided him, not wishing to be tempted. I had got into the habit of being frugal, and every ha'penny went into the strongbox for Ellen's eyes. But Prentice had a way of talking that made things seem easy, and made things that you knew were wrong seem right. While we were in Buenos Aires he persuaded me and three of my shipmates to go in on a lottery with him. A pound apiece was all we had to spend.

"Well, a pound was a lot for me, Mr. Holmes, but in a weak moment I said I would do it, and I wouldn't go back on my word once it was pledged. And do you know, we won. The pot was in Argentine money, but we converted it to British, and it came to five thousand pounds, more than I ever believed I would see in my life. We split it five ways, and told no one else. It was too much, you see, to be loose-tongued about.

"When I came home, I put the thousand pounds in the strongbox, where you found it. I had enough, now, to quit sailing and look about for a doctor for Ellen, and to see to it that my mother need never take in washing again. But I had signed up for my next voyage out before I won the money, you see, and when I told the captain I was pulling out, he begged me to sail. Two of the three shipmates who had won the lottery with me had already pulled out, and he was shorthanded. Well, he was a kind man, and had been good to me, so I agreed to sail one last time. I told Ellen of the lottery money, but not my mother, for I knew that she would be nervous with such a sum in the house, even with Robby there.

"It was when we got to Ceylon that I began to hear rumours from other ships that made me uneasy . . . about my two mates who had stayed behind turning suddenly jinxed. One was killed when his carriage lost a wheel and smashed into a tree. The other was found inland, dead in a railroad yard with his pockets turned out. And then, when I got back from Ceylon, there was Prentice, just happening to be down at the docks. He slapped me on the back when he saw me, so that someone would have thought he was my long-lost brother, and then he bought me one drink, and then another, at a pub a ways away from where I usually go, and when I woke I was in the icehouse. He told me that he was in debt and his life forfeit, and that he needed my thousand pounds to pay off his creditors. Well, you know the rest, Mr. Holmes . . ."

Five months later, Ellen McCadden had surgery on her eyes that partially restored her sight. The next year she married a young barrister from Lincoln's Inn, and a year after that her brother wed as well, and started his own business as a ship's outfitter. Ellen McCadden Forsythe's vision will always be somewhat impaired, but she sees well enough to watch her children and her brother's children grow and thrive. Hilda Blakey lives with her daughter now, in a handsome house just up the street from her son. Surrounded by grandchildren, and with her daughter's sight restored, the good lady has all that she ever desired.

HOLMES HAS NEVER once referred to what I believe I saw on that extraordinary night. Once, and only once, I mentioned it to him.

"I am absolutely certain of what I saw and heard," I said. It was an equally foggy night some years later, and we sat before the fire at Baker Street as we had on that other night. "As certain as I am that I see and hear you now."

"Well, it is not for me to dissuade you," he said. "I will only mention, again, that the dog was dead, and that what you believe you saw was therefore impossible. And when you have eliminated the impossible—"

"Yes, yes," I laughed. "I remember your tenet well. Nevertheless," I said, growing more serious, "how pleasant it is to think that it mightn't be impossible. Aren't we taught, after all, that love is stronger than death?"

"And that, my dear Watson, is why you are so good at turning my rigorous investigations into pretty romances." Laughing silently, he reached for the newspaper and stretched his legs out to the fire.

Selden's Tale

Daniel Stashower

"There's a convict escaped from Princetown, sir. He's been out three days now, and the warders watch every road and every station, but they've had no sight of him yet. The farmers about here don't like it, sir, and that's a fact . . . You see, it isn't like any ordinary convict. This is a man that would stick at nothing."

"Who is he, then?"

"It is Selden, the Notting Hill murderer."

—*The Hound of the Baskervilles,* Chapter VI

THE BEAST IS coming.

It comes as if guided by a huntsman's horn. I dared hope that I had eluded it at last, after so much time and so many desperate measures. I was a fool to return to this desolate, hell-blasted place. It is too late for me. Even now I sense the thing stirring in the blackness, alert to my fear. I suppose it was always my fate that I must face it here.

You will say that I have taken leave of my senses. Perhaps so, but in my wretchedness has come a comforting sense of resolve, and I must try to find some small consolation from this. There are strange, red depths in the soul of even the most commonplace man, and my life has been anything but commonplace. There is much I would erase, if I could.

Time grows short, Eliza. I know that it is only a matter of days, perhaps hours. My only regret is the pain that I have caused you. You have been more loyal than I dared hope. No brother could ask more. I know that I have been a source of sorrow and disappointment. Perhaps there may yet be a small token of redemption. Perhaps even now it is not too late.

You fear me. I saw it in your eyes last night. You believe that I am responsible for what happened to the old gentleman. I swear to you, Eliza, by those few remaining things that I hold dear, I would sooner have perished than bring harm upon that man or any in his line. You must believe this. You will.

I shall try one last time to explain myself. I never intended that I should sink so low, or that my offenses should place such a burden upon you and John. It is fair to say that no one who saw us in childhood would have guessed what life had in store for me. I flatter myself that I was an unusually bright lad, at least by the lights of our station in life, and I fully expected that I should follow Father into a life in service, perhaps even at Baskerville Hall. I was grateful to the old gentleman for taking an interest in me, and seeing to my modest education. I owed much to his kindness, and I should have been proud to remain in his household if Her Majesty had not formed other designs.

I do not pretend to understand fully the threat posed to Britain by the Boers and their politics, or why this presented such an intolerable affront. I simply went because I was told to go. I felt that it was an obligation I owed to Sir Charles. I hoped that I might justify his faith in me.

I have never spoken to you of my time in South Africa, and you have wisely respected my silence. I daresay that you did not recognize your brother in the withered husk that returned from that place. Certainly my injuries accounted for a large measure of the change, but there was something more, something so fundamental that it eludes me even now.

When men talk of war, they talk of great deeds and epic battles and acts of glory. When *I* think of South Africa, I recall only the tedium. At first, of course, I was anxious and full of nerves, well aware that the monotony of training and drill was simply the calm before the storm, but in time my fears gave way to an overwhelming sense of gloom. It crept into my bones like winter damp and left me restless and despairing.

One longs for companionship in these circumstances, and I found it in Henry Stallworth, whose family kept a farm in Dorset. We spent many long hours training together on a forward gunnery crew. He seemed to have an endless line of jokes and stories, and he was forever placing outlandish wagers which he had no intention of honouring. "Here's three shillings for the first man to climb that tree," he would say. "Here's three shillings for the first man to bag a leopard." It was all nonsense, but it took us out of ourselves and helped pass the long hours.

At length, our orders came. I prefer not to dwell on what followed, except to say that there was little about it that could be described in terms of valour. When the enemy struck, it came in the form of a shell from above. I never saw or heard it coming; I was aware only of a shadow passing overhead.

I no longer have any sense of how long I remained in the hospital unit. When I first awoke, my eyes were bandaged and the throbbing in my head was terrible. I drifted through the days and nights as though at a great remove. Doctors arrived to examine me and administer injections, but I paid little heed. Even the question of my own survival seemed of no great import to me.

I would not have survived without Stallworth. He had come through it worse than I. His leg was off below the knee, and for the first few days all I could hear was his moaning. After a time, he seemed to rally and some of his old vigour came back into his voice as he tried gamely to bolster our spirits. "We make a fine pair!" he would say. "Still, even with one leg I can still run circles around you, Selden. Here's three shillings for the first man to hobble out of here." I admired his pluck, but I was just as glad that my eyes were bandaged and I did not have to look upon that empty trouser leg.

Among the doctors who saw to us there was one who claimed experience in treatment of the eyes. His kindly, sad-eyed face, glimpsed briefly through a milky haze as he changed my bandages, was the only sight I knew during those long days. In the evenings he would come to us and tell stories of various kinds. I remember one in particular about an Egyptian mummy in a museum. Silly to think of us hanging on his every word like eager schoolchildren, looking like mummies ourselves in our bandages and gauze, but this doctor had a way about him. His stories took us away from our hurts for a time. Even Stallworth, who was usually so quick with a tale of his own, would fall silent in the presence of the doctor. Once, the doctor told us of his belief that our fallen comrades were not really dead—not dead as we understood the notion—but only transferred to a different place. A different plane of existence, he called it. It struck me as a right load of nonsense, but I could not fault him for thinking so. We all did what was needed to keep hold of our senses in that nightmare of a place.

At length, the day came when the bandages on my eyes were to be removed for good. The kindly doctor arrived and explained that I must not expect miracles; the vision would be slow to return and would likely never be entirely clear. I assured him that I would be glad for any result but total darkness, and sat forward eagerly on the edge of my cot as he unwound the long ribbon of gauze. Gradually the light began to seep in as the bandages fell away, and I became aware of the contours of the hospital tent taking on definition and substance, like shadows suddenly washed with color. The face of the sad-eyed doctor shimmered before me. I felt my heart lift.

"How's that, Henry!" I cried, blinking at the retreating darkness. "I believe I might just might claim those three shillings after all!"

The doctor's face clouded. "Who is Henry?" he asked.

"Stallworth, of course," I said.

"Stallworth?" asked the doctor.

"Henry Stallworth!" I cried. "The man who was lying there with his leg off! Where is he?"

But the cot beside me was empty. Indeed, it had never been occupied. I tried to rise but an orderly was called to restrain me. The
doctor explained, speaking urgently to be understood over my rising
panic, that from the first I had been isolated from the other patients.
It was thought that in my weakened condition I would not survive
exposure to the enteric fever that had cut a swath through the camp.

I suppose I must have seemed a raving madman then. I lashed out
against the orderly and demanded to know what had become of
Stallworth, insisting that I had spoken to him but a few moments
earlier. Through my hysteria, I saw the doctor give a sad shake of his
head, and another needle was produced.

And so it began. Where once I had needed the morphine for the
pain, now its absence became the pain. The visions it produced grew
more horrendous each day, but it was ever more necessary to my survival—more real to me than any bleak and solitary hospital tent. The
beast had come.

In time, what remained of me was shipped back to England. Whatever humanity I once possessed was left behind. I will not burden you
with a lengthy account of what became of me when I washed up on
England's shores once again. Some of it you will know, some of it can
never be known. What had once been medicine was now a lash that
drove me down a very dark path. They call me the Notting Hill murderer, but this is wrong, as it implies that there was a deliberate calcu-
lation to my crimes. There was not. My only concern was to satisfy my
craving. If someone stood in my path, I struck. If they died as a result,
it was of no concern. I was aware of my actions, but I had no more
control of them than does a falling leaf or a floating cork.

It soon reached a stage at which my every movement was attended
by violence, so that when the police captured me at last, my hands
were literally stained with blood. I am amazed that they did not
destroy me, as they would a rabid animal. It was only in prison, when
the needle was withheld by force, that I began to emerge from its
grip. Or so I thought.

The opportunity for escape came quite by chance—a sleeping
guard, a key ring within reach—and I acted more by instinct than
resolve. I daresay my plans were set before I emerged from the

shadows of the prison. Some measure of sanity had returned during my confinement, and I felt a crushing and irredeemable shame at what I had done. I resolved to go to sea and live out my days as quietly as possible. But first, Eliza, I wanted to take my leave of you, and bid farewell to the only home I had ever known.

It was a reckless decision. Had I been in my right mind I should never have brought such worry upon you. I wanted only to recover from the privations of my confinement and gather myself for the labours to come, but I know now that I should never have returned here. I had no idea what awaited me upon the moor.

I was exhausted when I first crossed the narrow granite bridge leading onto the familiar countryside. I kept out of sight as I fought my way through the dense scrub oak and fir. It would have been more direct to travel across the moor, but I dared not show myself in the open during daylight hours. I knew, also, that in my weakened condition I would not survive a journey through the Grimpen Mire. As a boy I thought nothing of leaping across the granite crests, venturing perilously close to the bright green bog-holes and thrilling to the knowledge that a single false step meant a hideous death. Now with my injuries and diminished vision, I knew that I could not trust myself to cross that treacherous landscape. Often enough as a boy I had watched with horror and fascination as one of the hapless moor ponies stumbled into a mossy bog, writhing and struggling, pulled down by a force beyond its comprehension. I did not relish exposing myself to the same fate.

Travelling in this stealthy, indirect fashion, it took many hours to reach safety. I recalled, of course, the many stone huts along the hillsides where we had played as children, and I knew that they would afford a perfect place of concealment. I chose the one closest to the moor, as it was largely obscured in the hollow of an outcropping. How many hours had we spent there in years past, huddled together in the gathering dusk, as I spun outlandish tales of the ghostly thing that was said to haunt the moors? The creature from hell. The Hound of the Baskervilles. Now, after the horrors of South Africa, the very idea of it seemed childish and quaint.

Creeping inside the familiar hut, I fell into a fitful slumber. I awoke, half-starving, as night fell. I had no other thought than to make my presence known to you, Eliza, in the hope that you would take pity on your wretched brother. Emerging from my hiding place I crept toward the Hall under the cover of darkness. There was no light showing from your window, so I circled back, intending to return later. As I retraced my steps I caught sight of movement by the Yew Alley, and realized that I had come upon the old gentleman in the midst of his nightly stroll.

I spoke earlier of the heavy debt I owe to Sir Charles. I knew of his habit of taking the air each night before retiring, but I assure you that I never intended to show myself to him. As he drew closer I sank back into the shadows, tracking his movements by the glowing end of his cigar. As my weakened eyes adjusted to the gloom, I could see that he was waiting for someone. He consulted his watch once or twice, and peered repeatedly in the direction of the moor gate. Not wishing to risk discovery, I eased toward a stand of trees, treading lightly to avoid detection. It was then that I saw the horror.

Eliza, I scarcely know how to describe it to you. It was our child-hood nightmare come to life—a savage black hound, but so large and sleek as to suggest a panther. There was something unearthly about it, a green aura that pulsed and flickered against the curtain of night, and from its muzzle there issued a distinct orange glow of hellfire.

Terror pinned me to the spot. My first thought was that my rav-aged brain had conjured yet another vision. In South Africa I had expected to find Henry Stallworth in the cot next to mine, and somehow my mind had produced him. Perhaps in some corner of my battered skull I had expected to see this spectral hound when I returned to the moors. Perhaps this horrifying vision was merely the product of my vile cravings.

In the next instant, however, I knew that the beast was all too real, for the old gentleman saw it too. He stood transfixed for a moment as the cigar slipped from his fingers. Then he turned and began to run. I bolted forward. I swear to you, Eliza, I was prepared to fling myself onto that beast in an effort to spare Sir Charles. I snatched up a fallen tree branch to use as a weapon and burst into the open, but the crea-ture did not advance. Behind me, the old gentleman clutched his chest and slipped to the ground, but I dared not turn my back on the beast. I held my ground as the hellish thing gave a low, menacing growl and lowered on its haunches, preparing to lunge. I raised the branch above my head and braced to swing, but the attack did not come. Abruptly, the hound turned and slipped into the darkness.

Dropping the branch, I turned to assist Sir Charles, but I could see at a glance that he was beyond help. Somehow I summoned the presence of mind to steal away before I was discovered, taking care to obscure the few footmarks I had left in the soft earth of the Alley. I struggled back to my stone hut and lay awake through the night trying to calm my nerves and make sense of what I had seen. Was it possible? Could the legend of the spectral hound be true? Was every male member of the Baskerville line truly fated to fall prey to this centuries-old curse? Even now I wondered if my damaged eyes and shattered nerves had somehow summoned the hound's likeness out of shadows. And yet, there was the old gentleman lying dead on the ground. I used to laugh when the villagers spoke of the Hound of the Baskervilles, but I will laugh no longer.

Two more days elapsed before I managed to alert you and John to my presence, and you know the rest. I suppose I appeared to you to be little more than a half-mad beggar in rags. I should not mind if that were the worst you thought of me, but there was more, wasn't there, Eliza? You tried to conceal it, even as you nursed my wounds and brought me food and clothing, but I could see the light of suspicion in your eyes. You never could keep a secret from me, dear sister. You believe that I had a hand in the death of Sir Charles. It was at that moment, seeing that shadow of doubt cross your face, that I realized how very far I have fallen in the world.

And yet I cling to the hope that it is not too late. Last night as I lay awake with my thoughts churning, I heard a strange sound drift across the moor. It began as a throbbing, plaintive wail but quickly gathered into a fearsome roar, filling the air around me. After a moment, it faded into silence.

I arose as if in a dream and walked out to the very borders of the Grimpen Mire. I had no light but the moon, and realized that I could easily blunder into one of the lethal bog-holes, but I was possessed by the need to know the source of that terrible cry. I pushed forward until at last, in the distance, I could see the retreating form of the gigantic hound, its hackles glowing with greenish light. But another figure seized my attention, the figure of a man—small and thin, with yellow hair—leading the creature forward into the fastness of the Mire.

In that moment, I understood. I know now that there is no curse upon the house of Baskerville, only a devious enemy of flesh and blood. I know also that there is no such thing as a spectral hound conjured up from the world beyond, for there is no world beyond. It follows, then, that the kindly doctor in South Africa was mistaken, and that my friend Stallworth is truly dead and gone, not merely transferred to a different plane of existence. I must accept that my visions of him emerged from the beast I carry inside me. My enemy is also flesh and blood.

So, tonight I will leave you forever. From my hut I can see a dark and resolute figure on the tor, a grim sentinel outlined against the moon, and I know that I must flee. I will not return to prison, Eliza. I will accept any judgment but that.

I have no wish to excuse my actions or the many crimes I have done. The yellow-haired man upon the moor picks his way among the bogs by means of a line of ash wands and yew sticks. They are stuck in the midst of firm ground to show him a path invisible to the untrained eye. I saw him hurtling along this treacherous path, veering from side to side at remarkable speed, avoiding certain death by the grace of these frail signposts. There were no signposts laid out for me when I set off those many months ago, Eliza. There were no ash wands and yew sticks to bring me safely home. I have wandered down a treacherous path, and even now I feel the pull of a force I can scarcely comprehend.

And so I leave here, Sister, in the hope of staying one step ahead of my demon. I am grateful for your kindness, and leave you with a small token of my affection—a modest bouquet of ash wands and yew sticks gathered from deep within the Grimpen Mire. It is quite possible that the man who placed them there will find himself inconvenienced by their absence. I would be willing to wager that he, too, may lose his way.

No matter. Here's three shillings for him.

THE ADVENTURE OF
THE ST. MARYLEBONE GHOUL

Bill Crider

NOVEMBER IS OFTEN a dreary month in London, with its dampness and its yellow fog that slides along the streets and creeps into the crannies of stone walls. But in one particular November the rooms I shared with Sherlock Holmes at 221B Baker Street were snug, and there was already a fire in the hearth as I enjoyed the breakfast provided for us by Mrs. Hudson. It was a breakfast prepared especially to keep off the chill of the outdoors: kedgeree of the English type, not unlike a dish that I had once eaten in India; toast and eggs; hot buttered oatmeal; freshly baked scones; and coffee contained in a silver-plated pot polished to such a shine that I could see my face comically mirrored in its rounded surface.

Holmes, not being an early riser, had not yet partaken of the food, and was, in fact, preparing his pre-breakfast pipe. He stood at the mantlepiece carefully packing his pipe with the tobacco that remained from all his smokes of the previous day, and when he had done so satisfactorily, he got the odorous mixture alight. After taking a few puffs, he sat on the sofa and began to turn through the pages of the *Times*. Often he turned first to the agony column, but today his attention was caught by something else, and I watched him as he read with mounting agitation.

"My dear Holmes," said I, wiping my fingers on a napkin, "you appear to be a bit perturbed. Allow me to speculate upon the reason why."

Holmes removed his pipe and set it on a nearby table. Then he turned his piercing eyes on me and said, "Do as you will, Watson. There have been times when you have surprised me with your ability to apply my methods. Perhaps this will be another of those times. What do you believe to be the cause of my supposed perturbation?"

"It is plain to anyone with eyes to see. It is something that you have read in the *Times*."

The paper rustled in Holmes's fingers, which were stained from some sort of chemicals, as they often were.

"Indeed," said he. "Anyone could have deduced that, Watson. Can you not be more specific?"

"I can," I responded with spirit, enjoying the game, for I felt sure of victory. "You are reading an article about the ghoul of St. Marylebone's cemetery."

"Very good, Watson. You have hit your target with the first shot. And how did you arrive at your conclusion?"

I relaxed in my chair and launched into my explanation. "I know that you prize rationality above all things, so that only something on the irrational side of things could cause you such disturbance. Therefore you must be reading something about the supernatural, and the only supernatural events of note concern the infamous ghoul."

"I am sometimes disturbed by things that are not entirely irrational," said Holmes.

I smiled. "But not in this case, I believe."

Holmes rustled the newspaper again. "You will concede, however, that there are other articles with irrational content."

"It is, after all, the *Times*," I admitted.

"And will you also concede that you arrived at your conclusion by devious means?"

"What do you mean by that, may I ask?"

"I mean that you reached your answer by having read the paper earlier today. That you saw the page which I was reading, and knew at once the kind of article that would catch at my attention."

"And if I did, would that not be a matter of deduction?"

"Not in the least. It would merely be a matter of glancing at the page of the newspaper and seeing the article."

"But that is not what I did," I protested. "I did read the article, of course, but I based my conclusion on both your agitation and my knowledge of your way of thinking."

Holmes rewarded me with a thin smile. "Very well, Watson. I believe that your deductive powers are indeed improving. You will soon prove to be my equal."

"You are jesting, Holmes, but I suspect you found little to jest about in your reading about the St. Marylebone ghoul."

"You are correct in that assumption."

"Deduction," I said.

"Deduction, then. At any rate, I confess that it does irritate me somewhat that our countrymen should be so gullible as to believe in the presence of some supernatural creature, and practically in our own neighbourhood, at that."

"You do not believe in the ghoul?" I said.

"The agents of the devil need not be of supernatural origin," said Holmes. "Flesh and blood will serve as well. Indeed, they often serve better."

"Having spent a bit of time in India and Afghanistan, I perhaps know more about such creatures than you do," I responded.

"Of the supernatural kind? I do not doubt it." Holmes folded the paper and took up his pipe. It took several puffs to get it going again, but when he had succeeded, he said, "Tell me what you learned of ghouls."

I did not have to gather my thoughts. My reading of the article had brought back to me some of the things I had heard during my military days.

"First of all," I said, "the word *ghoul* comes from the Arabic *al ghul.* It means something like 'to grab hold of.' "

"Your arcane knowledge amazes me, Watson," said Holmes. "Am I to assume, then, that ghouls are in the habit of grabbing hold of their victims?"

"I am not quite sure on that point," I admitted. "Ghouls may indeed have that habit, or it is possible the name comes from the fact that, unlike ghosts, ghouls have a corporeal existence. You could, if you wished, take hold of one of them."

"But I would not wish to?"

"Indeed not. Their faces are terrifying. Their skin is putrefying, and their breath that reeks past their yellowed fangs carries the foul stench of the rotting corpses upon which they feed."

"An unpleasant meal indeed," said Holmes, looking at the table where I sat. "Not at all like the repast you have before you."

"*Had* before me," I said, following his gaze. "I believe that I have done away with the lion's share of it."

"And you believe a ghoul would prefer a rotting corpse to such a thoroughly filling breakfast?"

I hesitated. "The ghoul seems like an unlikely creature, I know, and during the time we have been acquainted, I have learned that there is a logical explanation for all the things we have encountered, from vampires to seeming preternatural hounds. But I also know that the people who told me of the ghoul believed in it wholeheartedly. One man even swore that he grappled with one of the creatures that, before he interrupted it, had been feeding on the corpse of a recently buried child dug up from the ground with the thing's spiky talons."

"Talons, eh?" said Holmes. "Quite handy for digging, I am sure. But why, pray tell me, has *this* ghoul begun to plague the St. Marylebone cemetery?"

I thought about what I had read in the *Times*. There had been no explanation for the ghoul's presence, but rather a colourful, and no doubt exaggerated, description of the creature's supposed depredations.

"I don't know," I said.

"And we are to believe that this creature of the night has come here to London, sought out that cemetery in particular, and begun to haunt it?"

"*Haunt* is not precisely the right word. Ghosts haunt, but ghouls have other unpleasant habits. And it did not necessarily *come* here. It could have been here all along."

"Surely," said Holmes, "even ghouls must come from somewhere, have an origination. Whence this one?"

I could not answer his question, of course, and I confessed that I had never heard where ghouls might originate.

"That, then, is not a powerful argument in the favor of their existence," Holmes said. "But what's this?"

He rose, stepped to the window, which was closed against the morning chill and fog, and opened it. Only then did I hear the muffled sound that Holmes's keen ear had already detected, the sound of footsteps on the street outside. Then came a knocking on the outside door.

"Someone is in dire need of your help, to have risen and come here at this early hour," I said, exercising my deductive powers.

"Perhaps," said Holmes. "Or perhaps it is someone who has not yet been a-bed. But we shall soon find out."

In that, he was correct, for it was only moments later that Mrs. Hudson showed our visitor into our rooms. He was a short but stout young man with brown skin. He peered round the room, his liquid brown eyes appearing somewhat enlarged behind the lenses of his thick spectacles. He gave me the merest of glances before focusing on Holmes.

"Mr. Sherlock Holmes?" he said. He had a light, high voice.

"Yes," Holmes responded. He indicated me. "And this is my friend Dr. Watson."

"I am honoured," our visitor said. "My name is —"

Holmes did not allow him to finish, saying: "Benjamin Swaraj."

The young man was taken aback, though of course *I* was not surprised. I had seen Holmes perform similar feats all too often.

"You are the night caretaker at the St. Marylebone cemetery," Holmes continued, "and you have come here directly from your work as the night caretaker."

"Astounding!"

I was not quite as astonished as our visitor, having by now recalled his name from the article in the *Times*, though I confess I had no inkling of how Holmes had deduced that the caretaker was our visitor.

"Not astounding at all," said Holmes. "I see that your hands are calloused, as they might be from some use of a shovel; in particular, I note that callus on the outside of your forefinger. And the peculiar loam that adheres to the side of your left shoe is the type found in the St. Marylebone cemetery, where an article in today's *Times* states that you are employed."

Holmes had often told me that a man's hands and shoes could tell one a great deal about him, and once again he had proved his theories to be so.

"Furthermore," Holmes continued, "you are plainly of Indian descent. The name mentioned in the *Times*, your calloused hands, the soil on your shoe—all those things suggest that you must be the man referred to in the article. And you have come here directly from your work"—at this remark Holmes gave me a significant glance, which I pretended not to notice—"because you are in some distress about your situation with regard to the so-called St. Marylebone ghoul. It is all rather elementary."

"That may be," said Swaraj, his eyes wide, "but I doubt that any other man in London could have arrived at your conclusion based on the same evidence."

"Oh, there is perhaps one other," said Holmes. "Possibly two. But be that as it may, you did not come here to discuss my deductive abilities. Take our visitor's coat, Watson, and let us sit down to hear his story."

I did as requested, taking his hat and scarf as well, and when we had settled ourselves comfortably, Holmes asked Mr. Swaraj to begin.

"My father is a Parsee Indian, a convert to Christianity and a minister of the gospel," he said. "My mother is an Englishwoman. As you can no doubt imagine, this somewhat, ah, unusual domestic arrangement, at least in the eyes of some, has been a cause of some consternation. Not in ourselves, but others."

Holmes nodded, impatiently, I thought, as he waited for Swaraj to get to the meat of his story.

"I said that my father was a minister," Swaraj continued, "but things in his parish"—here he named a small community in rural Sheffield—"changed. It was fine for a long time. We had a garden full of roses at the rectory, and the hollyhocks were higher than my head. There were bees in the hollyhocks, of course, but we didn't mind." He shook his head. "But you don't want to hear about that. It's just that it was a happy place for us for a while, until things became difficult. But they did, unfortunately, and we left our home in the country and moved to London."

Holmes looked more interested now. "Difficult in what way?" he said.

Swaraj did not meet his eyes. "There were . . . incidents."

"What kind of incidents?"

"Unpleasant ones."

"Please be a bit more specific," said Holmes, and Swaraj turned his magnified eyes in my direction.

"Anything that you can say to me may be said to Dr. Watson," said Holmes. "He is a man of utmost probity."

Swaraj took a deep breath. "Very well. Obscene writings appeared on the walls of some houses in the parish. Small animals—pets— disappeared, and later were found killed in a heinous manner. Someone . . . something . . . had fed on them, or so it appeared. Blame fell on me."

"And were you involved in any fashion?"

"Oh, no. I would never do such disgusting things. I have heeded my father's Christian teachings since boyhood. But there were those who believed I was guilty. It was an intolerable situation."

"But someone held a grudge against you or your family for wrongs, real or imagined."

"Imagined, I assure you. My father is a man of unwavering Christian faith and beliefs, which he has instilled in my mother and me. Our only wrongs were their marriage and my existence. And so we removed ourselves."

"And the 'incidents' stopped."

"So I had thought. But now I believe they have commenced once more."

"The ghoul?" said Holmes.

"Yes, the ghoul. I cannot think what I have done to anger the foul creature, but it has followed me here, and now I shall lose even the lowly position I had managed to obtain for myself as a watchman and digger of graves."

"Surely you cannot be blamed for the crimes of a purportedly supernatural creature."

"Someone has told the owners of the cemetery about my past, and the presumed guilt has followed me just as the ghoul has."

"And you have no idea who might try to implicate you in such bizarre crimes?"

He shrugged. "There was more than one person in Sheffield who did not like the idea of a mixed marriage, much less a child of mixed blood."

"Undoubtedly," said Holmes. "Such people are to be found everywhere. Was there anyone in particular?"

"Stanley Forbes was one. He took delight in torturing me at school. He and his friends made my life . . . quite unpleasant."

Holmes nodded, knowing as much, or perhaps more, about schoolboy cruelty as anyone. "I can well believe it. You have not seen the ghoul, I suppose."

"I *have* seen the ghoul, Mr. Holmes."

"You have?"

"Yes, once."

"And it looks nothing like this Forbes?"

"Oh, no. Nothing at all. It is much more horrible. Like nothing living or dead that I have ever seen before."

"According to what I have read in the *Times*, the ghoul has opened graves and mutilated corpses in the cemetery where you work."

"It has, beyond question!" Swaraj exclaimed, growing excited. "*That* I have seen more than once. It is horrible. Horrible! The bodies were mangled and tossed about, their burial clothing ripped to shreds, their faces torn. It was a sight to frighten even the most valiant."

"I do not doubt it," said Holmes. "Nevertheless, I should like to see it for myself."

Swaraj shook his head. "As much as I covet your help, I do not recommend that you attempt to confront the ghoul. It is—"

"Horrible," said Holmes. "And frightening. I know. But Watson and I have seen many things that would equal the sight of a ghoul, if not surpass it. Is there any way to predict when the creature will strike?"

"It could come at any time. But most often it comes soon after a burial."

"When will there be another?" Holmes asked.

"Tomorrow," said Swaraj. "And if I fail to prevent the ghoul from desecrating the body this time, I will surely lose my employment. It would not be so bad if my father and mother were doing well, but when they came to London, my father could not find a church that would have him. He is working for a greengrocer, and the pay is small. The money I provide is necessary for the family's survival."

"Dr. Watson and I will stand watch with you tomorrow night," said Holmes. "We will see just what this ghoul can do, but you must tell no one that we will be there."

Although he protested that we need not come, Swaraj was clearly pleased to have company when next he confronted the ghoul, and he wrung our hands as he took his leave. When he had gone, I questioned Holmes.

"Are you quite sure you wish to accost this abominable creature?"

Holmes's eyes were alight. "Life has been a bit dull lately, Watson, and I can think of nothing that offers more of a challenge at the moment. Can you?"

I admitted that I could not, and Holmes went to the coal scuttle where he kept his cigars. He selected one, and I waited until he had lit it before I said, "You do not believe that the ghoul is a supernatural creature; but what if you are wrong?"

He puffed twice and smoke curled around his face. Then he said, "I have been wrong before, Watson, as you know."

"Seldom, I admit."

Holmes smiled and gave a small nod. "And I do not expect to be wrong this time. Supernatural creatures? They do not exist, my dear Watson, and you know it." He gave a few more thoughtful puffs and continued. "What do you know about cemeteries, Watson? And about ghouls of the human sort?"

I had to think for a moment before I grasped his meaning, but then I said, "You are speaking of people like Burke and Hare?"

" 'Burke's the butcher, Hare's the thief, Knox the boy that buys the beef,' " said Holmes. He was not much for poetry, but when it came to doggerel of the sort inspired by abhorrent criminal activity, Holmes was as knowledgeable as anyone in England.

"A catchy little ditty," he went on, "but not the thing I mean. While you are close, Watson, you are still wide of the mark. Burke and Hare were not ghouls in the strictest sense. As a doctor, you must recall that they sold the bodies of their murder victims to the anatomy school, to Dr. Knox, in fact, but they did not snatch the bodies from graves. I was thinking of some of the notorious sack-em-up boys, like the infamous Robert Crouch."

"Ah, of course. I see what you mean. The body snatchers. But there are no longer such people as Crouch to be found, not since Parliament passed a bill to provide surgeons with bodies from almshouses and morgues and such places as that."

"True enough, Watson. Not since the bill was passed in 1832, I believe. You studied legally obtained cadavers in the course of your training, I am sure. But what of cemeteries? I am thinking now about the ones in London itself."

I was certain that Holmes already knew the answer to the question he was posing, as he invariably did. But I happened to know a bit on the subject myself, as it was something that had been discussed during the course of my medical schooling. So I was pleased to be able to answer.

"There was a time," said I, "and not so long ago at that, when the burial grounds in London were mostly comprised of churchyards, and those had become a positive hazard to the general health. They were crammed so full of the dead that the very bones of the deceased could sometimes be seen protruding from the ground. Children walked above the bodies that had been shoved into shallow graves beneath the floors of schools and chapels, and the living breathed the noxious fumes of decay emitted by the dead. This was quite unhealthy for all concerned and led to the laws allowing the establishment of private cemeteries such as St. Marylebone."

"You do not disappoint me, Watson." Holmes carelessly flicked the ash from the end of his cigar. "You are a veritable trove of information. And you speak as if you were not horrified at all by the bodies and the decay."

"To a physician," I said, "there is nothing horrifying about death. It is part of the process of life."

"Yet some people fear their inevitable end, just as some fear those whose skin is of a slightly different hue, whereas both death and the difference in colouring among different peoples are perfectly natural."

"Ignorance is at the root of their fear," I said, "as it is at the root of most human fears."

"Well said, Watson. But we are not ignorant men, and therefore we have nothing to fear from ghouls. For if they are supernatural creatures, they do not exist except in the minds of the ignorant. And if they are human, we can defeat them."

"I suppose so, but are you saying that Swaraj is ignorant?"

"Not entirely ignorant, I am sure, but besides his father's teachings Benjamin may have absorbed some folkloric background as well. It is only logical that a father would tell his son a bit about the culture of his native land, and children love tales of ghosts and such things. And the father no doubt mentioned something of ghouls when the distressing incidents to which Benjamin alluded occurred."

"And I?"

Holmes favoured me with a thin smile. "You, Watson, do not believe in the ghoul any more than I do. Oh, you may pretend to believe, at least a little, and you may allude to your time in India and what you heard there, but I know that at bottom you are the one of the steadiest and most sensible of men."

"I thank you, Holmes for your belief in my good sense, but there are times, I must say, when I suspect that I am far more credulous than you seem to think."

"We shall see about that when we visit the cemetery tomorrow night," said he. He turned his cigar in his fingers and gazed at it thoughtfully. "It might be best, Watson, if you bring your pistol along."

"I most certainly shall," I said.

ALTHOUGH THE WEATHER remained foul, Holmes spent the rest of that day and most of the next outside our apartments. He did not discuss his whereabouts or offer any explanation, nor did I ask for one, being accustomed by now to his occasional unexplained absences.

The evening on which we were to visit the cemetery was as dismal as the ones that preceded it. The air was bitingly cold, and a greasy fog hung in the air, making halos around the gas lamps along the street as we made our way to the St. Marylebone cemetery. We seemed to be the only pedestrians on the dimly-lit streets, though we did pass an occasional cab rattling over the cobbles.

When we reached the gate of the cemetery, Holmes indicated that he would go ahead of me along the path that wound among the monuments and graves.

"All you need do is follow my lead," he said, "and I will take you to the grave where the late Jonathan Holden is now interred."

"Holden? The name is not familiar."

"There is no reason why it should be. He is simply the latest to be buried here. For that, and for other reasons, he is quite a likely candidate for a visit by our ghoul. Come along, Watson. We do not want to miss our appointment with that interesting apparition."

I followed him as he had asked, and as we wandered along, the way became gradually darker the farther we got from the street. There were no gas lamps inside the cemetery grounds, although their light would hardly have disturbed those sleeping there. Holmes reached into his Inverness and withdrew a dark lantern, which he lit, and by its weak beam we made our way along the path. We passed by low headstones and marble monuments depicting white crosses, praying hands, hovering angels, and risen youths, their outlines but dimly glimpsed in the deepening gloom. The fog wreathed the taller ones, hiding some of their bases from our view, and I fancied I could smell the newly turned earth of graves. I stopped to wipe the moisture from my face, assuring myself that it was simply the fog rather than the result of any anxiety I might be feeling.

"We have arrived," Holmes said, and I confess that I was momentarily startled.

The feeble light of the dark lantern revealed a mound of dark earth, and standing nearby was the figure of a man whom I assumed to be Swaraj. The man started toward us, and I put my hand into the pocket of my overcoat and gripped the pistol I had concealed there.

"I am glad that you have come," said Swaraj, for it was indeed he, as I could see when he got closer. "Still, I fear for your safety if the ghoul should make an appearance."

"It has appeared before, and *you* are unharmed," Holmes said, sliding the cover over the lens of the lantern.

We were plunged into an eerie kind of semidarkness. Though the sky was obscured and no trace of moonlight leaked through, the fog itself seemed almost phosphorescent, and I could still see things around me, though they were blurred as if in a dream.

Swaraj looked toward the fresh grave, then down at his feet. "I did not tell you the entire story."

"I was wondering about that," said Holmes. "If the ghoul is so vicious, how did you survive its terrors?"

"I ran," said Swaraj, his eyes still downcast. "I could not face it. It was too terrible."

"Tonight you shall face it," said Holmes, "with me and Dr. Watson at your side."

He looked round us at the strangely blurred monuments. After a moment he said, "There is a good one, Watson, not too far away, yet not so near as to allow the ghoul to sense our presence."

I looked in the direction he indicated and saw a large tomb, a formidable monument to the departed, no doubt white and shining in the light of day but now an oddly shimmering grey. The tomb's decorative statuary represented a body apparently being resurrected, breaking its bonds of earth and rising from the cold ground.

"We shall wait behind that admirable edifice," Holmes continued. "And if the ghoul appears, we shall confront it."

"But what of me?" asked Swaraj, looking up at last.

"Follow your usual pattern," said Holmes. "It should be as if nothing were different."

"I often sit somewhere nearby to watch over the grave since the ghoul has begun making its visits."

"Very well. Do that, and we shall remove ourselves."

With that, Holmes led me behind the tomb, and we endeavoured to make ourselves as comfortable as possible under the circumstances. Holmes never seemed bothered by cold and damp, but I confess that they seemed to seep into my joints. The hard ground and the harder tomb against which I waited did nothing to ease the stiffness that overtook me in the silent darkness.

I judged that almost two hours had passed when Holmes gave me a gentle nudge. I might have been dozing, for I jerked away from the tomb, my hand grappling in my pocket for the pistol.

"Not yet, Watson," Holmes whispered. "But soon, I think. Come along."

He rose up and crept to the corner of the tomb, and after he had peered around it, he motioned for me to follow, which I did, my joints protesting creakily. What I saw when I looked around the end of the tomb caused me to come erect at once, taking no notice of complaining joints.

Above the grave beside which Swaraj stood rooted in terror there floated the bulbous snaggle-toothed face of the ghoul, its mouth frozen in a horrific grimace. It swooped down toward Swaraj, who swung at it with a shovel that he had held concealed by his side. He missed his mark, and the head flew away with a chilling laugh before swooping again. Swaraj struck again with the shovel, missed again, and threw the shovel at the thing, which easily dodged it. Swaraj tried to hold steady, but his knees buckled and he collapsed to the ground.

"Now, Watson!" cried Holmes, and taking his meaning, I drew my pistol and fired at that dreadful, swooping face. My first shot missed, but Holmes was already off and running in the direction of the grave. I fired again and was more successful, but the result was unexpected. The face of the ghoul exploded into fragments that flew away and disappeared in the fog.

Holmes meanwhile had leapt over the grave and plunged past a small nearby obelisk. The sound of my shots was still ringing in my ears when I heard someone cry out, and there was the new sound of a struggle.

I started forward. Swaraj had already recovered from his fright and gone to join Holmes in his fight with the ghoul. When I reached them, I saw that they confronted not a creature of the night but a purely mortal enemy, though one who appeared as vicious as any ghoul could hope to be. A man with a Bowie knife was crouched with his back to a tomb. He held the knife loosely as he swung it in front of him, as if daring Holmes and Swaraj to come any closer.

"There is your ghoul, Watson," said Holmes as I approached. "Though I have never seen him before, I would wager that his name is Stanley Forbes."

"I believe you are correct," said Swaraj, leaning forward for a better look. "But why is he here, and what happened to the monster?"

"The monster was nothing more than a balloon," said Holmes, "painted to resemble a grotesque face. Your former school friend used an old medium's trick, dangling the balloon from a flexible fishing pole, which I am sure we will find nearby."

"You will find nothing," said Forbes—for it was indeed he—as he stepped forward, brandishing his knife.

"A knife is an effective weapon," said Holmes, "in certain situations. However, I believe our American friends have an aphorism about the foolishness of bringing a knife to a gunfight."

I exhibited my pistol. Forbes looked at it for a long moment. Without a word, he flipped the knife so that the blade and not the handle was in his hand. Then he hurled the knife at Swaraj, who ducked aside barely in time as it whistled by him. Forbes did not wait to see the result, but turned and ran.

"If you please, Watson," said Holmes, and I fired. The bullet struck Forbes in the right calf, and he went down on his face, sliding a few feet along the ground.

"And thus," said Holmes, "ends the career of the St. Marylebone ghoul."

THE NEXT MORNING over a late breakfast, I asked Holmes how he had known what we were going to encounter.

"Of course I was not certain," he said, buttering a muffin. "But it appeared to me that Swaraj was ripe for trickery, especially of the kind that takes place in the darkness. You must have noticed how nearsighted he is."

I said that I had, and Holmes went on. "He needed considerable assistance to see under the best of circumstances. At night he must have been nearly blind. Add to that the frightful appearance of the 'ghoul,' along with just the smallest bit of superstition on our client's part, and you have a situation that someone might easily take advantage of."

"Someone like Stanley Forbes," I said, savoring a sip of Mrs. Hudson's excellent coffee.

"Indeed," said Holmes. "His hatred of the Swaraj family, and of Benjamin in particular, led him to his bullying at school, and when that proved not to be enough to satisfy him, to other, more barbarous things. When the Swaraj family moved to London, Forbes was deprived of his pleasure, and followed them. This I learned when I took a trip to Sheffield by rail. I undertook to locate Forbes in London, but I was unable to do so in the short time I had. I was not bothered by my failure, however, for I knew we would encounter him at Holden's grave."

"But how could you be so sure of that?"

"Holden was a well-to-do man, and I had a few words with some of his family. They informed me that he was to be buried with certain personal items, including a valuable gold ring and pocket watch. Forbes, while mutilating the bodies to make it appear that they might have been fed upon, was actually robbing them."

"Ah, now I understand more fully your reference to human ghouls."

"Yes, the body snatchers did more than provide cadavers for the anatomists. They also enriched themselves with whatever tokens they found on the corpses. Forbes was doing the same."

"A wretched sort, that Forbes," I said.

"Yes," said Holmes. "It is too bad that ignorance, hatred, and superstition cannot be exploded as easily as a painted balloon."

I set my cup down and said, "That reminds me, Holmes. The laughter that I heard when the supposed ghoul was attacking Swaraj . . . how was that produced?"

"By Forbes, of course," said Holmes.

"But the direction of the laughter," I protested.

"It is all too easy, Watson, for some people to become confused, in the night and the fog, about the direction from which a sound emanates."

"Yet Forbes has vehemently denied the mutilation of the bodies."

"My dear Watson," said Holmes, sounding a bit peevish, "are you implying that there might have been someone else in the cemetery?"

"Or something," said I. "The laughter was, you must admit, positively ghoulish."

"I do believe that is the worst joke you have ever attempted," said Holmes. He pushed back his chair and stood up. "Now I believe I will play a few tunes on my violin, as there is nothing left to do on this dreary November day."

Within moments he was drawing his bow across the strings, and I seemed to hear again the laughter of the St. Marylebone ghoul.

THE COOLE PARK PROBLEM

Michéal and Clare Breathnach

R EALLY, WATSON, THIS time you've gone too far. What would the ladies of London say if they knew you had a secret admirer across the Irish Sea? And of such high station?"

Mrs. Hudson had just finished clearing away the breakfast things, and I had settled in with the *Telegraph*. Holmes was standing by the mantel, inspecting his collection of plugs and dottles and stuffing only the choicest remnants into his morning pipe. It was a fine day in late June of 1897—the day before the summer solstice, in fact—and I was looking forward to the English joys of strawberries and cream.

My recent illness—mild neurasthenia was the unanimous diagnosis of my London peers, although some in Edinburgh and Glasgow felt otherwise—coupled with the demands of my busy practice, had temporarily laid me low, and it was all I could do to concentrate my attention on the newspaper.

"What do you mean, Holmes?" I asked, brushing past "Court and Social" to get to the altogether weightier news of the recent test match at Lord's. Despite our long years of acquaintanceship, Holmes had never entirely accepted my weakness for the fonder sex, and enjoyed guying me about it whenever he could.

"I mean this," he replied, tossing me a letter from the morning post. I picked up the letter and began to examine the envelope as Holmes continued.

"Obviously a woman's hand. Note the precision of the rounded vowels, and the flair for the dramatic as the *o* soars towards the *n*. I had no idea you travelled in such exalted—might I say revolutionary—company." He finished stuffing his pipe, struck a match and applied the flame to the week's detritus; the resulting conflagration nearly seared his hawk-like nose. "It's just as well Lestrade is on holiday in Blackpool, for I don't think I could face the ineptitude of Scotland Yard at this hour of the morning."

The letter was addressed simply to "John H. Watson, M.D., Baker Street, London." As I turned it over to look at the return address, Holmes saved me the bother.

" 'Coole Park.' Handwritten, not engraved. Only an Irish peasant—or a lady of the highest rank—would deign to inscribe her own return address. *Noblesse oblige* and all that. But the real question is: what does Lady Gregory want?"

"Holmes, you astonish me."

"And you, Watson, are beginning to bore me. Surely you remember our, shall we say, unusual introduction to Lady Gregory's errant nephew during that lamentable unpleasantness in Liverpool the year before last?"

I had only the vaguest recollection of the tragic events surrounding the final sailing of the White Star Line's *Scotia,* but I remembered well the fair, clean-limbed youth who had sought my medical advice for a personal matter before boarding the steamship for America on its last, doomed voyage.

I was still lost in my remembrance when Holmes said, "Well, aren't you going to open it and end this hideous suspense? Or must I resolve this eternal boredom by reaching for the—"

Needing no further encouragement, I tore open the envelope. Sure enough, the epistle was from Lady Gregory, the Anglo-Irish aristocrat, authoress, and playwright, whose growing passion for the language and folklore of the Irish common folk was widely remarked upon in the better drawing rooms across London, if generally disparaged as a fool's errand.

As I read, Holmes mused: "The only thing drearier than an English country weekend is an Irish country weekend. Especially one provoked by tragic gratitude. Please don't confirm my worst fears."

"Alas, I must do exactly that," I told him, happy to have the upper hand for once. "A rather intriguing problem seems to have come up in County Galway."

Holmes snatched the letter from my hand, glanced at it, and then handed it back. Although he feigned disinterest, I could see by the subtle flare of his nostrils and the slight dilation of his pupils that the missive had piqued his interest. He threw himself back into his chair and resumed his pose of pantomimed lassitude.

"Ireland is a wretched country, Watson. A primitive, superstitious land of druids and priests battling for the souls of an ignorant and savage people, with hardly a beacon of reason on the entire island. It hardly needs be said that a man in your condition—"

This was too much for a Celt like me to bear, even from Holmes. "Now see here, dear fellow—"

"Still, it might prove amusing," he allowed, setting down his pipe and ringing for our long-suffering landlady. "And I suspect the food will be tolerable as well."

And so it was that the next morning Holmes and I found ourselves on the early boat train from Euston Station to Holyhead and thence by ferry across the Irish Sea to Dun Laoghaire, and overland by rail to Gort, where we were met at the station by a coach and four bound for Coole Park. Lady Gregory's man took our luggage with an unintelligible Irish mutter and pointed to the door of the carriage; hardly had we settled into our seats when he started the horses and off we went.

Sitting beside me Holmes shuddered involuntarily as we passed first one, and then another ruin, whose only epitaphs were some low stone walls and a gable or two, peeking out from behind the hedgerows. "Moriarty, of course, is Irish," he muttered at last, half beneath his breath.

"You suspect something?" I enquired.

"I suspect everything. Would you be kind enough to read Lady Gregory's letter aloud to me once more before we arrive?"

I extracted the letter from my breast pocket and laid it upon my traveling escritoire, a gift from a grateful patient I had cured of some trifling illness or other the year before. The new summer sun was still hanging high in the west as I read:

" 'My dear Dr. Watson. It is with considerable gratitude, mixed, of course, with sorrow, that I recall your discreet service to my family in the matter of my late nephew. For several years now I have wanted to return the favour by offering you the hospitality of Coole Park, but I realised that your professional schedule is a demanding one and so I hesitated until such time as I could entice both you and Mr. Sherlock Holmes with both boon companionship and a small mystery worthy of your friend's talents, which I of course have followed closely in your published writings. That day has now arrived. Friday next—"

"In other words, today," interjected Holmes.

" '—we shall be hosting here at Coole Park a gathering of intellect and ability that, I dare say, may well be unique in Great Britain. I flatter myself in thinking that I have some small eye for talent, but both my guests are men on the cusp of accomplishment, and without revealing their identity, I am sure that you and Mr. Holmes will agree when you meet them that our company is as fine as any to be found in the finest salons of London.' "

"I have no use for salons," growled Holmes. "Pray continue."

" 'But I promised you a mystery and you shall have it. For the past fortnight or so, one of the girls in service here has exhibited the most extraordinary symptoms of incipient hysteria. For nearly a week, the girl—Mary Sheridan is her name, the granddaughter and namesake of my childhood Irish nurse—is to be found sitting on her bed, stock-still, staring out the window at the roof. All entreaties for her to resume her duties have failed utterly, including those by Undershaft, my butler, and Mrs. Warren, our housekeeper, and we have begun to despair of her health.

" 'This is no mere medical matter. For the really strange element, my dear doctor, is that there is nothing whatsoever wrong with young Mary. Our local physician, Dr. Connelly, has examined her and pronounced her fit. She takes nourishment, albeit alone in her room. But she utterly refuses to leave her perch by the window, replying to all entreaties: "Don't you see them? One by one they are gathering, and when they are all here, then the Sidhe will be here too."

" 'You perhaps recall my saying that I have been gathering folktales of western Ireland, which I hope to publish some day under the rubric "Visions and Beliefs in the West of Ireland." Being familiar with the power of folklore, I have my suspicions about what poor Mary is referring to. And I must say that I—unlike some—take them very seriously. Coole Park is a magical place, where anything can happen.

" 'I realise it is highly unusual to call a man of Mr Holmes's stature into a case before anything untoward has occurred, or any crime has been committed. Nonetheless, I entreat you to come as quickly as possible to Coole Park, both to savour our hospitality and perhaps— if my suspicions are correct—to prevent a very great tragedy. Yours very sincerely, etc.' "

Holmes let out a sigh. "For an authoress," he said, "Lady Gregory has certainly left out the most important part of her narrative, without which I am unable even to formulate an early opinion. But then I suspect that very much was her intention. Mere fillips do not make a meal, but then, unless I am mistaken that is the locus of poor Miss Sheridan's fantasies looming just up ahead."

There is something about the homes of the Anglo-Irish aristocracy that has never sat quite right with me. A certain decadence, perhaps, an overripe lushness, an aura of unreality and impermanence that makes all the more poignant the desperate air of normalcy that surrounds them. Whenever I am in Ireland I cannot escape the feeling that England's first colony will also be her last.

Coole Park, however, was different. A three-storied Georgian villa with later additions and a sheltered entryway in the Irish style, it sat at the top of a small rise, overlooking a green field of yew trees, at the centre of which stood an enormous copper beech. Though the sun was still shining, a soft Irish rain greeted us as the horses cantered toward the great house; the only sound besides the beat of hooves was the cawing of the crows hovering above us or perched on ancient ruins which had been the dwellings of the original Irish inhabitants of this haunted realm, now reduced to a gable wall and some stone fences.

It was clear our arrival had been accurately forecast, for there, awaiting us, were two extraordinary men. One was lean and wiry, with keen blue eyes and the mien of a particularly hungry hawk; the other possessed a kind of poetic decadence, with the air of the repressed voluptuary about him. The first could barely conceal his physical agitation. Even in relative repose his entire being seemed to vibrate, while the second man (should one believe in humours) was of the phlegmatic type, utterly calm and unruffled.

Showing no signs of exhaustion after our long journey, Holmes bounded from the carriage, a glint of recognition in his eyes. "Corno di Bassetto, unless I am very much mistaken," he said.

The wiry man let out a small snort of gentle derision. "An easy deduction, and if I may say so, one unworthy of your reputation—if Dr. Watson's chronicles are reliable guides," he replied. Noting my puzzled expression, he continued: "Bernard Shaw, as I am more familiarly known," he said, extending a hand. As we shook, I saw him and Holmes exchanging quick, respectful glances, as well-matched duelists might just before engaging.

"An amateur violinist of Mr. Holmes's stature would surely recognise the scourge of London's musical life—my own good self," explained Shaw. Then, turning to Holmes, he said: "I gather from Dr. Watson's writings that you find Norman-Neruda's performance of that little thing of Chopin's quite remarkable, Mr. Holmes. But perhaps you could answer one small question: just what was that 'little thing' again? Since Chopin composed nothing at all for the solo violin."

Holmes smiled graciously. "Music, I fear, is one of the many things that are not Dr. Watson's forte," he said. "Surely you don't believe everything you read, Mr. Shaw?"

I felt the heat of Holmes's glance in my direction, but fortunately the other man extended his hand. He was a handsome young fellow who wore his hair brushed straight back, and his wire-framed glasses gave him an older, more sophisticated air than his youth would have otherwise suggested. "Yeats," he said, introducing himself.

Looking back, it is hard to credit that I recognised neither of these gentlemen. The great plays of Shaw were yet to come, while William Butler Yeats was still known largely as a minor Irish poet and folklorist.

At that moment, a woman appeared in the doorway. Severely beautiful, she was dressed in a simple, homespun style, as befitted the lady of the manor, and I recognised her at once as Lady Gregory.

"Gentlemen, I see that you have already introduced yourselves," she said. "You, John Watson"—the smile she gave me upon remaking our acquaintance was one that I shall long remember—"and you, Mr. Sherlock Holmes. You are both very welcome in Ireland."

A butler and housekeeper suddenly materialised behind her. "Undershaft and Mrs. Warren will show you to your rooms. If there is anything you need, please don't hesitate to ring. Shall we say downstairs, in the dining room, in an hour?"

As Holmes and I followed the servants up the beautiful hewn mahogany staircase, Lady Gregory called out: "By the way, there's no need to dress for dinner, gentlemen. Here in County Galway, we pride ourselves on our informality."

The short hitch in my tread did not escape our hostess's attention. "I hope our Irish ways do not offend your sense of decorum, Doctor," she said.

Holmes immediately rescued me from any embarrassment. "Watson may be the last civilized man in England, but even he is prepared to pull on a pair of Wellingtons at the command of a lady such as yourself, Lady Gregory." Holmes gave our hostess a brief bow. "Until later, then—when I very much look forward to meeting Miss Sheridan."

AFTER THE LONG journey, Holmes preferred to stretch his legs rather than recline, and so after a few brief moments of rest I found myself accompanying him on a brisk ramble across the grounds of Coole Park. The woods were dark and deep, and I could not escape the feeling that we were being observed by otherworldly shades.

Holmes, however, looked neither to the left nor the right, but instead concentrated his attention on the path ahead. "Do you see it yet, Watson?" he asked at one point. I looked around, but could see nothing but brambles and thickets. "I refer to the reason we have been called to this strange and wonderful place."

I could not say that I did, and told Holmes so.

"I mean, a letter arrives on our doorstep from a woman we briefly met several years ago, with an invitation to spend a country weekend in Ireland. What on earth could possibly explain such an occurrence?"

I suggested coincidence as the most reasonable explanation—that our small service to Lady Gregory's family, and our discretion, had caused her sudden outburst of generosity—but Holmes would have none of it.

"These are deep waters, indeed," he said, shaking his head. "And if what I am beginning to suspect is true . . ." He stopped, and relit his pipe. "But come, Watson, else we are late for dinner." Holmes said nothing more as we wandered back in the direction of the great house.

"RIDICULOUS!" EXCLAIMED SHAW over a second—or perhaps it was the third—glass of tawny port. The meal had indeed been splendid, with Irish lamb and roasted new potatoes and a selection of Coole Park's justly celebrated wines. We were sitting in the dark-paneled dining room, with its exquisitely wrought table of Spanish oak and a huge stone fireplace in which roared a welcome wood fire. Normally, Irish fires were small, mean things fired with peat instead of wood; the "turf," as they call it, which tended to smolder rather than spark. But this was a proper, hearty English fire.

"I can state categorically," continued Shaw, "that there are no such things as Sidhe, the Good People, or—"

" 'Them,' as we respectfully say," finished Lady Gregory. Abstemious to a fault, she sipped a glass of clear water. "And, Mr. Shaw, I am appalled that you, Irish-born, are so skeptical about the existence of the fairies. Perhaps if you had more imagination—"

"Skeptical?" exclaimed Shaw. "Worse than that, I'm afraid. In

religion, I'm an agnostic on his way to outright atheism; if there is a
God, He has yet to manifest Himself to me. But fairies? If, as our
guest Mr. Holmes here has so famously said, that one can infer the
existence of a Niagara from a single drop of water, then from a positive waterfall of non-evidence, one can be absolutely certain about
the non-existence of fairies!"

There was a moment of silence as Undershaft poured each of us
gentlemen another glass of the excellent port. In the silence, I could
distinctly hear the cawing of some nearby crows. Lady Gregory
caught his eye, and gestured to the fireplace; Undershaft threw on
the last split log as Yeats broke the silence.

"Oh, don't be such as ass," he said to Shaw. "The Age of Reason
has produced at least as many monsters as the Dark Ages ever did,
and who is to say that these Catholic Irish don't, in their own way,
understand the ways of the world equally as well as Rousseau,
Voltaire or, or . . . you yourself? Some of us have the souls of poets,
and some the souls of musical critics."

Shaw flashed a glance at Holmes, obviously expecting a natural
ally on the subject. While I, as a medical man, had seen enough of
the inexplicable so as not to entirely discount the possibility of the
miraculous, I knew that Holmes relied instead upon the precise meas-
urement of the depth to which the parsley had sunk into the butter,
or the distinctiveness of the ash from a Trichinopoly cigar. To suggest
otherwise was to visit Cloud Cuckoo-Land.

I was not disappointed. "Thanks to the deplorable efforts of
Watson here," and he gestured in my direction, "it is well known that
my taste in literature runs more to Horace than to Houseman," said
Holmes. "Reason, ratiocination—these are the watchwords of the
modern man."

"You see," said Shaw, turning triumphantly to Yeats. Yeats, however, lit a cigar and instead addressed his remarks to our hostess.

"I gather Mr. Shaw has never met Biddy Early," he said cryptically,
"or, indeed, even heard of her. If he had, he might well be singing a
different ditty. *Tra-la-la-lira-lira-lay*—"

"Biddy Early?" I ventured.

"The Wise Woman of East Clare," supplied Lady Gregory. "She is supposed to dwell on Dromore Hill, in Kilbarron, near Feakle. My nurse often spoke to me of her. Some call Biddy Early a witch. Others, an extraordinary woman given the gift of healing, and of prophecy."

"Who 'died' more than a decade ago," added Holmes, surprising me once more by his encyclopaedic knowledge.

"Who was *said* to have died," corrected Yeats. "But the back roads of Ireland shelter many a mystery, Mr. Holmes." Holmes's expression, however, proclaimed his absolute rejection not only of Biddy Early's putative talents, but indeed her very existence.

"This is not England, Mr. Holmes," said Lady Gregory, and she was about to continue when at that moment a scream, such as I had never before heard and never wish to hear again, broke the stillness of the evening.

SUCH WAS MY introduction to Miss Mary Sheridan. I cannot recall whose foot first stepped upon the upper landing, but suffice it to say that in a few moments all four of us men had raced up two flights of stairs, where we found Mrs. Warren holding a lantern and pointing down a narrow hallway into the servants' wing. The oriental rugs on the ground floor and residence floors had been replaced by matting, and mere candlelight, not gaslight, illuminated the corridors.

We charged down the hallway to the girl's room with Holmes in the lead; with nary a knock, he threw open the door, where a most extraordinary sight met our eyes.

Sitting on the bed was a comely young woman just a few months past her majority, attired only in a simple cotton shift that displayed her youthful figure to full advantage. Our intrusion, however, could not distract her from the objects of her attention, which lay outside the room through the open window and beyond to the roofline of the main house.

"Do you see them?" she whispered. "Hurry, before they vanish!"

We strained our eyes through the falling night—and there, silhouetted against the darkening sky, was a sight I shall never forget. Hundreds of ravens were perched on the roof, radiating malevolence but utterly still, as if awaiting the call of some unseen mistress. I had never witnessed so many blackbirds gathered in one place. I glanced over at Shaw, whose flinty expression betrayed his bemusement, and then at Yeats, who had a far more serious mien. There was no time for further reflection because just then Miss Sheridan suddenly arose from her bed and dashed towards the window. It was only Holmes's quick thinking and strong arms that prevented her from throwing herself upon the cobblestones several stories below.

As if in response, the hideous birds began beating their wings. Straining against invisible bonds, they seemed on the verge of taking flight as the girl shouted. "Don't you see?" she exclaimed, her eyes wide with fright. "They're leaving! We must stop them!"

With an animal cry she disengaged herself from Holmes's grip and reached for the sill. Just as she did, the crows took wing, turning the purple sky black as they wheeled in formation, screeched in unison, and bolted for the unknown. With a final scream, the girl collapsed sobbing to the floor. "They have her now."

Holmes gestured to me and I sprang forward in order to give the poor simple girl some medical attention. Calling for some water and a damp cloth, I loosened her nightshirt and began to sponge her down. The prompt administration of a sedative soon had the desired calming effect. The fear drained out of her eyes, replaced with a dull resignation and an overwhelming sense of grief.

"She's gone," she murmured.

"Who is gone, child?" whispered Holmes solicitously.

"My lady," came the reply.

This was patently ridiculous. We had left Lady Gregory sitting safely at table in the dining room. "No," Holmes said. "She is down-stairs, awaiting our return and your safe recovery."

Mary gave no reply. Instead, she scanned the faces of her attending gentlemen, finally settling on Yeats. "Tell them, Mister Will. Tell them."

"An old Irish superstition," Yeats began, his eyes cast downwards. "A tale told by the village women to frighten children." Young Mary kept her gazed fixed on Yeats as he continued. "When magpies gather along the roofline, keeping a vigil as it were, the local people believe that someone is about to carried off by the fairies. It's a ridiculous notion, but in the course of my own researches I have learned that folk belief is often a very powerful—"

He got no further, because at that moment, Mrs. Warren appeared in the doorway, trying but failing to conceal her agitation.

"Milady is gone," she said. And with that, Mary let out a deadly sigh and sat bolt upright in her bed, cackling like a madwoman.

AT FIRST GLANCE, the dining room was in the same state as when we had left it, the wine in the goblets. But Lady Gregory was nowhere to be seen. Undershaft was summoned. A thorough search of the great manor house and its outbuildings failed to turn up a trace of the stately home's mistress, and carriages sent out along all the nearby roads failed to spot her.

Holmes himself, as I had so often seen him do, attacked the scene with the utmost concentration, examining the surface of the oriental carpet beneath the table, tracking across the floor, surveying thresholds and window transoms for any clue, however small. Once or twice I thought I heard him give a small grunt of satisfaction, as he often did when he was onto something, but a glance at his face revealed nothing.

And so, after two fruitless hours, we gentlemen gathered in the library to discuss the extraordinary events of the evening.

"If Lady Gregory is having us on," I remarked, standing near the fireplace and cradling my second brandy, "then I must say I find her sense of humour wanting." The embers were dying, and an Irish chill had descended upon the great room.

"I assure you, Doctor, Lady Gregory is not given to jokes, practical or otherwise," retorted Yeats. "On the contrary, she has the utmost respect for your professional talents, and her . . . concern for your health and well-being has been ever in the forefront of her mind these past few days."

I had wished he might continue, as I could sense, rather than see, that he was concealing something from us, or rather that he wished to say more but could not bring himself to do it. Whether he would have found the courage is moot, because at that moment, Shaw spoke up.

"The great Sherlock Holmes—the apostle of reason and a rationalist after my own heart—stumped." Shaw stuffed his pipe, lighted it, and continued: "It seems that Dr. Watson's reports of your exploits may have been greatly exaggerated."

I was about to spring to the defence of my companion's honour, but Holmes calmly held up his hand. "Before you say anything rash, Watson, let me say to Mr. Shaw that I entirely agree. I have long said that your embroidered accounts of my exploits have put me in the unhappy position of having to satisfy a public ever more ready to believe the most outlandish claims for my ability. It should, indeed, have been a simple matter to pick up Lady Gregory's trail and deduce from the physical evidence where she might have gone. But as you saw, I was entirely unable to find anything."

"So what do we do?" I asked. To which Holmes gave the most extraordinary reply: "We await developments." And with that, he flung himself into a wing chair, closed his eyes and began to brood. To the untrained eye, he might have been asleep.

Yeats tried to rouse him, to no avail. "It's no use," I said. "When he gets like this, he's completely impervious to outside stimuli. He's turning over all possible explanations in his brain, eliminating the impossible and—"

"And that's just his problem," said Yeats. "He's eliminating what he thinks is impossible. But this is Ireland; what is impossible in England is not only possible here, it's commonplace. Isn't that right, Undershaft?"

The invisible butler stepped out of the shadows to agree with Yeats. I could see Holmes's eyelids flicker as Yeats continued. "Would you mind sending Miss Sheridan down, when she is able?"

A few minutes later, the soft tread of bare feet on the stairs drew our attention to Mary Sheridan, the girl whose plight had enticed Holmes and me here in the first place. Somewhat recovered from her bout of hysteria, her nightclothes primly buttoned, she took a chair and looked expectantly at Yeats.

"You know what's happened to Lady Gregory, don't you, Mary?" he said. In response, the child nodded her head severely. This was too much for me, and I blurted out: "Then for God's sakes, tell us where—"

Yeats cut me off. "You don't know where she is, do you?" This time, Mary shook her head sadly. "But you know the name of someone who does."

At this, Holmes opened his eyes, staring intently at Mary Sheridan. Even before the girl spoke, Holmes had snatched the words out of her mouth.

"Biddy Early." Shaking off his lethargy, he stood smartly and looked at Yeats, Shaw, and me.

"But my dear Holmes," I ejaculated. "You yourself said earlier—"

"That whenever you eliminate the impossible, whatever is left, no matter how improbable, must be the truth. Let us pay the lady a visit without delay."

Yeats turned to Undershaft. "My good man—a carriage to Kilbarron at once."

FROM COOLE PARK to Kilbarron was a trip of some several hours, but neither the lateness of the hour—it was now well past midnight—nor the effects of our long journey from London had the slightest effect on Holmes. Shaw snoozed, Yeats was silent, I dozed, but Holmes sat bolt upright in his seat, turning the problem of Lady Gregory's disappearance over in his mind. At last, he said, "Watson, I propose to speak to you in your capacity as a medical man."

"Of course, my dear fellow."

"What do you know of hysteria?"

It was a delicate subject. I had lost my own dear first wife in part to this malady—a story I am not yet prepared to share with the world—but I had also seen and, occasionally, treated it in other women as well. "You are speaking of the sexual aspect, I suppose."

"Indeed I am."

"In that case . . ." and I launched into a rather clinical description of what damage the suppression of the female sexual impulse could do in extreme cases. I was finishing my catalogue of ills and possible treatments when Holmes spoke.

"You see it clearly, don't you?" When I had to confess that I did not, Holmes continued. "No, I suppose you cannot. There are really only three possibilities. The first is that Lady Gregory, for reasons known only to her, lured us here for an elaborate practical joke—"

"Lady Gregory does not joke," interjected Yeats. Holmes nodded at him curtly.

"—the purpose of which I cannot begin to imagine."

"And the second?"

"The second is that the poor woman really has miraculously vanished—a proposition that I am not prepared at this time to accept. The third," and here he lowered his voice, "the third is something so sinister that I cannot even begin to contemplate it."

"You think Yeats and I had something to do with this," said Shaw, who had only been pretending to sleep.

"I did not say that," said Holmes testily. "I think nothing of the kind."

"Of course you do " said Shaw, more combative now. He rose to a full sitting position and looked squarely at Holmes. "Else why would you have brought us along on this wild-goose chase? I mean, it's obvious, isn't it?" And he looked directly at me.

I had no idea what was obvious, but Holmes had clammed up again, like a Buddha, and we rode in silence through the dark Irish night.

I MUST HAVE dozed, for the next thing I knew, the carriage had stopped, there was a glint of sunlight on the horizon, and I could hear Holmes and the others conversing in low tones. Dismounting, I stepped outside. The most remarkable sight met my eyes.

Framed against a lightening eastern sky, high up on a cold rocky outcropping, was a simple Irish hut—"cottage" would be too grand a word—with smoke from a kitchen fire curling from its chimney. A blunt, rectangular structure, it was built entirely of whitewashed stone and boasted only one door and not a single window. But this was not the most extraordinary thing about it.

On all sides save one the house was surrounded by what can charitably be described as a blasted heath. This was not the lush green Ireland I had come to know, but a landscape of singular desolation.

The grey of the omnipresent limestone was the dominant colour, limestone hills that soared and stretched away as far as the eye could see. What little vegetation survived were tufts of grass and poor mean whitethorn bushes whose berries looked inviting until one realised that they were viciously protected by sharp, nearly invisible thorns. The only ameliorating feature was a small lake just beyond the house, but even that looked cold and uninviting.

I broke out of my reverie as Holmes strode toward the door of the hovel. I could see him taking a mental inventory of the surroundings, glancing around at the ground and scanning the roof line, no doubt formulating some sort of working hypothesis.

"I've always wanted to see this," whispered Yeats under his breath, "a legend come to life."

And then the door opened.

The figure of a woman was just barely visible in the doorway: small, somewhat squat, dressed simply in the regional style of blouse, skirt, and apron. If this was Biddy Early, and she really was a witch, then a most unprepossessing witch she was.

I had expected Holmes to indulge his innate skepticism fully, and to approach the woman with an admixture of disbelief and contempt. I had underestimated, however, the degree to which Holmes's decency would dictate his actions.

Holmes and the woman conversed briefly in low tones; Holmes earnestly, the witch calmly. Then Holmes turned to us and, with a curious expression on his face, said: "Miss Early asks if we would kindly join her for a cup of morning tea."

THE INTERIOR WAS spare and harsh: a packed dirt floor, a crude kitchen arranged around the lone fireplace, in which burned a flaming turf fire, and a bench off to one side—a bench, I learned later, that the Irish call a "settle bed," which opens up into a kind of box in which the witch slept. In the throes of my exhaustion, even such rude bedding as this looked inviting.

The mistress of the house was just as plain as her surroundings. Homely, of indeterminate age, she looked at us and said, "I'm Biddy Early and you're very welcome in my house."

We five took our tea—served in ancient but immaculate tea cups—and stood as the witch took the lone seat at her simple pine table and began to speak in a soft voice, thick with an Irish accent that was often difficult to make out. Nevertheless, I herewith offer my best efforts at a reasonably accurate translation in contemporary parlance:

"The English gentleman"—she meant Holmes—"has asked me whether I know anything of the disappearance of Lady Gregory," she began. "I do." We moved closer to catch her words. "The fairies have carried her off."

I expected Holmes to scoff—Shaw did, and loudly—but instead my friend listened attentively. The old woman looked at Shaw.

"It is a simple matter, for those who believe," she said. "Your Dublin ways are not ours here on the Burren, Mr Shaw. Scribble though you like, without belief in things you cannot see—or even dream of—you will never amount to more than what you are now, poking fun at the work of your betters." How she knew Shaw's name and profession I could not imagine, but I had seen Holmes pull such a parlour trick often enough that I knew it was possible.

She looked my way. "You, Doctor—what do you believe in? All your books and learning surely cannot account for the miracles you encounter daily in the course of your work." (I had to admit—to myself, at least—that she was right.) "You know the truth, but you cannot bring yourself either to admit it, or write it."

I felt a chill pass over me as the witch spoke. Not believing in such personages, I could hardly bring myself to use that word, even in my mind, but there was something about Biddy Early's unearthly countenance—serene and wise, yet with an undercurrent of sudden, violent danger—that demanded it.

She turned to Yeats. "And you, fine sir, our poet. You have sensed the truth on your rambles through the wicked wood of Coole Park. You have felt the presence of the things you cannot see, heard the voices of those whom you cannot name. And yet you seek them, seek to know them. But how can you know them when you deny their existence? Your soul wants to believe, but your mind battles it. Let yourself go, Mr. Yeats. Embrace your destiny."

She paused. It did not seem right to break the silence, but Holmes could not contain himself. "I have asked you three questions," he said, " and you have replied to one. I pray you to address the other two."

The witch thought for a moment. "Your second question again, please, fine sir."

"Supposing you are correct, and that the 'fairies,' as you call them, have indeed carried her off, is there a way to ensure Lady Gregory's safe return?"

This question Biddy Early answered with a nod of her head. "But only if you believe."

"And the third?" Holmes leaned forward expectantly. I had watched him often enough to know when the actor in him was coming out, and I could tell that he was playing along with her, as a thespian might when undertaking a new scene.

Instead of replying, Biddy Early finished her tea and stood up. Looking at Holmes, she said: "That I cannot answer."

"Why not?" enquired Holmes.

"Because that is a question only you can answer. Your world is not my world, English sir. Your world does not even admit the existence of mine, much less honour or learn from it. In time, perhaps, you will understand. But this is not the time. For you are not the man you will become." She looked around the room. "None of you is."

She went to a cupboard and opened it. The sole item on the shelf was a small bottle, which she handed over to Holmes. "Take this back to Coole Park," she said, handing it to Holmes, "and tonight, at the exact hour and minute of her disappearance, drink it down. All of you."

"And?" blurted out Shaw, the blunderbuss.

Turned away to tend her fire, which had begun to dim, Biddy Early ignored him; fired by just her glance, the fire once more burst into bright, searing flame. "Remember," she said over her shoulder as we made ready to depart, "the fire must never go out. No matter what, the flame must always endure."

•••

THE FOUR OF us rode in silence back to Coole Park. I tried but failed to elicit from Holmes his third question, which the witch had refused to answer.

On the journey back, I began to feel that this had all been a horrible nightmare—an hallucination, perhaps, from which we would eventually awaken. Any remaining hopes we had for Lady Gregory's safe return, however, were immediately dashed by Undershaft. I shuddered to think that the poor woman might have had to spend the night in those lonely woods—if something worse had not happened to her. All in, I retired to my room.

I must have slept very soundly, for the next thing I knew there was a loud knocking at my door. I knew that knock up to be Holmes's.

"Come, Watson, come," he said, brushing past my door. A glance out the window at the setting sun told me to hurry. Was it just twenty-four hours ago that our hostess had so mysteriously disappeared? Hurriedly, I made my toilet and left the room.

As I descended the stairs, I happened to glance out the window. As before, row upon row of hideous crows were perched on the roof in silent, sinister menace. In the distance, I could hear young Mary, sobbing alone in her room.

"Ah, Watson, you're just in time," said Holmes as I entered the dining room. The places were laid out as they were the night before, with Holmes, Yeats, and Shaw arranged as before; Lady Gregory's chair was, of course, vacant. As I took my seat, I noticed that Holmes was holding the mysterious bottle Biddy Early had given him. "Shall we try the little experiment?"

I could sense Shaw's agnosticism, but as I glanced at Yeats, I could see his eyes shining through the thick lenses of his spectacles as Holmes held up the flask. "What we are about to test, gentlemen," he said, "is the superiority of pure reason over superstition. I confess that just a scant day ago, I would have doubted whether this would even be necessary. And yet, during the course of my investigation both here and in Clare, certain things have come to my attention that demand we follow the witch's instructions to the letter."

For the life of me, I could not imagine how Holmes could use the word "witch" so uncritically. My friend's capacity to astonish me was ever infinite. "In precisely"—he glanced at the clock on the mantel as it ticked inexorably towards the hour—"three minutes, we shall drink this concoction, and here is what will happen." We all leaned forward in our seats.

"Absolutely nothing," said Shaw. "Some vile peasant spirits—what are they called, Mr. Yeats?"

"Poteen," he replied. "Brewed from the potato."

"Quite. 'Poteen' will slide down our throats. We shall feel a slight burning sensation. And then we will continue to sit here, no wiser or more illuminated than before."

"Do you think so?" asked Holmes quietly. "For I cannot help but think that Lady Gregory has gathered us here for a purpose."

"Are you suggesting that she has arranged her own disappearance?" I exclaimed as Holmes turned towards me.

"Well, that is the question, isn't it?"

"This is ridiculous," barked Shaw. "We should have long since called the authorities."

"There may be higher authorities present than you think, Mr. Shaw," replied Holmes, signaling to Undershaft, who nodded and opened the door.

Holmes paused a moment, perhaps for dramatic effect, and then, when his keen ears detected the sounds of bare feet upon the stairs, he continued: "Lady Gregory is safe and very near. Isn't that right, Miss Sheridan?"

Standing in the doorway, young Mary cast a furtive glance in my direction and then looked at Holmes. She had the kind of wild stare that I associated with hysteria, or extreme battlefield fatigue; I had seen something very much like it in Afghanistan. "Yes, sir," she replied. "She is coming. I can feel her."

"Precisely," said Holmes, indicating Lady Gregory's empty chair. "Please sit down." Gingerly, the girl sat down, her bare feet barely reaching the oriental rug beneath her chair. "Now, Mary," he said, "tell us what you know of what happened."

"I told you, sir."

"I want the truth, Mary. Lady Gregory has never left this house, has she?"

Mary looked round wildly, as if seeking allies. But not even Yeats was forthcoming; instead, the poet was focusing intently on the girl's face and manner. "A terrible beauty . . ." I heard him mutter under his breath as Mary said: "I don't know what you mean, sir. The Sidhe—"

"The Sidhe be d——d!" exclaimed Holmes, shoving the cup of strange liquid before the girl. She reacted as if she'd just seen a ghost, throwing herself back in her chair and nearly knocking it over. I caught her up in my arms as she screamed.

"No! No! It's forbidden!"

"Why? Why is it forbidden?" Holmes's voice rang insistently in our ears.

Mary's eyes darted about. "Because of the flame. The flame—"

"Nonsense!" cried Holmes. And at the very moment the clock struck the hour.

The ensuing events occurred with such rapidity that it is difficult for me to reconstruct them accurately for this narrative. Holmes thrust Biddy Early's eldritch brew at Yeats, who drank and in turn passed it to Shaw, who gave it to me. I, too, took a sip from the unholy chalice and pushed it across the table to Holmes. He swept the flagon up in his hands, tossed back the remaining drops, and slammed it back down on the table.

"There," he said. "You see?"

For one tense moment, nothing at all happened. And then—

The crows screamed and beat their wings en masse in a ferocious, evil symphony. The fire, which had not been relit by human hands, magically flared to life. A strange glow appeared over the gathering, a Pentecostal umbra that distorted the visages of all those present; the witch's liquid, which had gone down tastelessly, began to burn, and I felt the room starting to spin.

Visions such as a solid Scotsman as myself should never hope to see danced in my head. Before I lost consciousness I caught sight of Holmes's face—a sight I shall never forget. He seemed to be staring directly into the void—and the void was staring back. He gripped the tabletop so fiercely that a piece of it snapped off in his hands. The thunderous sound of a million flapping wings echoed in my ears as I heard Holmes speak:

"The flame, Watson," he hissed through clenched teeth. "The unconquerable fire . . ."

I AWOKE IN my bed, with the sun streaming through the open curtains. At first I had no memory of the terrible events of the night before, only a vague sense of surprise at where I was. Then, what recollections my fevered brain had managed to retain flooded back to me. As I sat up with a start—

"Good morning . . . Doctor." I looked, and there was Mary Sheridan in the doorway. She was dressed in her servant's clothes, her face scrubbed and her hair clean, and it was with some difficulty that I recognised her at first. She was smiling coyly, as if we shared some sort of secret, and I thought I detected a faint blush on her comely visage. "Lady Gregory begs your indulgence . . ."

I could scarcely credit my senses. What had the foolish girl just said? "Lady Gregory?" I croaked. "But—"

"But as the other gentlemen are occupied with their work this afternoon, she wonders if you would be kind enough to join her at luncheon."

"Of course," I said, staring at her. "Are you feeling all right, Mary?"

The child blushed more visibly and moved back a shy step. "Never better, sir." As I continued to stare at her—rather rudely, I'm afraid—she said, "You'd better hurry, sir. It's nearly half twelve. And sir . . ."

"Yes?" I said, starting to rise.

"Thank you."

"I TRUST YOU are feeling refreshed, doctor," said my hostess as I came down to lunch. We were sitting out of doors, enjoying the fine day. "No doubt you have a thousand questions. But they can wait for another time. I need the company of at least one of my guests. A glass of wine?"

I shook my head and reached for the seltzer instead.

"You are probably wondering where the others are," she said. "Shaw has told me he has begun work on a play, something I have been encouraging him to do for years. He's much too good a writer to be wasting his time writing musical criticism. And Mr. Yeats is redoubling his researches into Irish history, which I've long urged him to do. Up to now, his poems and plays have lacked depth, been on the surface. There is so much here in this country that we don't understand, and yet we can learn from."

After what had transpired, I could only nod helplessly in agreement.

"And your friend, Mr. Holmes—I understand that he has secluded himself today to begin work on—what did he call it? A 'trifling monograph' on a subject he prefers not to speak about at this time. All in all, an inspirational evening, don't you agree?"

Lady Gregory let out a small laugh. "Coole Park has that effect on people," she said. "As I warned you, this is a magical place. You would be astonished to hear of the visions that come unbidden to my guests—and change their lives. Change all of our lives."

As my hostess spoke, she noticed that I was gazing upon the huge copper beech directly across the lawn.

"The autograph tree," she said. "Every one of my guests who is an artist, a poet, or a writer has carved his initials into that ancient trunk. The Celts, you know, believe that trees are sacred; this is my tribute to them, and to the eternal renewing power of art. Come, let me show you."

We walked over to the tree. Sure enough, the side facing the house was carved full of initials, like some weird druid monument. "Marvelous, isn't it?" She paused a moment, then continued. "I am but a poor writer, Doctor. Yes, I compose my plays and my poems to the best of my abilities, collect my folklore, and I do what I can to contribute to the reawakening in this wonderful land. But I know my limits; others will be far greater writers than I could ever hope to be."

I began to politely demur, but she cut me off. "And I know my strengths, too. I know people. I sense what they are capable of. I transform them—not into something different, but into what they really are."

"A kind of magic," I said.

"Call it a belief. There is a mighty stirring in Ireland, Doctor—a mighty stirring. The fairies move in mysterious ways. All we can do is move with them."

I could contain my curiosity no longer. "Lady Gregory—I beg your pardon but—what happened yesterday?"

She looked at me blankly. "I have no idea what you mean, Doctor."

"I mean Mary Sheridan's hysteria, your mysterious disappearance, our trip to County Clare to see Biddy Early—"

She laughed and cut me off. "Biddy Early is a legend," she said, "dead now, if indeed she ever lived. And I . . . I was here, with you and the other gentlemen. And you, Doctor, went nowhere, except to bed." Was that the hint of a smile she gave me?

"You mean—"

"I mean that you were exhausted from your long trip. Your attention to poor Mary during her emergency in the night was very much appreciated. I have no idea what you did, but this morning the glow is back on her cheeks and she is once more the hale and hearty lass we all love. And I am very glad you slept as long and soundly as you did. From what Mr. Holmes had told me . . ."

To my surprise, she suddenly produced a sharp hunting knife. For a moment I could not imagine its purpose, until she nodded in the direction of the copper beech. "Would you like to join them? My very own Sidhe?"

Tempted as I was, I knew that no mere Boswell deserved a place alongside his Johnson. "I am but a mere doctor, Lady Gregory," I said. But she would have none of it.

"Join them," she urged. "For you are also a Scotsman and a Celt. The heart of a storyteller beats within your breast. Embrace your destiny."

I took the knife in my hand and moved toward the tree.

I DID NOT see Holmes, nor the others, the remainder of the day. Instead, I roamed the spacious grounds, and wandered through the dark woods down to the river, alone with my turbulent thoughts and emotions. It was as if I were alone in this mysterious Hibernian world, listening as it spoke to me. Then something caught my attention.

A small lake was disappearing before my eyes, sinking into the ground from which it had sprung. The Irish call such a thing a "turlough," a temporary, illusory body of water which appears after a heavy rain, then slowly vanishes. I watched it until it was completely absorbed into the earth, leaving no trace of its existence.

Returning to the house, I had undressed and was about to retire for the evening when I heard the sound of billiard balls click-clicking from one of the rooms below. Pulling on my smoking jacket, I found Holmes in the billiard room, puffing on a Trichinopoly and contemplating the angle of an impossible shot.

Before I could say anything, Holmes read my mind, as he had done so many times in the past. "Even the impossible may yet be rationalised, with world enough, and time," he said. "The limits of the powers of reason have yet to be fully tested. And I intend to test them."

We contemplated the table in silence for a moment. Then I said, "Holmes, I simply must know. What was the third question you asked the witch?"

He looked at me levelly across the green baize. " 'Witch?' A curious word, Watson, with which to refer to a great lady."

Great lady? My companion was often hard to follow at the best of times, but now . . . I was completely baffled. For a brief moment, I wondered whether he missed his pipe or his syringe more.

"The greatest living Irishwoman," said a voice over my left shoulder. I turned to see the speaker, Shaw, entering with Yeats, who was carrying a notebook. The pair of them settled into a couple of wing chairs by the fire; Holmes and I remained standing by the billiard table. "With aspirations of becoming a playwright. Something I have tried my hand at as well, with indifferent success if the truth be told." Shaw fidgeted anxiously. "But I now find myself curiously . . . emboldened. Inspired. After all, a man cannot remain a critic forever."

"Indeed," added Yeats, "Lady Gregory and I are very seriously contemplating the establishment of an Irish Literary Theatre, to be located in Dublin. Edward Martyn and George Moore are joining us here at Coole Park next month to further the discussion. Never underestimate the power of art to change the world. Or even Great Britain."

To this remarkable and somewhat provocative statement Holmes said nothing; instead, he let his gaze fall upon Yeats, who opened his notebook and read aloud:

Dim Pairc-na-tarav where enchanted eyes
Have seen immortal mild proud shadows walk;
Dim Inchy wood that hides badger and fox
And martin-cat, and borders that old wood
Wise Biddy Early called the wicked wood.

His voice trailed off. For a time the only sound was the licking of the flames in the fireplace. Finally, Holmes spoke, and at last answered my question.

"The fire must never go out, gentlemen. No matter what, the flame must always endure. Call it the light of right reason, or the voices of the fairies—the lure of the Eternal Feminine. But we underestimate its power at our peril."

He bent down, lining up his shot. Exhaling softly, he drew the cue back, and then, with a sudden swift movement, let fly. I counted the cushions as the ball rolled along its preordained path. As it slowed to a stop, I could hear Holmes mutter softly under his breath: "Art in the blood . . ."

TWO DAYS LATER, we were back in the well-loved rooms on Baker Street. Mrs. Hudson was in her place, the Queen was on her throne. All was as it was before. We never spoke of the Coole Park problem again.

Miss Sheridan and I, however, maintain a vigourous and stimulating correspondence.

"Some Analytical Genius, No Doubt"

Caleb Carr

IN THE GENERATIONS since Sherlock Holmes first bemused, then annoyed, and finally endeared himself to Dr. John Watson through his "bumptious style of conversation" and his deceptively unregulated habits and behavior, it has become commonplace among those who ply the ever more degraded trade of literary critic to declare that Arthur Conan Doyle did not really *choose* to make his hero so extremely idiosyncratic. Rather, he was *forced* to paint Holmes with such broad strokes in order to avoid the enormous sense of inferiority, and hence hostility, that the great detective's scientific genius would almost certainly instill in readers of the tales. Crime writing analyst and sometime Holmesian, Stephen Knight offered a succinct summary of the effects of Conan Doyle's supposedly deliberate efforts along these lines when he declared that "Holmes isn't only a man of objective science: he's also aloof, arrogant, eccentric, even bohemian. His exotic character humanises his scientific skills: a lofty hero, but crucially a human one."

But this argument in favor of the purposeful portrayal of Holmes as an eccentric is even less perceptive than it is convincing. True, Conan Doyle was never shy about acknowledging that he considered the Holmes stories as much a speculative business venture as an experiment in literature; and yes, this fact has led too many modern analysts—for whom the declaration of a pecuniary motivation is tantamount to a confession of artistic bankruptcy—to conclude along with Knight that it was Holmes's scientific interests and observations that were the original and "genuine" part of his character, and that the more outlandish aspects of his behavior were a rather mercenary exercise in commercialism, an added feature that would make the audience "like" him.

But one need not be a creator of literary sleuths or an analyst of such efforts to see where such criticism stumbles. Indeed, one simple method of finding its flaws is to look at Conan Doyle's subsequent creations. Long after success of every stripe far beyond his original imagining had been granted to Sir Arthur, he persisted in creating new characters who (though never as popular as his great detective) were also both renowned geniuses and "bumptious" in much of their behavior. From the heights of Professor Challenger's *Lost World* to the depths of the eponymous *Maracot Deep*, as well as in a raft of his natural and supernatural tales that dotted various realms in between, we come upon this same matching of brilliance with eccentricity repeatedly in Conan Doyle's work, until finally, in 1922, he joined the ranks of the brilliantly odd himself, with his publication of *The Coming of the Fairies*, an assertion of the genuineness of the famed Cottingly photographic hoax.

In short, as man and as author, the creator of Sherlock Holmes understood that the qualities of intellectual genius and personal oddity are not artificial in their pairing. They are natural and complementary parts of the modern creative genius, scientific and otherwise. Indeed, in the crowded, anonymous, conforming social orders that have dominated the Western world (and much of the rest of the globe) since the rise of industrialism, it is the nondescript, the personally ordinary genius, that is the aberration, not the outlandish variety.

Yet Conan Doyle's instinctive understanding of this fact—his clear recognition of the sometimes terrible irreconcilability between the ultimate individuality of genius, and the ultimate regimentation of what Charlie Chaplin would so brilliantly illustrate as the unchanging fundamentals of *Modern Times*—did not significantly lead him down a path toward the discipline already well on its way to making both an art and a science out of the study of the human mind and its eccentricities: that of psychology. Indeed, Conan Doyle's profound interest in spiritualism later in his life indicates that, if anything, he sought explanation for any apparently inexplicable aspects of human behavior in quite another—and most unscientific—direction.

There is, of course, enormous irony in this fact. For just as psychology has led to many of the most important advances in forensic science in our own time—most notably, perhaps, through the technique of psychological profiling that has made the pursuit of such elusive characters as serial killers possible—so the discipline was already, in Conan Doyle's time, making important and pioneering contributions to criminal detection. Like any good writer, of course, Conan Doyle had an instinctive and refined command of the essential elements of psychology. Yet that understanding went pointedly unacknowledged by the author himself, a man who may have seemed more Watson than Holmes to the public, but who was quite aware of his intellectual strengths, and believed he applied them to the issue of spiritualism as much as he did everything else.

We can speculate as to the personal reasons why such a notable lack of any stated appreciation of a young but well-established field—one which had such a deep bearing upon his principal livelihood of criminology—should have marked Conan Doyle's character. The troubling fact of an unbalanced and alcoholic father who was eventually deemed ill enough to live out his days in the Montrose Royal Lunatic Asylum in Scotland, for instance, would more than account for any personal or professional reluctance to explore the topic openly. But whatever its origins, Conan Doyle's aversion was strong enough to endow his greatest creation with his own lack of interest in psychology. Indeed, he gave Holmes a positive disdain for matters of the mind generally, even down to the question of motivations for crimes. Nor was it enough, apparently, to have Holmes proclaim that he could solve any case through physical evidence alone. It was necessary for the great detective to say that he *preferred* such a route, despite, again, the enormous advantages that could have been gained through even a cursory knowledge of how the beginnings of psychology illuminated behavioral motivation, which, after all, is the very essence of criminality.

And yet, almost inevitably, there are moments in many of the Holmes stories when Conan Doyle's enigmatic hero displays—*must* display, given his profession—a self-contradictory yet distinct interest in the mental forces that drive human actions (particularly, of course, those that drive women). Indeed, Holmes's intellectually pure and purely intellectual facade is not without cracks on a number of levels, a message that Conan Doyle hints at (perhaps subconsciously, perhaps not) in various ways and from the very start of the tales. In *A Study in Scarlet*, Watson reveals that Holmes's command and appreciation of those disciplines constituting the humanities is "nil," but this is not the most crucial revelation that the doctor makes. Even Holmes's mastery of the sciences, Watson goes on to tell us, is uneven. His understanding of botany is pronounced "variable," and his knowledge of geology only "practical." True, his command of chemistry is "profound," but we are quickly informed that his skill at anatomy is "accurate, but unsystematic." Yet we have still not reached the most important revelation on Watson's list.

That place belongs to something that would not, at first blush, seem to even belong on the inventory. Watson labels it "Sensational literature," of which the doctor rates Holmes's knowledge to be "Immense." He appears to know every detail of every horror perpetrated in the century. The importance of this item cannot be overstated. It was in "sensational literature" that one was most likely to find, in British society of the late 1880s and early 1890s, many spectacular yet semi-scholarly studies that we would today categorize under the heading of "forensic psychology." Perhaps the most significant British example of this nexus between the serious and the spectacular was the work done by one noted alienist of the age, Forbes Winslow the younger, concerning the Jack the Ripper murders. (Winslow's father had likewise been a mental health specialist with a particular interest in forensic issues, though he did not share his son's taste for the sensational or the spotlight.)

Immersing himself in the details of the Ripper's crimes, and haunting their scandalous locales to a degree considered morally suspect in many circles, Winslow produced a deliberately shocking, celebrated account that nonetheless bore more than a passing resemblance not only to detective work but also to the beginnings of psychological profiling. It is almost impossible that Conan Doyle could have been unaware of Winslow's work; and it seems even less likely that he would have been similarly blind and deaf to the labors of France's Doctor and Professor Alexandre Lacassagne—a far more professional but less showy "amateur" detective—who did yeoman and inventive profiling and sleuthing service during the quest to catch "the French ripper," Joseph Vacher, who was finally guillotined in 1898 after an amazingly long and public career.

Why should it be so probable that Conan Doyle, the celebrated author of detective fiction, should have been conversant with at least the basic professional vocabularies of Winslow and Lacassagne? There was the fact that he was himself a doctor, of course. But even more pertinently, there is the fact that his father had first been committed to a mental institution in 1881—years before either the English or French Rippers began their savage work, and more than five years before the first Sherlock Holmes story appeared in *Beeton's Christmas Annual.*

Conan Doyle would later attempt—with transparent dismissiveness—to fix responsibility for his father's deterioration on an "unworldly and impractical" attitude as well as on alcohol. But the truth is, Charles Doyle may have taken to drink to alleviate the equal perils of epilepsy, severe depression, and artistic failure. (He was an accomplished but largely unrecognized painter, who sought to compensate for the lack of enthusiasm for his youthful creations by turning to architecture, with almost as little success.) And Arthur Conan Doyle, as the eldest son in the family, perforce played a role in his father's commitment. Some Doyle biographers believe that Arthur's first act, on returning to the family home in Scotland from boarding school was to sign the papers that initially consigned his father to professional care.

Throughout the years of his medical studies at Edinburgh University,

Conan Doyle endured the profound tragedy of a father who was for-ever in and out of several kinds of mental and alcoholic institutions before being finally committed for good and all to the Montrose Royal. We cannot say with certainty that the deep disturbance and embarrassment of coping with such a parent would have drawn Arthur, as a medical student, to instructors of a diametrically opposing mental constitution. But we *can* say that, of all his teachers, the young Conan Doyle was most deeply impressed, emotionally and intellectually, by the man that he would later cite as a general model for Sherlock Holmes: Dr. Joseph Bell. Vigorous, logical, disciplined, and a master of theatrical deductive reasoning, Bell was certainly an accomplished detective.

But he was a detective of *physical*, not mental, disorders. And as the careers of Winslow and Lacassagne would soon demonstrate, the approach of the new century was bringing with it more and more evidence that it was diseases and disorders of the mind—not neces-sarily the side effects of any physical disorders—that were respon-sible for many of the most intractable criminal behaviours. For Conan Doyle to have been unaware of such developments would have represented a kind of willful ignorance. As was the case with his detective hero, it seems that the entire subject of psychology—espe-cially psychological pathology—made him so profoundly uncom-fortable (even if for reasons that we shall never be able to state with certainty) that he had to assume an attitude of feigned detachment.

Mind you, none of this analysis should be interpreted as com-plaint. Without this discomfort on the part of the master of the genre, the success of other authors of detective fiction such as I would likely have been impossible.

If Holmes's pointed avoidance of, and aversion to psychology, like Conan Doyle's own, was an almost embarrassing case of protesting too much, it does not change or detract from the fact that both characters were highly successful geniuses, artistically as well as pop-ularly. Nevertheless, the strong element of eccentricity in both would also have made them ideal subjects for psychological study, even if they refused to practice such *formally* themselves. And by the time of my own youth (no small portion of which was spent first reading, then studying and restudying not only the texts of the Holmes stories but what was handed down to my generation as the definitive theatrical interpretation of the great detective—the films of Basil Rathbone), psychology and psychiatry had become so pervasive, indeed so common in everyday life that even young students of Conan Doyle could almost instinctively comprehend this perhaps shrouded but no less important aspect of Holmes's often, and inarguably, peculiar behavior.

I had scarcely left high school, in fact, before one modern author, Nicholas Meyer, exploited the lucrative commercial possibilities inherent in this situation. Hurling himself down the slippery slope of "reinventing" a master's work, Meyer, in his novel *The Seven-Per-Cent Solution*, posited an encounter between a cocaine- and childhood trauma-stricken Holmes and Sigmund Freud. Yet for all the timely cleverness and initial popularity of Meyer's concoction, its failure to keep faith with Conan Doyle's original tales almost predestined it for a transitory sort of notoriety. Ultimately, we learn as little about literature as we do about history when we attempt to solve riddles by simply rearranging facts. The pertinence that the discipline of psychology earned by going so obviously deemphasized, and almost unmentioned, in the Holmes tales and in Conan Doyle's account of his own life remained intact in all its ambiguous glory in the original works well after Meyer's attempt to make it explicit had faded.

It retains that ambiguity today, as it should, for—at the risk of offending the priests and priestesses of deconstructionism—that is how Conan Doyle wished it. And as I continued to study the original stories and novels well past boyhood, I came to realize that somehow, strangely, this silent but important role of psychology does not *detract* from Holmes's status as the first great scientific detective in literature. It *enhances* it, precisely because it is so powerful and yet so ambiguous. It allows room for those uncomfortable with such subjects to ignore it, if they wish; or those interested in it can track its every subtle appearance and influence (or lack thereof) throughout the stories and novels. Eventually, however, I began to seek out fiction that would more explicitly investigate both the rise of psychology—specifically, early American psychology—and its entrance into the field of criminology.

The tongue-in-cheek cleverness of Meyer's work, to say nothing of the far more objectionable literary and film "reinventions" of the Holmesian world that appeared at roughly the same time and continued during the two decades that followed, was not so much inadequate as unrelated to this curiosity. Among modern mystery writers, only Thomas Harris came close, in his first two Hannibal Lecter novels, to dealing with the relationship between psychology and crime in a way that transcended the sophomoric—and even at that, Harris's works were rooted very firmly in the present. The characters and setting that I was looking for simply did not seem to exist in fiction.

There are similar moments in most writers' careers, when they realize that the book they want to read hasn't yet been written. To observers, these seem moments of unique opportunity—for the writer is, apparently, being given the chance to create the desired volume her- or himself. The writer, of course, immediately asks a very different set of questions: Why *haven't* others thought of it before? Or *have* they, and then thought better of the whole thing? If the writer's inspiration and conviction are strong enough, this moment of doubt is brief; and if the writer can look to a long-admired member of the profession for, if not precedent, then at least guidance—even unintentional guidance—then the doubt can be weakened further still.

This was the role that Conan Doyle and Sherlock Holmes played in the conception of what would become my own first crime novel, *The Alienist.* In attempting to bring to life a late nineteenth-century psychologist who becomes his own form of "amateur detective," I intended to pay homage to, and recognize the works of, all the forensic and consulting psychologists that Conan Doyle so carefully failed to mention in his own works. But at the same time, I had no desire to reinvent Sherlock Holmes, even in a veiled form, nor would mine be an attempt to demonstrate any shortcomings of the great detective's character, or that of his creator's. Rather (at least ideally), the two fictional creations and intellectual approaches would be complementary, not contradictory, for one can pay homage far more effectively by filling some of the available creative space around a beloved character than by trying to crowd the same territory through imitation or reinvention.

The essential mechanics of my intended complementary approach were simple. Holmes took great pride in declaring that he not only could but *preferred* to solve crimes without troubling himself over the personal details of the victims or others involved in the case. But modern investigation has shown us that there are now—and were then—many crimes in which few if any physical leads present themselves; and that, for much if not most of Holmes's career, many of the methods used to identify those few clues (blood typing, fingerprinting, etc.) remained too controversial or inconsistently executed to be recognized as evidence in a courtroom. In other words, while I did not dispute that there were cases that could be solved on the basis of physical evidence alone, I knew that there were also many cases that could be broken only through methods that did not depend upon physical evidence; and that foremost among these latter methods was forensic psychology.

Further, the turn of the nineteenth century had already seen successful forays into what would one day become the most successful of all techniques in criminal psychology—profiling. Like Conan Doyle, I could make a plausible scientific (and historical) case for my protagonist's revolutionary methods. And as in the example of Holmes, those methods would mean that my protagonist would also perforce be an eccentric genius of what might seem deliberate proportions. But they would not, in fact, *be* deliberate, any more than I believe they were in Conan Doyle's case. As I soon learned for myself, eccentricity is no contrivance when it is contained in a character of sufficient intellectual acumen. It is (especially in the modern, psychologically regimented world) simply natural, so natural that the modern genius who lacks it somehow seems not a genius at all, but rather an artificially well-adjusted poseur.

The remaining portions of my own creative undertaking represent a story for another time. My purpose here is simply to note that my own development of a personal alter ego, the New York alienist

Dr. Laszlo Kreizler, was never intended as any sort of reinvention of Sherlock Holmes—that, in fact, Dr. Kreizler could not have found the success he has (surprising to no one more than to me) had I ever felt, or indulged in, anything but continued and, indeed, augmented respect for the integrity of Conan Doyle's work as I grew older. One cannot, after all, create a complementary image if one dishonors the integrity of the figure alongside which that complement is shaped.

Given my ever-strengthening enthusiasm and respect for the character of Holmes, it is less surprising to me now than it was when the project was first proposed that I should find writing my own Sherlock Holmes tale as gratifying as I have.* There has been no question of needing to reinvent Holmes, of needing to supply that "different something" that so many writers apparently feel must be grafted on to a character who is, after all, the single most recognized name in all of world fiction. Who can have the temerity to reinvent such a global icon, and then expect the reinvention to be more than a novelty item? Rather, if we, as modern mystery writers, elect to elaborate on the Holmesian canon at all, it must be to demonstrate the enduring integrity of Conan Doyle's techniques and their pertinence to modern crime fiction—to maintain a kind of professional faith, and show that, even (perhaps especially) through those subjects that he treated with such enormous ambiguity as he did psychology, Conan Doyle inspired and influenced us all.

It is, of course, the paradoxical nature of all faith that only by assiduously honoring the integrity of what *has* been—the old—can we successfully invent what *will* be—the new. In crime literature, as in any literature or art or architecture, to "reinvent" the specific works of great masters is to engage in triviality, however facile, just as to ignore the influence of such masters is to engage in mere narcissism. Both qualities, facility and narcissism, are much at work in contemporary American society. Intellectuals and academics work tirelessly to deconstruct masterworks, in the hope that they will reinvent the meaning of such achievements in a more "just and proper" form, and are shocked to find that, instead, they merely drain these

---

* *The Italian Secretary*, published by Carroll & Graf, May 2005.

works, and the culture and societies of which they were or are symbolic, of all meaning.

Small wonder, then, that crime fiction should have come to inhabit such an important position in our culture. It is one form that the deconstructors have, for the most part, been content to leave to the occasional interloping and meaningless reinventor. The majority of deconstruction's practitioners feel no compulsion to put the work of our profession's greatest originating genius through such destructive intellectual rearrangement, and we are free to learn from every original nuance and ambiguity of Conan Doyle's work.

For how long will this be the case? How soon can we expect the first serious deconstructive assault on the Holmesian canon? It is impossible to say. But one suspects that, whoever the authors of such an attempt might be, they will find themselves with an unexpectedly vigorous fight on their hands, for, more than Hemingway, Twain, or even Dickens, Conan Doyle is the member of the literary old guard who possesses the most extraordinarily diverse and international constituency. And if ever there were two characters who could form a seawall against which the mad tide of modern literary theory would break harmlessly, it is Holmes and Watson. Indeed, one anticipates the mere idea of such a contest with a kind of relish. After all, far more dangerous professors than those currently prowling the halls of academia have tried their luck against the eccentric lodgers of Number 221B Baker Street.

No Ghosts Need Apply?

Barbara Roden

"Rubbish, Watson, rubbish! What have we to do with walking corpses who can only be held in their grave by stakes driven through their hearts? It's pure lunacy. . . . This agency stands flat-footed upon the ground, and there it must remain. The world is big enough for us. No ghosts need apply."
   —*Arthur Conan Doyle, "The Adventure of the Sussex Vampire"*

THIS PASSAGE, WRITTEN in 1924, is one of the better-known sayings of Mr. Sherlock Holmes; and there are undoubtedly a good many admirers of the great detective, then and now, who breathed a sigh of relief when they realised that whatever the beliefs of his creator, Holmes himself would remain the resolutely rational character he had always been. Not that elements of the mysterious— or even the supernatural—are absent from the Holmes canon: as early as 1891 the detective found himself embroiled in the Gothic affair of "The Speckled Band," while 1901 saw him involved in the mysterious case of *The Hound of the Baskervilles,* the adventure which contains the most tantalising hints of a solution which cannot be arrived at without recourse to the supernatural. Among the later cases, both "The Sussex Vampire" and "The Creeping Man" (1923) appear to hint at events that are not of this world; but all, of course, is rationally explained at the end. It should be noted, however, that while the solution to the mysterious events plaguing the Baskerville family at the time of Holmes's investigation proves to be a rational one, the great detective does not enquire closely into the apparently supernatural events described in the "Legend of the Hound of the Baskervilles" as read by Dr. Mortimer, which do seem to admit of a decidedly non-rational explanation.

The temptation for Arthur Conan Doyle to allow his most famous creation to embrace—however subtly—the occult must have been a strong one, given his own firm belief in the spirit world. Wisely, he resisted this urge; although he was not so strong-willed with another great creation, the larger-than-life Professor Challenger, who becomes a convert to the Spiritualist cause in the now largely unread novel *The Land of Mist* (1926). Conan Doyle doubtless realised that for Holmes to endorse the supernatural in any way would have been a contravention of much that was known and loved about his creation. Fortunately, other authors have not feared to tread where Conan Doyle held back; thus we have that offspring of the mystery tale and the ghost story, the psychic detective tale.

That such a hybrid should have come into being is not surprising, given the Victorians' love for the ghost story, for many ghost stories are really mystery stories in which the supernatural plays a part. Victorian supernatural fiction follows, for the most part, a fairly well-worn path: a spirit returns to earth seeking either revenge or pardon for past deeds (or misdeeds), and much consternation ensues until the spirit is granted what it seeks, whereupon it departs this world. However, before the ghost is identified as such, some detective work is usually involved. Then as now, characters in fiction mirror real life inasmuch as they are generally unwilling to embrace a supernatural explanation until all rational avenues have been ruled out. So the mysterious figure seen in the garden, the unexplained footsteps and rappings, and the whispered sighs are all attributed to a variety of rational causes until someone puts two and two together and realises—according to Holmes's famous dictum—that when you have eliminated the impossible, whatever is left, however improbable, must be the truth.

However, while the ghost story and the mystery story were born within a few years of each other, they had very different childhoods. The first ghost story, in the modern sense of the term, is generally acknowledged to be Sir Walter Scott's "Wandering Willie's Tale," published as part of his 1824 novel *Redgauntlet*, while the first modern mystery story is Edgar Allan Poe's 1841 tale of "The Murders in the Rue Morgue."

Once the short ghost story had been unleashed upon the world, it proved immediately, and immensely, popular, flourishing in the pages of the monthly magazines which sprang up to cater to the increasingly large number of people who had the ability to read and the free time in which to do so. The mystery story, however, failed to set the literary world alight, and limped along for several decades, attracting the odd novelist (Wilkie Collins, Emile Gaboriau), but not garnering anywhere near the same attention that had been afforded the ghost story.

All this changed in 1891, when the first Holmes short story, "A Scandal in Bohemia," was published in the pages of *The Strand Magazine*. Its success was immediate, and the mystery story—until then something of a sickly child—went through a metamorphosis which changed it overnight from a ninety-eight-pound weakling into a literary heavyweight. The readers of *The Strand* and the other monthly magazines of the day suddenly could not get enough mystery stories, and a flood of literary detectives poured into every available market. Each magazine needed its own series of mystery stories in order to compete with Holmes in *The Strand*, and writers were not slow to take advantage of the situation. However, it soon became apparent that there was only one Sherlock Holmes and that other writers needed to distinguish their detective creations from the Master in some way. Thus it was that there were lady detectives, blind detectives, thinking detectives, comical detectives, foreign detectives, medical and scientific detectives, backwoods detectives, and eventually and inevitably, occult detectives.

It was in 1898 that the two genres finally met and married, as it were; but just as the roots of the mystery story can be traced back prior to Edgar Allan Poe, so too can prototypes of the psychic sleuth tale be discerned several decades before the genre sprang fully formed into existence. The first budding of the idea came about in 1869, when Joseph Sheridan Le Fanu's short story "Green Tea" appeared in Charles Dickens's weekly magazine *All the Year Round*. Le Fanu is acclaimed today as the father of the modern English ghost story, the writer who liberated the genre from its Gothic trappings and introduced a more psychological, realistic aspect which would be further developed by twentieth-century writers, and "Green Tea" is one of the most famous, and chilling, ghost stories ever written. The story is narrated by Dr. Martin Hesselius, described as a "medical philosopher," a man who takes as keen an interest in his patients' spiritual health as he does in their physical health. He befriends and is subsequently consulted by The Reverend Mister Jennings, a man who is being pursued by a very specific apparition: one that takes the form of a malignant monkey. Although Hesselius listens patiently to Jennings, and declares at the end of the story that he has met with some fifty-seven cases of the kind, in none of which he has failed, he is singularly unsuccessful here: Jennings, driven to despair by the persecution of the creature haunting him, takes his own life. Hesselius attempts, somewhat disingenuously, to excuse his failure in this case by declaring that Jennings was never really a patient of his, and goes on to state that he has no doubt that, given time, he could have cured Jennings of his malady; but we shall never know the truth of the matter. The good doctor appears briefly in three further Le Fanu tales—"The Familiar," "Mr. Justice Harbottle," and the early vampire classic "Carmilla"—but only as the person presenting the narratives which follow, all of which are penned by other hands and in which Hesselius himself plays no part. He is thus not truly representative of the psychic detective, as we see almost no evidence of his methods, deductions, or actions; the term "psychic consultant" might be more accurate.

The next development along the road towards the psychic detective came in 1882, with the founding of the Society for Psychical Research (SPR) in England. The SPR rose out of the ashes of a group with similar aims, the Psychological Society of Great Britain, which had been formed in 1875 and dissolved in 1879 following the death of its founder. The purpose of the SPR was to encourage a rigorous, scientific approach to the investigation of psychic or paranormal phenomena in order to establish the truth (or otherwise) of such occurrences. The group's researches took in several areas of the paranormal, including telepathy, mesmerism, mediums, the physical phenomena associated with séances, and of course apparitions. In 1884 the SPR successfully (and famously) exposed Madame Blavatsky and the Theosophical Society, bringing the SPR and its aims to public attention; one result of this fame was the subsequent appearance of the SPR (or a thinly disguised query) in the pages of many a ghost story written between 1885 and the Second World War. Arthur Conan Doyle, who had been interested in paranormal phenomena since the early 1880s, joined the SPR in 1893, and was a vigorous supporter of the group for many years despite his feelings that the organisation assumed a somewhat "supercilious" air towards Spiritualism. He includes a mention of the group in his 1899 ghost story "The Brown Hand," in which the narrator mentions a night he spent in a haunted house while a member of "the Psychical Research Society."

A further step towards the creation of a fictional psychic detective came in 1897, when Bram Stoker's *Dracula* was published. Stoker knew of Le Fanu's work, particularly his vampire novella "Carmilla," and was thus aware of Dr. Hesselius and the assistance he provided to those suffering from spiritual manifestations. It is, therefore, entirely possible that in addition to drawing on the vampire aspects of "Carmilla" for his own vampire novel, Stoker drew on Hesselius when he created Abraham Van Helsing, the man whose knowledge of all things to do with vampires enables him to unmask and ultimately defeat Count Dracula. However, to call Van Helsing a psychic detective would be a misnomer. He displays a detailed knowledge of vampires, which he puts to effective use; but vampires are physical creatures, very much of this earth, and little in what we are told about Van Helsing leads us to believe that he is concerned with, or knowledgeable about, more spiritual, unearthly matters.

In 1896, a year before *Dracula* was unleashed on the world, a nineteen-year-old writer named Hesketh Vernon Hesketh-Prichard had come up with an idea for a series of detective tales centering on a character named Flaxman Low. He conceived of Low as being a detective very much in the Sherlock Holmes tradition: cerebral, widely read in his field of interest, keen-eyed, able to discern the meaning of clues and signs which others cannot decipher, and always ready to be consulted by those who see him as their court of last appeal. The main difference was that, while Holmes confined his investigations to this world, Low would use his deductive skills to solve problems of a supernatural nature; and thus was the true psychic detective born.

Hesketh-Prichard's interest in writing a series of detective stories almost certainly received a boost after he met Conan Doyle in February 1897, at a dinner given by the *Cornhill* magazine. According to Hesketh-Prichard's biographer, Eric Parker, "Conan Doyle took a fancy to Hesketh at once, and when they left the house after dinner walked about the London streets with him talking into the small hours of the morning. The elder man, perhaps, did not guess at the time what the encouragement meant to the younger . . . That walk began a friendship of many years." The first six Flaxman Low tales were completed in the months following this meeting, with Hesketh-Prichard receiving some assistance from his mother, Kate, who probably (in light of her son's subsequent distinguished literary career) did little more than add a bit of polish to her son's efforts.

The stories began appearing in *Pearson's Magazine* in January 1898 under the byline of "E. and H. Heron," with a second (and final) series of six tales beginning in *Pearson's* in January 1899. They purported to be accounts of the haunting of "real" places, a conceit bolstered by the use, at the beginning of each story, of a photograph of the house or locale in question. That Low is a completely new sort of detective is made clear in a preface to the first story, where he writes "I think I may say that I am the first student in this field of inquiry who has had the boldness to break free from the old and conventional methods, and to approach the elucidation of so-called supernatural problems on the lines of natural law." Reference to others preceding Low in "this field of enquiry" makes him sound like one in a line of psychic detectives, but the truth, of course, was that Hesketh-Prichard was breaking entirely new ground. He could hardly draw on other psychic sleuths for inspiration while writing his tales, for the simple reason that there weren't any; instead, he turned to Holmes to provide him, and his character, with inspiration. Throughout the Low stories there are echoes of the great detective, his cases, and his methods; for example, this passage from "The Story of Yand Manor House" could have come from any of the Holmes tales:

> "By the way, Sir George, who lived in this house for some time prior to, say, 1840? He was a man—it may have been a woman, but, from the nature of his studies, I am inclined to think it was a man—who was deeply read in ancient necromancy, eastern magic, mesmerism, and subjects of a kindred nature. And was he not buried in the vault you pointed out?"
>
> "Do you know anything more about him?" asked Sir George in surprise.
>
> "He was, I imagine," went on Flaxman Low reflectively, "hirsute and swarthy, probably a recluse, and suffered from a morbid and extravagant fear of death."
>
> "How do you know all this?"
>
> "I only asked about it. Am I right?"
>
> "You have described my cousin, Sir Gilbert Blackburton, in every particular."

Or consider this passage, from "The Spaniards, Hammersmith":

> "I can recall," replied Flaxman Low thoughtfully, "quite a number of cases which would seem to bear out this hypothesis. Among them a curious problem of haunting exhaustively examined by Busner in the early part of 1888, at which I was myself lucky enough to assist. Indeed, I may add that the affair which I have recently been engaged upon in Vienna offers some rather similar features."

Like Holmes, Low has, it seems, spent a good deal of time reading up on cases from the past, on the assumption that there is nothing new under the sun. The similarities between the Holmes stories and Low's cases are most marked in the two final cases in the series, where Low describes his encounters with the villainous genius Kalmarkane in terms that make it plain that Hesketh-Prichard had a copy of "The Final Problem" within easy reach of his writing desk: "The very extraordinary dealings between Mr. Flaxman Low and the late Dr. Kalmarkane have from time to time formed the nucleus of much comment in the press. This is partly the reason for the narration of the present story, which may safely be said to be the first true account of those passages which have provoked so much contention."

In addition to creating the character of the psychic detective, and showing others how such stories might be written, Hesketh-Prichard also came up with the interesting idea of not always providing a supernatural explanation for the events that his detective investigates. Two of the stories in the second series are rationalized at the end, in a neat inversion of Sherlock Holmes's supposedly "supernatural" cases; an innovation that lends a series of psychic detective stories the charm of surprise and keeps readers on their toes, wondering whether or not everything will be explained away naturally at the end. However, this idea came too late to save the series, which ended after the second set of stories was published. Perhaps the world was not yet prepared for this novel idea; indeed, during the next nine years only one author seems to have treated the idea of a psychic sleuth with any kind of seriousness, and that was Harold Begbie, a prolific journalist and novelist, who in 1904 penned a series of six short stories for the *London Magazine* featuring Andrew Latter, a man who is able to solve seemingly inexplicable crimes through the medium of a dream world that can only be travelled to—and through—by someone who is "aware." Latter has this ability, and while the crimes he solves are rooted in this world, with no element of the supernatural about them, his actual solving of them takes place via the medium of this dream world in which all is made clear to him, and him alone.

1908 saw the publication of one of the landmark volumes in the genre of the psychic detective story: *John Silence*, by Algernon Blackwood, an English writer who had already made a name for himself as a writer of superb supernatural tales (his stories "The Willows" and "The Wendigo" are frequently cited as being amongst the best examples of the genre ever written). *John Silence: Physician Extraordinary* was Blackwood's most popular collection and contains five stories centering round the eponymous hero (a sixth Silence story, written about the same time, did not appear in print until 1914). The book's subtitle makes it clear that Silence is very much in the tradition of Le Fanu's Hesselius: a doctor who is as much, if not more, concerned with his patients' psychical health as he is with their physical health. (Silence is often referred to—to his chagrin—as the "psychic doctor.") Blackwood, who had long been interested in arcane lore and was himself a member of the Hermetic Order of the Golden Dawn (the preeminent magic order in Great Britain in the late nineteenth/early twentieth century), had originally intended to explore the theme of the occult in a series of essays, but was persuaded to turn them into fiction instead, a change of mind which explains, in part, why the stories are not completely successful in terms of structure and plotting. Indeed, it must be said that the character of Silence has something of a dampening effect on the stories in which he takes an active part; he is prone to lecturing, and the stories do slow down, if not grind to a halt, when he takes centre stage. Critic Jack Sullivan has noted of Silence, "Whenever the good psychic doctor appears on the scene, we can expect some heavy going. We suspect that Dr. Silence can indeed 'conquer even the devils of outer space'—by boring them into a catatonic state." At their best, however—in the stories "Ancient Sorceries" and "Secret Worship," tales in which Silence is largely relegated to the role of listener, and occasional interpreter of events—Blackwood's tales of psychic detection stand at the very forefront of the genre, and provided a model for many of the authors who would follow.

Silence is not averse to Sherlockian touches, as this passage from "The Nemesis of Fire" shows:

> "You remember the sensation of warmth when you put the letter
> to your forehead in the train; the heat generally in the house
> last evening, and, as you now mention, in the night. You heard,
> too, the Colonel's stories about the appearance of fire in this

wood and in the house itself, and the way his brother and the gamekeeper came to their deaths twenty years ago."

I nodded, wondering what in the world it all meant.

"And you get no clue from these facts?" he asked, a trifle surprised.

I searched every corner of my mind and imagination for some inkling of his meaning, but was obliged to admit that I understood nothing so far.

"Never mind; you will later."

However, Blackwood's interest lay more with the psychic than with the detective part of the equation, and one of the main influences Silence had on the genre was to demonstrate how it could be moved away from the classic Sherlockian detective tale, with the emphasis placed more on healing psychic wounds or breaches than on solving a crime in traditional Holmesian manner (although elements of mystery continued to be a staple of the occult detective tale). It did not take long for other writers to seize on Blackwood's template. Where Flaxman Low had been content to keep occult jargon to a minimum, preferring the language of more conventional detectives like Holmes, Silence did not hesitate to give voice to the theories and modes of expression with which his creator was intimately familiar.

William Hope Hodgson's Carnacki was something of a hybrid of both characters: an occult detective who was equally familiar with the jargon of the paranormal and the methods of more mundane sleuths. Hodgson's creation made his debut in the 1910 collection *Carnacki, The Ghost Finder*, and it is Carnacki who is credited, in Ellery Queen's *Queen's Quorum*, as the first psychic detective (this despite the superior claim of Hesketh-Prichard, and even Blackwood, both of whose creations appeared in print some time before Carnacki). However, it is hardly surprising that Carnacki made a more lasting impression on Queen than did Flaxman Low and John Silence, for Hodgson's stories are inventive and engaging; indeed, one could almost describe them as romps, so firmly are they in the tradition of "boys' own" tales of breathless adventure and hair's breadth escapes. That all will work out is attested to by the form of the tales, which is consistent throughout: Carnacki invites a group of friends to his Cheyne Walk, London house to hear of his latest adventure; the fact that their host is present to give all the details shows that he emerges unscathed. The stories themselves—written by their author as a commercial alternative to his more visionary, poorer-selling works—have a period charm, and are punctuated by Carnacki's talk of electric pentacles, the Unknown Last Line of the Saaamaaa Ritual, Aeiirii and Saiitii developments, and the Barrier which separates the Ab from the Normal. This could, in some hands, become an annoying distraction; but Carnacki tells of his adventures in such an engaging way—and without trying to gloss over the fact that he more than once finds himself in a "tremendous funk"—that it is a reluctant reader indeed who is not pulled along for the ride.

If Hodgson's creation gets his psychic jargon from Blackwood, then he inherits his detective skill from Hesketh-Prichard and *his* model, Conan Doyle. Carnacki is shown carefully examining the scene of each of his cases, applying Sherlockian methods of observation and deduction, including such newfangled aids as photographic equipment. The sleuth notes: "I am as big a sceptic concerning the truth of ghost-tales as any you are likely to meet— only I am what I might term an unprejudiced sceptic. I am not given to either believing or disbelieving things 'on principle' . . . I view all reported 'hauntings' as unproven until I have examined into them." In keeping with this philosophy, Hodgson is careful to give Carnacki one or two cases which, despite their supernatural trappings, turn out to be caused by human agency, an effect which pays off spectacularly in what is arguably the finest of the Carnacki tales, "The Horse of the Invisible." In this story, the explanation—supernatural or logical?—is left to the reader to decide, with Carnacki giving evidence to support both views, but declining to make a final pronouncement one way or the other. It is one of the finest demonstrations of the great ghost story writer M. R. James's dictum that the best supernatural stories should leave "a loophole for a natural explanation; but, I would say, let the loophole be so narrow as not to be quite practicable."

Despite the general popularity and success of the Silence and Carnacki stories, the psychic detective genre did not receive much attention from writers in the years immediately following the debut of the tales. One of the handful of exceptions was the Australian-born writer Max Rittenberg, whose accounts of the cases of Dr. Xavier Wycherley, "the Mind-Reader," appeared in such magazines as the *English Illustrated Magazine* and the *London Magazine* beginning in 1911. Another exception was the series of eight stories about Aylmer Vance, Ghost-Seer, written by the prolific husband-and-wife writing team of Alice and Claude Askew, which appeared in the pages of *The Weekly Tale-Teller* in July and August 1914. This timing is particularly noteworthy. The Askews were extremely popular writers, who usually wrote short story series in groups of six or twelve tales, so there would likely have been more Vance stories (at least another four) had not events of August 1914 diverted the world's attention from more frivolous matters.

As it was, the appalling tragedy of the Great War—"the war that was to end all wars" that cost the lives of millions—led many people, both during the war and after, to take an interest in the occult and the supernatural in an attempt to answer the simple question: "What happens after death?" Millions of young men suffered leaving their parents, wives, and children groping for answers, and turning, in their search, to channels that they might otherwise have overlooked or ignored. It is almost certainly no coincidence that, while Arthur Conan Doyle had been interested in spiritualistic matters since the 1880s, it was not until the war years that he embraced the cause of spiritualism and declared publicly his whole-hearted belief in it.

Conan Doyle was by no means the only writer who interested himself in these matters; as has already been noted, Algernon Blackwood was a keen student of the occult, with the Silence stories reflecting his own outlook and experience. Until the war, he had been the only writer to use psychic detective stories as more personal vehicles; other writers looked on the genre as something lighter, an interesting outlet for their talents but nothing of any significant personal importance. In the years between the wars, however, the genre attracted several authors whose interest in spiritual matters was more than casual, and who looked at psychic detective tales as a way to bring this interest to the attention of the public in a more palatable, and popular, form than a series of articles. The first such author was Rose Champion de Crespigny, who in 1919 wrote six stories featuring Norton Vyse, Psychic, which ran in the *Premier Magazine*. That there was an interest in—and, probably coincidentally, a market for—this type of story was acknowledged in an introduction to the first Vyse story, written by the editor of the *Premier*, David Whitelaw: "Never has the lure of the occult been more in evidence than now, and the stories . . . are sure of a big welcome. They are ghost stories, and *more* than ghost stories."

Vyse is a psychic detective, yet *more* than a psychic detective; he is also a psychometric sleuth, or one who can intuit past events, and even foretell the future, by touching objects or people associated with them. Interestingly, Conan Doyle had himself touched on the idea of psychometry in his 1903 story, "The Leather Funnel," in which two men, both of whom are interested in the occult, are able to "see" the past history of a woman associated with the funnel of the title when they go to sleep with the object itself beside them. Vyse's method is explained somewhat more scientifically: he holds the object to his forehead, and de Crespigny makes much of the conjunction of glands—the pituitary and the pineal—at the base of the brain, which, says Vyse, "has an important relation to the action of the inner senses."

As this passage suggests, de Crespigny was not averse to utilizing psychic jargon in her stories; but she was a good writer who knew her craft, and who had the good sense to understand that the reading public would not sit patiently for a series of lectures. The Vyse stories are well written and well plotted, and the detective himself is an engaging character, willing to explain his methods to those who are interested, but not averse to standing up for himself and his beliefs in the face of skepticism:

"I go by common sense—good old common sense [said the visitor] . . . You can't go far wrong if you stick to that."

"You can't go far in any direction if you stick to so-called common sense," Vyse rejoined; "we should still be in the Stone Age if the dreamers hadn't flouted 'common sense' through all the ages. Common sense said iron couldn't float, that man could never fly,

that every new invention or discovery outside the range of his comprehension must come from the devil. Common sense has done a
lot of climbing down in its day. . . ."

The following year—1920—saw several additions to the psychic
detective family. Moris Klaw, the "Dream-Detective" created by the
prolific Sax Rohmer, is a dealer in antiques who is able to assist the
police in solving baffling crimes by using his ability to reproduce,
from the atmosphere, the last images seen by the murder victims. He
calls it "the art of the odic photograph," and allies it with his belief in
the "Cycle of Crime" and his theories about the indestructibility of
thought. We are once more in the world of jargon, for Rohmer, like
de Crespigny and Blackwood, was also a dabbler in the occult, an
interest which finds its way into a good many of his tales. The Klaw
stories, which began appearing in 1913 but were not collected
together until seven years later, are themselves something of a mixed
bag, but they do include more features of the classic Sherlockian
detective story—not least in the way Klaw works with the official
police—than many of the other psychic sleuth tales of the period.

The Broken Fang and Other Experiences of a Specialist in Spooks by Uel
Key contains five stories that concern the adventures of the occult
detective Dr. Arnold Rhymer, who occasionally collaborates with
Scotland Yard. Most of the tales have a background theme of war
and espionage, in addition to vampires, zombies, dream journeys,
mind control, reincarnation, and possession. As can be deduced
from this summary, the Rhymer stories are not great literature, and
can descend into silliness and sensationalism. However, 1920 also
saw a more serious addition to the genre in the form of Ella Scrymsour's stories about Shiela Crerar, notable as being one of the few
female psychic sleuths to grace the literature. The six Crerar stories
appeared in *The Blue Magazine*, and detail the occult experiences of
the young heroine, who, left penniless following the death of her
father, decides to make use of her psychic powers. She places an
advertisement in *The Times*, stating that she will devote her abilities
to "the solving of uncanny mysteries and the 'laying of ghosts' " and
is soon embarked on her first case, the solving of the mystery known
as "the Kildrummie Weird." The stories are well told, and Crerar

makes for an interesting and feisty heroine not afraid to shy away from the physical dangers inherent in dealing with the supernatural.

The next author to turn seriously to the psychic detective story was Dion Fortune, the first of whose tales about Dr. Taverner began to appear in the *Royal Magazine* in 1922 (they were later collected, as *The Secrets of Dr Taverner*, in 1926). The stories proved immediately popular. Like Algernon Blackwood, Fortune was a member of the Order of the Golden Dawn, but she pursued her interest in the occult a good deal further, joining, and then eventually clashing with, many of the major mystical and Theosophical organizations of the day before founding a group called the Fraternity of the Inner Light.

Fortune wrote a good deal of nonfiction on various sociological, sexual, and mystical subjects, much of which is hard going today. Fortunately for all concerned, her fiction is a good deal livelier. Although she can never fully rid herself of a tendency to lecture, she has a good grasp of plotting and narrative. Her motives in writing the Taverner stories were similar to those of Blackwood with John Silence: a desire to place before the public a subject in which the author was interested, but which would likely not have much appeal if cast in the form of a lecture. In her introduction to the book edition, Fortune wrote:

> These stories may be looked at from two standpoints (and no doubt the standpoint the reader chooses will be dictated by personal taste and previous knowledge of the subject under discussion). They may be regarded as fiction, designed, like the conversation of the Fat Boy recorded in the *Pickwick Papers*, "to make your flesh creep," or they may be considered to be what they actually are, studies in little-known aspects of psychology put in the form of fiction because, if published as a serious contribution to science they would have no chance of a hearing.

In addition to the appearance of Fortune's Dr Taverner, 1922 also saw the publication of one of the few novels to feature a psychic sleuth: Jessie Douglas Kerruish's *The Undying Monster*. Kerruish's foray into the genre is notable for another reason: the psychic sleuth in question, Miss Luna Bartendale, is, along with Ella Scrymsour's Shiela Crerar, one of the very few female psychic detectives. The novel—a suspenseful tale of the curse that has hung over the Hammand family for generations—takes the form of a traditional mystery story, with a solution that has its roots in ancestral memory and the transformation of men into beasts.

The idea of psychic detective stories as a means for their authors to explore issues which interested them personally is a theme which runs through many of the works mentioned; but a major change was about to shake the genre, with the advent of the most popular—and prolific—of psychic detectives, Jules de Grandin, the dapper French phantom fighter created by American author Seabury Quinn. The first de Grandin adventure appeared in *Weird Tales* in 1925, and he would go on to become that magazine's most popular character by far, with Quinn writing ninety-three tales featuring his creation between 1925 and 1951.

De Grandin was accompanied by the faithful Dr. Samuel Trowbridge, who acted as both assistant and biographer. Most psychic detectives had, until now, been cast in the "lone wolf" tradition, with no one person to act as "Watson" on a consistent basis; so Quinn's de Grandin tales were something of a throwback to the Holmes-Watson partnership which influenced so much later detective fiction, not least the Hercule Poirot stories of Agatha Christie. This is only fitting, as the French de Grandin has invariably, and inevitably, been compared with the Belgian Poirot: not only because of the similarity in accent and mannerism, but because both characters first appeared in print, and achieved their greatest fame, at approximately the same time. Unfortunately, while his adventures remain popular, de Grandin as a character has not stood the test of time quite as well as Poirot. Where Christie managed to keep control of her character, reining in his more flamboyant traits, Quinn, who was writing for *Weird Tales*, felt no such constraint, and the exuberant Frenchman, with his odd turns of phrase, somewhat tenuous (at times) grasp of English, and recurring catchphrases can become rather tiring if his adventures are read *en masse*.

De Grandin's pulp origins are at once his blessing and his curse.

The curse came in the form of the demands and expectations of Quinn's publisher and his readers: Quinn noted that *Weird Tales* was fond of having nude, or semi-nude, women on the cover, and thus took care to include at least one scene in most de Grandin tales where a female character is fully or partially unclothed, in order to appeal to readers and to increase the chance of that story being selected as the subject of the cover illustration. The pulps, too, were not noted for the literary quality of the writing that appeared within their pages; and there is a sameness and predictability to the de Grandin adventures which does not work in their favor. Yet Seabury Quinn was a good writer, who had read extensively in the fields of the occult and mysticism, picking up along the way a vast historical knowledge of the way in which belief in the supernatural has become a part of mankind's sociological fabric. This knowledge lent his tales of ghouls, zombies, werewolves, ghosts, and demons something deeper and richer than was common in pulp magazines, and ensured that de Grandin was never in danger of running out of supernatural entities to vanquish.

De Grandin's armory included many of the traditional ghost-fighting tools—silver bullets, holy water, incantations—familiar to readers of earlier tales of psychic detectives. But he was also not averse to using more modern methods, such as radium and high-powered weapons, a trait he had in common with Hodgson's Carnacki, who in 1910 used such cutting-edge devices as photography, wireless radio transmitters, and even an early sort of television. All in all, the de Grandin tales marked the coming of age of the psychic detective story, blending a traditional Holmes-Watson partnership and the elements of the classic detective story with a modern approach to the supernatural. The immense popularity of the stories in the pages of *Weird Tales* ensured that psychic detectives, who had been in some danger of being taken over by earnest devotees of the occult anxious to spread their message, or of becoming the subject of short, soon-forgotten runs of tales in ephemeral magazines, became a legitimate literary subgenre.

In 1927, British author A. M. Burrage produced a series of ten stories about the occult detective Francis Chard, which were published in the pages of *The Blue Magazine*. Burrage is one of the best, and best known, writers of ghost stories of the early twentieth century, and several of his tales are among the classics of the genre. He was a prolific author, able to turn his hand to almost any kind of fiction, so it is hardly surprising that he should have tried his hand at psychic sleuth tales. He had actually made an initial foray into the genre in 1920, with two stories featuring occult sleuth Derek Scarpe which appeared in the *Novel* magazine; but for some reason the usual six- or twelve-story series did not materialize and Burrage did not go back to the format for another seven years. When he did, he produced a series of stories which were firmly in the tradition of the classic mystery story, with Chard accompanied by his friend and chronicler, Torrance. Although Chard is well versed in the ways of the supernormal, he is described as approaching every individual case "with the cautious step of the complete skeptic"; an approach which is shown to be eminently sensible when he encounters cases where the "haunting" proves to have a natural explanation. The Chard cases are not as substantial as some others in the genre; but Burrage was in the very first rank of the storytellers of his day, and his psychic detective tales are eminently readable and mercifully free from the jargon that permeates so many other similar stories.

Burrage's Chard stories, however, mark the end of the Golden Age of the psychic detective story. The interest in all things spiritualistic, which flowered in the years surrounding the Great War, had begun to fade by the end of the 1920s, and tales of occult detectives were not immune. Apart from the de Grandin stories, which appeared with almost alarming frequency in the pages of *Weird Tales*, there was little activity in the genre until 1937, when British author Jack Mann wrote a novel entitled *Grey Shapes*, featuring his detective Gregory George Gordon Green, more popularly known as Gees. An aristocrat who spent a short time in the police force after leaving university, Gees is not initially presented as being particularly adept in occult matters; but he frequently stumbles across cases that involve the irrational, and by the time *Her Ways Are Death* was published in 1940, he is described as being very high in occult advancement.

Mann was an exceedingly popular writer in his day, and the character of Gees was sufficiently attractive to the reading public that he appeared in several novels that rapidly devolved into a formulaic series in which Gees's slightly scuffed, unlucky in love, and ready-with-his fists gumshoe encountered a string of malevolent beings, including werewolves, elementals, witches, reincarnated souls, evil priests, and the misguided humans who made use of them. But Mann continued the tradition of psychic detective as popular enter-tainment set by Quinn's de Grandin, and is also one of the few authors in the genre to use the format of the novel as opposed to the short story. The fact that Gees was formerly a policeman also meant that the stories were heavy on the detective element, with a dogged sleuth investigating his case in time-honoured Sherlockian fashion.

In 1938 the American writer, and member of the Baker Street Irregulars, Manly Wade Wellman, introduced his occult sleuth Judge Pursuivant in the pages of *Weird Tales*; in the final story of the series, "The Half-Haunted," published in 1941, Pursuivant finds himself consulted by Jules de Grandin. Another of Wellman's psychic detec-tives, John Thunstone, made his first appearance in *Weird Tales* in November 1943; Wellman continued to chronicle the character's adventures in the magazine until 1951, then rested him until the 1980s, when he returned with further adventures, this time pre-dominantly in novel form.

The Second World War did not inspire the same interest in the occult as had the Great War, but in 1943 Dennis Wheatley wrote four stories about psychic investigator Neils Orsen, which appeared in the collection *Gunmen, Gallants and Ghosts*. The stories owe much to Dion Fortune's Dr. Taverner series, in that the tales were fiction based on fact, and the main character of Orsen was based on Wheatley's friend Henry Dewhirst. In 1945 Margery Lawrence pub-lished *Number Seven, Queer Street*, featuring the adventures of her psy-chic sleuth Dr. Miles Pennoyer. Lawrence was one of the many authors of psychic detective stories who was also a believer in the occult; yet where authors such as Rose Champion de Crespigny and Dion Fortune never seemed quite able to overcome a tendency to preach, Lawrence was first and foremost a storyteller, and a very good one at that. She can lay claim to being one of the most over-looked writers of ghost stories of the last century, and this has had the effect of throwing Pennoyer somewhat into the shadows—a pity, as his adventures make for some of the best and most compelling reading in the genre.

Like Fortune's Dr. Taverner and Wheatley's Neils Orsen, Miles Pennoyer is an amalgam of several real people who were known to Lawrence in the occult circles in which she moved. The Pennoyer tales are a throwback to the Holmes adventures: instead of Baker Street, Pennoyer lives on a quiet street near the Thames, officially called Queen Street, but soon dubbed "Queer Street" on account of Pennoyer's odd methods and clientele. He is accompanied on his adventures by his friend Jerome Latimer, a successful novelist, who recounts Pennoyer's adventures; and, like Holmes, Pennoyer has traveled in Tibet and other mysterious parts of the globe, and remains a confirmed bachelor, despite (or because of) one cherished but doomed love affair.

The Pennoyer tales are not as heavy on pure detection as are some earlier efforts, but Lawrence was adept at setting a scene, creating an atmosphere, and ensuring that her characters became more than mere two-dimensional figures going through the motions for the sake of the plot; and the character of Pennoyer himself is an interesting one, far more colorful and human than the somewhat ruminative John Silence. The character was successful enough that a further collection, *Master of Shadows*, appeared in 1959, and one final Pennoyer tale was published posthumously in 1971. In the meantime, another psychic sleuth—in many ways the most distinctive of all—had appeared, when Manly Wade Wellman's John the Balladeer made his first appearance in the story "O Ugly Bird" in *The Magazine of Fantasy and Science Fiction* in 1951.

In addition to being a prolific writer, Wellman was also a folklorist, and his stories of John the Balladeer, or "Silver John," as he is better known, are among the finest cycles of tales in the genre of the supernatural story. They were gathered together into book form in 1963 as *Who Fears the Devil?*, published by the legendary Arkham House. John, like Wellman, is a folklorist who roams what are presumably the Ozark Mountains, tracking down old songs and odd bits of folklore, accompanied only by his silver-stringed guitar, living on his wits, and defeating the powers of evil and healing the afflicted by virtue of his goodness and his knowledge of rural occult lore and Appalachian mythology. In some hands, the character could come across as cloying and saintly, but Wellman makes Silver John a living, breathing, complex character, and the people and situations he stumbles across are far from run-of-the-mill; indeed, no less a critic than E. F. Bleiler comments that the stories in *Who Fears the Devil?* are "unusual, original, and well-developed."

Apart from Silver John, there were few new psychic sleuths appearing in the 1950s; an exception was Edward D. Hoch's Simon Ark, a possibly immortal investigator who made his first appearance in *Famous Detective Stories* in December 1955, and whose adventures Hoch has continued to chronicle over the intervening decades. Eight years later, another enduring psychic investigator made his début, Joseph Payne Brennan's Lucius Leffing, probably the best-known psychic investigator of the second half of the last century. Brennan suffered somewhat from being born too late. Whereas a previous generation of writers had been able to hone their skills in a plethora of magazines publishing supernatural, horror, and weird fiction, by the time Brennan came along the pulps were finished and general circulation magazines were dwindling and dying, leaving authors in every genre with fewer markets for their tales, with writers in specialty markets particularly feeling the loss. Despite these drawbacks, however, Brennan was able to establish Lucius Leffing as one of the most popular characters in the genre, who appeared in nearly forty adventures that appeared over a period of almost three decades.

Where other psychic detectives depended upon psychic powers, knowledge of spells, and all manner of gadgets and paraphernalia designed to deal with the unquiet dead, Leffing was a detective in the classical mode, utilizing observation, deduction, research, analysis, a vast knowledge of arcane lore, and an ability to accept the incredible and deal with it in a matter-of-fact way. He is a reminder, in some ways, of Flaxman Low, who started the entire psychic detective genre in 1898, and who likewise depended on Sherlockian observation and deduction, research and analysis, in order to penetrate those mysteries that others could not fathom.

One common feature of many psychic detective stories—more so than in either the pure detective or pure ghost story—is a concern for the spiritual well being of the client. This can be traced back to Le Fanu's Dr. Hesselius, and the idea that the psychic sleuth is saving souls as much as lives drives a good deal of the fiction in the genre. John Silence, Dr Taverner, Miles Pennoyer, and Silver John are particularly concerned with this aspect of the fight between good and evil, which is something familiar to devotees of Sherlock Holmes, who eschewed the supernatural explanation but recognised the importance of the spiritual as well as the actual. "I suppose that I am commuting a felony," he said in "The Blue Carbuncle," "but it is just possible that I am saving a soul."

And so we come full circle, back to Sherlock Holmes, the detective who sparked off the mystery story and who was instrumental in the birth of the psychic detective. This overview of psychic sleuths has by no means been an exhaustive one; there has been no space in which to mention the strange cases of Cosmo Thaw or the wonderfully named Mesmer Milann, Mediator, or those of Godfrey Usher or Barnabas Hildreth (who might, it is hinted, be an immortal Egyptian priest), or Douglas Newton's two contributions to the genre, Dr Dyn and Paul Toft, or Costello, Psychic Investigator, or Manly Wade Wellman's later contributions to the genre, Lee Cobbett and Hal Stryker. The most recent of these creations date back to the late 1970s, so it is only fair to ask: is the psychic detective still with us? Apart from a few years immediately following the Great War, psychic sleuths have never been thick on the ground, and certainly there has been little in recent years to rival the output of Seabury Quinn or Margery Lawrence or Joseph Payne Brennan; yet the genre is still alive and well. British mystery writer Jacqueline Winspear has recently created the character of Maisie Dobbs, who uses her psychic abilities to assist her in solving mysteries and providing comfort to her clients in late 1920s England, while American author Jessica Amanda Salmonson's Penelope Pettiweather, based in the Pacific Northwest, is a more traditional occult detective, using her knowledge of ghosts and hauntings to investigate mysterious happenings and try to provide peace for the departed. Ralph Tyler, the creation of British writer Mark Valentine, made his first appearance in 1984, while Australian author Rick Kennett has written several stories about Ernie Pine, the reluctant ghost-hunter. And there has even been pastiche in the form of a series of stories written, together and separately, by Kennett and British writer Chico Kidd. Both realised, late in 1990, that although they were separated by several thousand miles, they had begun writing pastiches of Hodgson's Carnacki stories. They began comparing notes and sharing ideas, and the end result was a book of tales, *No. 472 Cheyne Walk*, in which Carnacki is able to expand on some of the unrecorded cases to which he makes tantalising, if incomplete, reference during the course of his better-documented investigations. This is yet another idea pioneered in the Holmes tales. Conan Doyle's creation has a good deal for which to answer, even if he did stay resolutely flat-footed upon the ground. No ghosts need apply? Perhaps not to Holmes. Thank goodness other detectives have been ready, willing, and able to step forward to fill the gap.

The Author is indebted to Jack Adrian for his assistance in the preparation of this article.

CHANNELING HOLMES

Loren D. Estleman

IT'S CUSTOMARY FOR writers writing about their personal interest in Sherlock Holmes to begin with the details of their first experience of him. I can't, because I can't recall a time when he wasn't known to me on some level.

In all the vast panoply of immortal literary characters, I can think of only four who have entered the dictionary with definitions of their own. To "create a Frankenstein," be called "a real Jekyll and Hyde," or address someone as "Sherlock" requires no explanation, even for an immigrant learning the English language. (Jekyll and Hyde, of course, present the problem of whether to consider them as two characters or one.) Yet Sherlock Holmes stands alone as a pictorial icon as well, and one that crosses all boundaries: class, generation, and geography.

One's image of Frankenstein (or rather his monster) depends on whether he grew up watching Boris Karloff, Christopher Lee, or Robert DeNiro. *Dr. Jekyll and Mr. Hyde* has been reprinted and filmed so many times, and imagined by so many different illustrators and actors, that no two people can be selected at random to agree on their appearance. But everyone can identify the eagle-beaked profile in the fore-and-aft cap with the calabash clamped between his teeth.

It doesn't signify that the cap and curved pipe appear only in illustrations, and not in any of the fifty-six short stories and four novels that Sir Arthur Conan Doyle wrote involving Sherlock Holmes. Our image of Christ is wholly a creation of Renaissance painters working sixteen hundred years after the Crucifixion. Neither Mark nor Matthew nor Luke nor John saw need to describe his Lord. The human imagination paints impressions; the retina takes pictures.

So I was aware of Holmes at an early age. Reading would come later, and seeing him on-screen in between. I think it was during my sophomore year in high school that the Detroit CBS affiliate ran a week-long screening of the Universal Sherlock Holmes series on the "Late Show," introduced by Basil Rathbone, its star. I swindled my parents into letting me stay up late four school nights in succession to watch the films. As has often happened during a movie-loving life (Martin Scorsese's *The Age of Innocence* introduced me to the works of Edith Wharton in my forties), I became infatuated with a character on celluloid, then continued the affair on paper. Bleary-eyed on the morning of the fifth day, I stumbled into the school library and checked out *A Study in Scarlet* and *The Sign of Four.*

Sign was a revelation. It was there I learned that Sherlock Holmes occupied his mind with cocaine when not engaged on a case. This was just after the Summer of Love (which I spent painting my parents' vacation cabin in northern Michigan), many years before dope-smoking Presidents, heroin-shooting movie stars, and line-snorting junior executives; the three-martini lunch was as stimulated as Corporate America ever got. My school system had only recently substituted "Community" for "Agricultural" in its name. There was talk of upperclassmen passing around joints in the parking lot during football games, but I was inclined to dismiss this as urban legend. We had only one hippie, who was stranger to us than the foreign-exchange student from East Pakistan. The prospect of a detective who injected cocaine catapulted me into the world of the *noir* antihero, and a forbiddingly intoxicating environment for a boy of sixteen.

I should state that entertainment wasn't my aim. My aspiration was to make my living as a cartoonist, and I had made inroads by drawing, stapling together, and selling comic books to my fellow students at fifteen cents a pop. (Comic books were then selling in drugstores for twelve cents, but I felt my time was worth more.) A trailer for the film (movie, again) *A Study in Terror,* pitting Sherlock Holmes against Jack the Ripper for the first (but far from the last) time, had started me thinking about doing something similar in comics form, and since I'd recently read Bram Stoker's *Dracula* for the first time, I thought it fitting that these literary contemporaries meet; they were in London at the same time, after all.

Sherlock Holmes vs. Dracula sold very quickly, as one copy ought to, and I only hope whoever bought it still has it, as it must be worth something by now as the earliest version of my all-time best-selling novel, and I'd like all my childhood friends to prosper. The story was facile, not at all canonical either to Stoker or Conan Doyle, but the appropriateness of the match was still with me ten years later when Nicholas Meyer's *The Seven Per-Cent Solution* soared up the *New York Times* list and I'd shifted my career objectives from graphic arts to writing.

By this time, I was far more familiar with the literary Holmes. (Reading *The Return of Sherlock Holmes* in the woods, I put down the book to shoot my first and only deer in 1972, then picked the book back up and finished the story before dressing the carcass.) In 1976, I had joined The Arcadia Mixture—which is the Ann Arbor scion of the national Baker Street Irregulars, and had sold a freelance piece on the group to the *Ann Arbor News.* To supplement my knowledge, I reread Stoker's *Dracula,* outlined the plot thoroughly, created a parallel timeline with the Holmes stories as calculated by respected Sherlockian scholars, and pored over a shelf of material on Victorian England. Every writing day began by reading a Sherlock Holmes story or a fragment of one of the novels. With the Doylean/Watsonian language patterns fresh in my mind, I wrote:

> I need hardly consult my notebook for 1890 to recall that it was in August of that year that my friend Mr. Sherlock Holmes, with some slight assistance by me, set out to unravel the single and most terrible bone-chilling mystery which it has been my privilege to relate. . . .

Sherlock Holmes vs. Dracula, or The Adventure of the Sanguinary Count, was published by Doubleday on July 15, 1978, the day that a reviewer for the *New York Times*—writing about someone else's book—said was the absolute worst date to bring out a novel of any kind, as everyone was away from home on vacation and certainly not inclined to spend one precious moment of vacation browsing in a bookstore. Despite this, my book sold 20,000 copies, which is still considered more than respectable for a hardcover book by an unknown author. Paperback rights went to Penguin, which distributed it throughout the English-speaking world. The BBC bought broadcast rights and aired it on radio. It was reissued in translation in Sweden, Denmark, Holland, and Spain. Penguin published it in a new mass-market edition ten years after the first, and just as it was passing out of print in America, the Book-of-the-Month Club picked it up for trade paperback. At present, ibooks, a division of Byron Preiss Visual Publications, is distributing it in both trade paper and mass-market editions. It was optioned twice by Hollywood (which approached Pierce Brosnan and Alexander Godonuv for the two leads), and very nearly pirated by a studio, which abandoned the project under threat of legal action. In twenty-eight years it has never been out of print. To put its longevity into perspective, consider that the original hardcover price was $7.95.

The book is more famous than its author. When strangers ask me what I've written—which is a polite way of saying they've never heard of me—I get perverse pleasure from seeing their eyes light up when I mention this one title out of fifty. Fans of Sherlock Holmes and Count Dracula could populate a good-size country, and I tapped into both groups. I'm prouder of having pleased the late Dame Jean Doyle, Sir Arthur's daughter, who acknowledged my respectful approach by exempting me from the temporary ban she placed on Holmes pastiches when it appeared her father's memory might be lost in the avalanche of imitators. I think this was because I avoided parody.

Next came *Dr. Jekyll and Mr. Holmes,* which I think the better book; but iconography. aside, Jekyll and Hyde don't claim more than a fraction of Dracula's following, and between sharing the Book-of-the-Month Club omnibus edition with *Sherlock Holmes vs.*

Dracula and its current incarnation as an ibooks trade and mass-market paperback, that book was out of circulation for seven years, and for a dozen years before that. I'd entertained the notion of doing a trilogy, to be closing out with a pairing of Holmes and Sax Rohmer's Dr. Fu Manchu, but gave up on that when one critic snarked, "Estleman is no doubt busy writing about Holmes and Fu Manchu." I dislike making even prescient snipers feel good about themselves. (Years later, Cay Van Ash, Rohmer's friend and biographer, published *Ten Years Beyond Baker Street*, fulfilling the prophecy with no assistance from me and laying that demon to rest.) I never gave any serious thought to *Sherlock Holmes Meets Frankenstein*. Abbott and Costello wrung that one dry.

I keep my hand in. The editors of the book you're reading invite me from time to time to submit Holmes pastiches at short-story length, and I had fun writing an introduction to the Bantam Books two-volume omnibus edition of the complete Sherlock Holmes. I think often of doing a third novel-length pastiche, and in this I've been encouraged by some booksellers, but as yet no publishers. For now, these small projects help me stay in touch with my Watsonian side.

These days, I find it less necessary to bone up by reading the originals, whole sections of which I've committed to memory, like a lay preacher who memorizes the books of the Old Testament in lieu of actually becoming holy. I merely switch gears, from twenty-first century to nineteenth and from America to England, and I'm off again among the yew hedges, cockney constables, and disgraced family crests; delightedly enmeshed in the *recherché* vocabulary and dependent clauses of John H. Watson—I hesitate to claim of Conan Doyle, whose erudition and crowd-pleasing instincts are far more advanced than mine. I do lay claim to a certain advantage over some others who make the attempt. I spend only half my time writing contemporary suspense. The other half I spend writing historical westerns.

If that last sentence appears to be a non sequitur, you're thinking of the wrong kind of western. In the westerns I like to read and am privileged to write, no one ever says, "Slap leather, ya sidewinder!" or anything remotely similar. Nor did anyone ever speak that way on the authentic frontier. The average sixth-grade-educated pioneer had a better grasp of grammar (taught at the end of a hickory stick) than does the average college graduate of today—as well as a larger vocabulary—and used both, in journals and letters and presumably in speech, since people tend to speak the way they write letters. The Old West townsman would no sooner drop his *g*'s or double his negatives than he would wear a flannel shirt to the theater. This was, it must be remembered, the Victorian period; even gunslingers like Wyatt Earp and Wild Bill Hickok wore evening dress, and Calamity Jane changed out of her greasy buckskins into taffeta and a bustle for a night on the town. A lifetime of correcting the errors of Max Brand and other pulp-western hacks has prepared me for the formal cadences of Dr. Watson's reports to his readers. With this experience at my back, and once I get caught up in the rhythm, it often seems that I am channeling Holmes and Watson rather than just writing about them in a borrowed style.

There is a great deal of talent on display in the post-Doyle Sherlockian era, no small amount of which precedes this essay. When it errs, it seems to do so on the side of conservatism. Pasticheurs who fall short of the ideal belong to two camps: those who fear their inability to measure up to the originals, and those who feel superior to them and consciously write below their own level in order to maintain what they consider a mediocre standard. Both camps fail miserably. Had Conan Doyle continued to write about Holmes after publishing the valedictory *Casebook of Sherlock Holmes*, he would certainly have been determined not to repeat himself, as some timid imitators do, and would have given Holmes greater challenges and new venues, both to keep his own senses sharp and to continue to attract reader interest. The breadth and quality of his body of work, from *The Lost World* and *The White Company* to the hilarious and impeccably researched *Adventures of Brigadier Gerard* (and we mustn't exclude his still highly readable history of the Boer War, for which he was knighted), are evidence enough, if any were needed apart from the endurance of Sherlock Holmes, that a cloned and healthy Conan Doyle could write rings around the poseurs looking to make a fast buck off a tour of the slums. Even his writings on spiritualism, which brought him ridicule from his detractors and apologies from his admirers, make a forceful case for the existence of the supernatural matched only by the essays of St. Thomas More.

The Supernatural. That's the crux of this anthology, and the cross borne by the courageous and possibly foolhardly talents who have accepted the challenge. For all his desperate efforts to establish communication with the world beyond the pale, Conan Doyle never asked Sherlock Holmes to join him in its embrace. At the very time he subscribed publicly to the evidence of fairies, Holmes, in "The Adventure of the Sussex Vampire," intoned: "This agency stands flat-footed upon the ground, and there it must remain. No ghosts need apply." The conspirators in this compendium, then, are forced, as I was in *Sherlock Holmes vs. Dracula*, to convince Holmes of incorporeal fact, and in so doing persuade him to set aside the precepts of a lifetime. Tough room, but if you win Holmes, you win the reader. In my case, *Dr. Jekyll and Mr. Holmes* had at least the imprimatur of chemical possibility—a Holmes specialty—and in our own time, the evidence of schizophrenia, steroids, and psychotropic drugs to testify to its premise. I don't know that I ever made a sufficiently compelling case re: vampires to sway Holmes. That I leave to the reader, who must also be the judge of the success of my contribution to this collection as well as that of the others.

One thing, at least, defies discord. Sherlock Holmes is forever green, and startlingly cutting-edge for all who discover him for the first time. If it weren't for him (and, possibly, Jack the Ripper), we might dismiss the late colonial British Empire as a stagnant pool of repressed passion, extra-Freudian piety, and the right fork for the right course. Through Conan Doyle's gimlet eye and razor nib, we know that it was a time of stupendous scientific achievement, sweeping social change, artistic beauty, and crime to raise the hackles on the neck of the most jaded familiar of Jeffrey Dahmer, O.J. Simpson, Osama Bin Laden, Martha Stewart, and the lyrics of Eminem. It was the time of Charles Darwin, Sir Richard Francis Burton, the aforementioned Sigmund Freud, Susan B. Anthony, Vincent Van Gogh, Kaiser Wilhelm, and weapons of mass destruction. It was also the time of Sherlock Holmes; and if Sir Arthur Conan Doyle had not invented him, God would have had to.

ABOUT THE AUTHORS

LOREN D. ESTLEMAN has published more than fifty books in the mystery and historical western genres and mainstream fiction. He has received fifteen national writing awards, including four Shamuses, four Golden Spurs, and three Western Heritage Awards. In addition, he has been nominated for the Edgar Allan Poe Award, the Silver Dagger Award, and the National Book Award. His first Sherlock Holmes pastiche, *Sherlock Holmes vs. Dracula, or the Adventure of the Sanguinary Count,* has been in print for twenty-seven years. His latest Amos Walker detective novel is *Retro.* In 2002, Eastern Michigan University named him an honorary Doctor of Humane Letters. He is also the author of *Writing the Popular Novel,* and has reviewed books for the *Detroit News,* the *Washington Post,* and the *New York Times.* He lives in rural Michigan with his wife, author Deborah Morgan.

JON L. BREEN, a contributor to five previous volumes of Sherlock Holmes stories, is the author of six novels (including the Dagger Award-short listed *Touch of the Past*), three short story collections, and two Edgar-Award-winning reference books, *What About Murder?* and *Novel Verdicts.* Breen, editor or coeditor of half a dozen anthologies, is a review columnist for *Ellery Queen's Mystery Magazine* and *Mystery Scene* and a frequent nonpolitical contributor to *The Weekly Standard.* His most recent book is *Kill the Umpire: The Calls of Ed Gorgon* (Crippen & Landru, 2003). A retired librarian and professor of English, he lives in Fountain Valley, California, with his wife and first-line editor Rita.

GILLIAN LINSCOTT is best known for her series of eleven novels tracing the career of the suffragette detective, Nell Bray. *Absent Friends* won the UK Crime Writers' Association Ellis Peters Historical Dagger for best historical crime novel in 2000. Before turning to writing full time, she had an eventful career as a journalist, including reporting from Northern Ireland for the *Guardian* and from Parliament for the BBC. She takes time out from writing to ride horseback, climb mountains, ski and trampoline. She lives in Herefordshire, England.

CAROLYN WHEAT's short stories have earned her an Agatha, an Anthony, a Macavity, and a Shamus award, and her novels have been twice nominated for Edgar awards. Her book *How to Write Killer Fiction*, was an alternate selection of the Writers Digest Book Club. She is currently working on a book about detective archetypes, the first of which is—who else?— The Great Detective himself, Sherlock Holmes.

A member of The Baker Street Irregulars, H. PAUL JEFFERS is the author of two acclaimed Sherlock Holmes novels, *The Adventure of the Stalwart Companions* and *Murder Most Irregular*, a history of Scotland Yard (*Bloody Business*) and fifteen mystery novels. Among his nonfiction books are histories of the Great Depression, Jerusalem, and the San Francisco earthquake of 1906; and biographies of Theodore Roosevelt, Grover Cleveland, Mayor Fiorello La Guardia, Diamond Jim Brady, Theodore Roosevelt, Jr., and Eddie Rickenbacker. He lives in Manhattan in an apartment that friends have described as a shrine to the Sleuth of Baker Street.

COLIN BRUCE is both a professional writer and a mathematical physicist who performs research for the European Space Agency. He is the author of two books explaining science and math in Sherlock Holmes stories: *The Einstein Paradox, and Other Science Mysteries Solved by Sherlock Holmes* and *Conned Again, Watson: Cautionary Tales of Logic, Math, and Probability*, have been published worldwide in many languages. His latest book, *Schrödinger's Rabbits: The Many Worlds of Quantum* describes a puzzle deeper than any man-made mystery, whose implications are more terrifying than any ghost story.

PAULA COHEN's investiture in the Adventuresses of Sherlock Holmes, to which she has belonged since 1975, is Lady Mary Brackenstall; she has complementary addictions to opera and all things Victorian. Her first novel, *Gramercy Park*, which combines her passions, was published in 2002 by St. Martin's Press. Born and raised in Brooklyn, New York, Paula lives there still with her husband, Roger, and their cat, Hodge.

DANIEL STASHOWER is the author of the Edgar Award-winning *Teller of Tales: The Life of Arthur Conan Doyle*, as well as numerous novels and short stories. He is a member in good standing of the Baker Street Irregulars.

BILL CRIDER is the author of fifty published novels and numerous short stories. He won the Anthony Award for "best first mystery novel" in 1987 for *Too Late to Die* and was nominated for the Shamus Award for "best first private-eye novel" for *Dead on the Island*. He won the Golden Duck award for "best juvenile science fiction novel" for *Mike Gonzo and the UFO Terror*. He and his wife, Judy, won the "best short story" Anthony in 2002 for their story "Chocolate Moose."

"MICHÉAL BREATHNACH" is the Irish *nom-de-plume* of Michael Walsh, the former music critic of *Time* magazine and the author of the novels, *Exchange Alley, And All the Saints,* and *As Time Goes By.* The setting of Coole Park and the legend of Biddy Early was suggested by his daughter, Clare Walsh, a junior at the Hotchkiss School in Lakeville, Connecticut. The Walsh family has recently rebuilt their ancestral home on the Burren in County Clare, Ireland, where the Sidhe are always welcome.

Novelist and military historian CALEB CARR is the critically acclaimed, best-selling author of the Alienist series, *The Lessons of Terror, Killing Time,* and *The Devil Soldier.* His books have been translated into over twenty languages worldwide. He is also a contributing editor to *MHQ: The Quarterly Journal of Military History,* and the series editor of the Modern Library War series. He was educated at Kenyon College and New York University, is a former employee of the Council on Foreign Relations in New York, and currently lives in upstate New York, where he teaches military and diplomatic studies at Bard College. His latest book, *The Italian Secretary,* published by Carroll & Graf, is an elaboration on the Sherlock Holmes canon in which the famed detective investigates a pair of gruesome murders.

BARBARA RODEN's two great literary loves are Sherlock Holmes and ghost stories. With her husband Christopher she runs Calabash Press, which specialises in books relating to Holmes and Arthur Conan Doyle, and the World Fantasy Award-winning Ash-Tree Press, which specialises in classic supernatural fiction. She edits *All Hallows,* the journal of the Ghost Story Society, and has contributed dozens of articles to Sherlockian publications in Canada, the United States, and Great Britain. In 1990 she was named a Master Bootmaker by The Bootmakers of Toronto, and she is investitured in the Baker Street Irregulars of New York as "Beryl Stapleton."